THE EXETER INCIDENT

DAVID WATKINS

D & T
PUBLISHING

For Luke, forever dancing in thunder

PART I

SUNDAY MAY 23RD

12:01 AM

CHARLIE MONROE GLANCED at his watch and groaned, his considerable bulk sagging. Looking around the room again, taking in the amount of blood, he knew he wasn't going to bed anytime soon.

"This is a mess," Danielle Brent said as soon as she entered. It was a massive understatement. "It looks like a fox has got all the chickens."

He didn't reply. Danni was just talking, filling the silent house with noise to take the edge off. They were both dressed from head to foot in white coveralls, and under strict instructions not to touch anything. The two uniforms – first on the scene, poor bastards - sat outside, in an ambulance, having a cup of coffee with the paramedics. Charlie would speak to them later, but right now he would much rather be *with* them.

A teenager's idea of a party lay on the table: popcorn, crisps, chocolate, a jar of processed salsa, twenty cans of the ever-classy Stella, one nearly empty bottle of expensive vodka, and an equally expensive, but full, gin. Charlie wished he could afford those sorts of drinks.

The dead were all teenagers, so there would be a problem if, or when, the parents turned up. Somebody back in the office was trying to track them down, but none were answering. Charlie was glad he wasn't making those calls.

The forensic guy – fat, bald, smelly – said there was only one dead person in this room, but, for the life of him, Charlie couldn't see where. Apart from the head, of course. Girl, approximately fifteen, on the table, in the bowl of popcorn. There were no traces of the rest of the actual body anywhere. The trail of blood had started just inside the doorway and whilst it looked like the girl had bled in the hallway, it seemed she had exploded in here. Red gore coated every conceivable surface. There were two more bodies upstairs so, with a sigh, Charlie started the ascent, feeling every second of his forty-five years.

This is not why I became a police officer, he thought. *This is not why I became a detective sergeant.* Charlie had been to many crime scenes in his career, seen many murder scenes, but none like this.

Danni trudged up the stairs behind him, babbling away. She was ten years younger, and two years on the team had not dampened her enthusiasm. It was all crap, so he tuned her out.

He pushed open the door to the first bedroom. The techs had not been in there yet. He leaned in from the doorway and shook his head at the sight. Here, too, blood covered everything. It even dripped from the ceiling. Nine pints in a human woman on average. Nearly five litres: enough to paint a room that size, and it looked like someone had given it a good go.

Danni touched his arm, and he jumped.

"Sorry Charlie," she said and smiled at him. Her face lit up with the smile, despite the surroundings. Condescending or genuine? He never could tell. Probably why his wife was moving out.

"This is bad." His turn for massive understatement.

"Yeah, don't go in the bathroom. The kid in there was taking a dump when he got got."

And that was it. Why did she insist on talking like a bad American TV show? She had a Home Counties accent and sounded ridiculous.

"Great."

"Whoever did this, took the head off, and threw it into the loo." She sighed, bewilderment writ large across her face. "So, is this a nutjob? Ex-boyfriend? Serial killer?" She paused, tilting her head to the side in that alluring manner of hers.

Charlie thought back to all the other murders he'd ever investigated. The sheer devastation in the house and the amount of blood was incredible. He always found it hard to believe any human capable of such rage, but his years on the force had only highlighted just how crazy people were.

"No," Charlie said. "This is something else. Something new."

12:02 AM

Kennedy watched the humans from the end of the road. So many bright lights: so beautiful. He wanted to study them, perhaps take some back to Father as a souvenir. He dismissed the idea - too many people. Father might not be happy if *they* found out about them now, not after so long in hiding.

Father would ask about the lights, and then Kennedy would have to tell him where he saw them. Explain why the humans had vehicles with lights. That would mean revealing he had eaten again, and Father would not be so forgiving this time.

With huge reluctance, he turned away and slunk into darkness.

12:15 AM

Danni peeled off the overalls, revealing a smart trouser suit, and was given a mug of coffee by a uniform. The fresh air in the street outside the house was a welcome relief from the stench in the house.

"Cheers," she said, earning herself a smile. Charlie took a cup from the man without a word. *Why is he so miserable?* Danni shook her head slightly and caught Charlie looking at her. He turned away to avoid eye contact. "What's our next move?" she asked, more out of a desire to break the silence than necessity. Charlie was a hard man to get a conversation out of at the best of times.

"Usual," he shrugged. "Back to the office. Cross reference the MO, check what flags up here or abroad. Work the neighbours, see if anyone saw anything." He sipped his coffee and pointed at the houses. "This is a decent part of town; we shouldn't get the usual stonewall."

Danni nodded. The uniforms were already knocking on doors and getting sworn at by tired people. The commotion had woken some; the rest were soon awake with the noise and lights.

The press would be here soon, and the news full of soundbites. Statements would be logged, and Danni and Charlie would spend most of tomorrow trawling through them. A murder case like this would need a large team and by tomorrow morning, there would be at least twenty officers assigned to the case. Forensics would be on site for a lot longer tonight and tomorrow, eking every bit of evidence and DNA from the scene. In the meantime, there would be CCTV to watch.

"Ok, let's bounce," she said, silently resolving to stop watching The Wire.

01:23 AM

Mike Baxter inched closer to the edge of the warehouse roof. He felt a tug on his jeans, warning him against going any further. He ignored it, looking through the viewfinder of the video camera.

"Got you," he muttered.

"Quiet," the woman behind him whispered. "They'll hear you."

Mike resisted the urge to point out she had said more than him and turned the camera on. He focussed on the two men in the distance and started filming.

His partner, Linda Carter, tensed, and he imagined her terse lips and stern expression, due to him ignoring her. Actually, he imagined a lot more than that, but forced himself to focus on the job at hand. Below him sat a large white lorry, parked but with engine running. The driver was one of the men he was filming, but Mike wasn't interested in him.

The other man was Jason Hamilton, ex-military, now a businessman. He had his fingers in many pies, but mostly focussed on property in and around Exeter. He was a regular in the tabloid press, always stepping out with whatever pretty young thing was the flavour of the day. Hamilton's past was mostly secret, but as far as Mike had worked out, he'd been frontline in most of the conflicts of the previous decade. His largely redacted military background was not why Mike was filming him.

That reason was *in* the lorry.

People.

Hamilton was bringing them into the country illegally, and he and Linda were about to get proof. This was a story which would be worth thousands and possibly win them some awards.

He held the camera as steady as he could, despite his rising excitement, and, with his free hand, gave his partner the thumbs up. The driver was leading Hamilton to the back of the truck. Earlier, he had placed a small microphone on the wall of the warehouse. It was a white dot, about the size of a penny, and yet had a fifty-metre range. He could hear the men breathing as they opened the doors.

"This is it," Linda whispered.

Mike didn't reply as he focussed on the scene unfolding in front of him. Also, he was still annoyed she had turned him down that morning. What did she expect though, walking into his hotel room, wearing just a towel? *Seriously, talk about mixed signals.* He'd got as far as touching her arse before she slapped him. Too devoted to her dick of a husband, that was her problem. She hadn't mentioned it since, so Mike had stewed all day.

"What are you doing?"

The voice was so loud, and so close to his ears, that Mike started and nearly dropped his camera.

"Hey... hey, sweetheart, what are you doing up here?" Linda said, standing and turning in one smooth motion.

That made Mike turn. Lights dotted the roof in regular intervals, but he and Linda were in a dark zone between two sets. Ten feet away from him, bathed in a neon glow, stood a small child. He was dressed in dark clothes and looked like he could spend an hour in a shower and still not be clean. The boy's accent was weird, too posh for his appearance, as if he'd learned to talk listening to Radio 4.

The boy tilted his head towards Linda. "You are pretty."

Linda blushed, despite the strangeness of the situation. "Uh, ok," she paused, trying to gather her thoughts. Her mouth was dry. "Honey, I don't know where you came from, but there are some bad men down there and they know we're here now, so they'll be coming for us. You need to hide."

"No." The boy smiled at them both. Mike grabbed Linda's shoulder, but she shook free.

"Please, poppet-"

Screams reached them from below, then gunfire. The noise was incredible, echoing from the tall buildings surrounding them. Mike looked down into the car park and saw some men running away from the warehouse. Five of them sprinted across the car park, occasionally firing over their shoulders at something Mike couldn't see.

He turned back to the boy. "We really need to go. You coming, little man?"

Another scream pierced the air as the gunfire faded. Mike looked again and one man was on his back, wrestling with a figure. The screaming turned into a gurgle and then stopped. The figure was up and running again in seconds.

"The Scouts are with me," the boy said.

"Scouts? Here?" Mike frowned. Whatever was happening here had nothing to do with boys in short trousers and sexually dubious older men.

"Mike, I think we should go." Linda edged away from the boy. Another scream filled the air, followed by more gunfire. It sounded like a war zone, not a city in Devon.

"That's a good idea." Mike stepped backwards, keeping his eyes on the child. He didn't want to turn his back on him again.

"You can't leave," the boy said. "I want you to stay with me." He held his arms out, like he was on the cross. For the first time, Mike noticed his eyes were black pits: no white in them at all. The dark was astonishing, even against the night sky.

"What's wrong with your eyes?"

The boy's expression changed to a sly smile. "What's wrong with yours?"

"Run," Linda screamed. They turned and fled as a low buzzing filled the air. It increased in pitch and they sped up. She hadn't run that fast since school. Pressure built at the back of her head, like being deep underwater or on a plane. The edge of the warehouse roof was rapidly approaching. Static electricity crackled around them and the noise rose in pitch, like a jet engine before take-off.

"Jump!" She yelled as they ran out of roof.

They leapt off the roof and heard an explosion of compressed air behind them. The drop was nearly ten feet to the level below but seemed further. Mike landed heavily and rolled, wincing as his ankle twisted. He ended up on his back, looking at the night sky just in time to see what looked like a black line shoot overhead. It momentarily blotted out the stars as it passed over them.

"What the hell was that?"

Panting, Linda stood and watched the roof, but the boy didn't appear. "That was the scariest kid I've ever met."

"Did you see the black stuff?" Mike said.

"What black stuff?" Linda's chest felt tight, her breathing laboured.

"It was like a wall. I can't describe it, really. Just... weird."

"Mike," Linda said, and he followed her point. The boy stood on the edge of the roof, looking down at them the way a cat would a mouse.

The expression on the boy's face terrified Mike, making the hairs stand up on the back of his neck. The pain in his ankle disappeared as more adrenaline flooded his system. They turned and ran again. In front of them, a door led into the warehouse. Mike yanked it open and ran inside, not waiting to see if Linda had followed him.

Strip lighting ran the length of the hundred metre building and the harsh light momentarily blinded him. He was on a metal walkway high above pallets which lined the floor, creating corridors between them. Blinking to clear his vision, Mike ran on, heading for a door at the end of the walkway. A bang from behind him made him spin, raising the camera like a club.

"Woah," Linda said, raising her hands. "Nice to see chivalry isn't dead."

"Sorry," Mike mumbled. With the immediate danger over, he felt ashamed of his actions. Adrenaline coursed through him, making him jumpy.

"What *was* that?"

"I don't know," Mike said. "You're right, that kid was scary as hell, but I don't know why."

"Me neither, apart from he was up there at midnight and its way past his bedtime."

Mike shuddered. "Did you see his eyes? Black, no white at all."

"I kind of hoped I'd imagined that."

"Well," Mike tried to smile, but his mouth wasn't up to the task, "you didn't."

"What now?"

"We've got to get out of here. Through the door." He nodded to the end of the walkway. "We can worry about everything else in the morning."

"Yeah. Story has gone."

"I think we have a new one."

"Creepy kid out at midnight? Come on, Mike."

"What about the screaming? There are dead men out there." Mike shuddered at the memory of the scream gurgling to a stop. "What were they shooting at?"

"I don't know, but can we just get out of here?"

He couldn't argue with that. Mike jogged to the door, wincing at the sound his boots made on the metal walkway. Also, now the immediate danger had passed, adrenaline was fading and the pain in his ankle returned with a vengeance. At the door, he put his finger to his lips. Linda nodded and he opened it.

They crept forward, trying to keep sound to a minimum. Stairs led down from their position, deeper into the brightly lit stairwell. Mike led the way, trying not to show his limbs were trembling. The reality of the situation was hitting hard now that they were somewhere familiar and well lit. Who was the kid? What about the black *thing* that appeared? He thought of the cross-shape the kid had made with his arms. It hadn't looked like he was carrying anything, so had the line come out of him? However absurd the idea, Mike knew he didn't want it to touch him.

His ankle throbbed, but he forced himself to ignore it. Perhaps Linda would take care of him when they returned to the hotel. That brought a brief smile to his lips. He would be in the bath, foot raised, she would walk in, bringing him a beer, slipping her dressing gown off-

"Mike!"

Her whispered call broke his reverie. A man sat on the floor at the bottom of the stairwell. His shirt was dark with blood and an assault rifle lay across his legs. He was staring, slack jawed, at the door which led to the rest of the warehouse.

Jason Hamilton.

"Is he-" Linda stopped as Hamilton looked up at them. His eyes were half closed, and his breathing ragged. He chuckled as they got closer.

"Why am I not surprised to see you two?" Weariness tinged his deep voice.

"What's going on?" Linda asked. "Who attacked you?"

Hamilton shook his head but didn't answer.

"Was it those on the lorry? Who've you brought in?"

Hamilton gazed at her, raising one eyebrow.

"We know what you're doing. All the people you smuggle in. The refugees you ship out to slavery farms up North." She put her hands on her hips.

"Probably not a great idea to tell him everything, seeing as he has a gun," Mike muttered.

"You're going to prison for a long time, you bastard," Linda said.

Hamilton laughed, blood trickling out of his mouth as he did so.

"Somebody fought back, didn't they?"

"Believe what you want. No-one is getting out of here tonight."

"What?" Mike said, wincing at just how high-pitched it had come out.

"I'm not stupid, Hamilton."

"Thing that attacked us, not human." Hamilton's panting was getting worse.

"You bring these people into the country and you don't think they're human? You're a bigger scumbag than I thought," Linda snarled.

"Christ, I'm going to die surrounded by idiots."

"Did you smuggle kids in?" Mike asked.

Hamilton shifted his gaze to Mike and shook his head. "He was waiting for us. This kid. With the thing with the teeth and the-".

He groaned, clutching his side as the words died on his lips. After a few moments of groaning and coughing, Hamilton continued. "The kid, he fired something at Smithy. Like nothing I've ever seen."

"A boy killed your man?"

"No, he obliterated him. Nothing left at all, not even a pile of ashes. This black stuff came out of the child, then bam, no more Smithy."

Linda looked at Mike, a frown on her face. She remembered what Mike had said about the boy.

"The kid was really pleased with himself." Hamilton gasped again, his face contorting with pain. "Then he looked up at the roof and ran away."

"The kid heard us," Mike whispered.

"More of them came, the things with the tails."

"Tails?" Linda laughed.

"Don't go near them. Dangerous," Hamilton said.

"How many are out there?" Linda nodded at the door. Things with tails? Pain had made him delirious, surely?

"Don't know. Shot one with all the teeth. He went down. Not before he did all this." Hamilton waved a hand over his own torso and winced.

"Can you walk?"

"What?" Mike said.

"We're not leaving him." Linda crossed her arms, her lips a thin line. "He comes with us."

"No way."

"We can't leave him here," she said.

"Why the fuck not?"

"This scumbag needs to do some serious time."

Hamilton chuckled. "Your man is right."

"He's not my man."

Mike wanted to crawl back into the shadows at those words. He felt his face flush hot with embarrassment and turned his head away from her.

"Look at me. Too much blood. I'm not making it through the night."

"So we get you to a hospital."

"Not in time."

"We're not leaving you," Linda said. "You have to pay for what you've done. You're not dying, anyway, this is a scam."

Hamilton laughed again and winced. "I fucking wish, princess."

"Come on, I'll help you up."

"Linda, I really don't think this is a good idea."

"I'm not leaving him, Mike. He faces justice for the shit he's done. End of."

Linda took the gun from Hamilton, who looked anxious as she reached for it, but then relented as she passed it to Mike. Up close, she could see how pale he was, and just how much blood was pooled on the floor around him. *Maybe it's not a scam.*

"I've never fired a gun in my life," Mike said.

"It's dead easy. Point it where the bad guys are, pull the trigger," Hamilton said. Blood seeped through his fingers where he clutched his side and his breathing had developed a wet crackling that really didn't sound good to Mike. Hamilton leant on Linda, but he was too heavy for her and they made slow progress along the corridor.

"You're the bad guy," Mike said.

Hamilton grunted. "Not tonight, Baxter, not tonight."

"You know who I am?"

"I know both of you. You're not subtle in following me. You stand out like James Bond." He looked at Linda, who was the same height as him, although their builds were very different. "Listen, if this goes bad, if they're still out there, leave me or they'll get you too."

"Who are *they*?"

"No clue, Baxter, no clue." Hamilton paused. "The kid, though, keep an eye out for the kid – he's the worst."

"Why don't we hide and call the police?" Mike said. Worry gnawed away at his stomach, making him feel nauseous. *Why the hell are we bringing this guy with us?* "That makes much more sense than dragging his sorry arse out through a warehouse filled with things that are trying to kill us."

"He'll bleed out before they get here."

"The cops won't get here for hours. That's why we chose this place."

"Bullshit," Mike said. "There's nowhere in Exeter that's hours away from the police."

Hamilton laughed. "You pay them what we do, there is."

Mike shared an uneasy look with Linda. Part of him wished he had the statement on camera.

Linda fished her phone out of her pocket and dialled 999. She lowered Hamilton to the floor, and he leaned against the wall, breathing hard. Mike ignored her conversation and opened the door a fraction. He peered through the crack into the gloom of the warehouse. He saw piles of boxes, riding high on pallets stacked up to the ceiling far above them. A light flickered in the distance, creating a near strobe effect inside. Ahead of him, pallets formed a passage, stretching halfway into the huge room and ending under the flickering light. More man-made corridors ran parallel to that one, and most were shrouded in almost complete darkness. Many of the lights were not working, their bulbs probably smashed by gunfire. Beyond the lines of pallets, the space opened into the loading area for lorries. This was blocked from outside by large doors, but he could see one was open. An exit.

"Police are on their way," Linda whispered in his ear.

"Your husband?"

"He's back home. I should call him."

"Don't," Mike said, and instantly regretted how quickly the word came out. "Do you want him charging down here? There could be anything out there."

A roar drowned out Linda's answer: a blood-curdling screech reverberating around the stairwell.

"We need to go," Mike said far more calmly than he felt. His legs were shaking, and he hoped Linda wouldn't notice. He ran back to Hamilton and pulled him to his feet. Hamilton grunted and held his stomach. He was very pale, and his blood-soaked shirt stuck to him.

"Hurry," Hamilton gasped. The noise had changed his mind about being left behind.

Linda yanked the door to the warehouse open and stepped into the dimly lit space. It was cold and she started shivering. She turned back to Mike, beckoning him forward.

Mike slipped Hamilton's arm around her shoulder, but then he faced the stairwell, taking a couple of steps towards it. He could hear footsteps – heavy footsteps. The sound of something *big* rapidly approaching. Sweat broke out on his forehead as he lifted the rifle, aiming towards the noise.

Linda's cry made him turn back to her.

"He's too heavy," she whispered. Sweat glistened on her brow, clear even in the gloom. Mike rushed forward and caught Hamilton's other arm. They moved forward again, still too slow to get away.

Boxes exploded next to them and a shape barrelled into them. Linda stumbled forward, yelling as she fell, but Hamilton took the full force of the blow. He howled and thumped into Mike. They tumbled into the boxes piled on the pallets. Mike rolled clear and got to his feet. His mind couldn't quite process what was in front of him.

The shape was a man, but a grotesque one. Scars criss-crossed his face, and his long hair seemed to start halfway across the top of his head. Two ears, both slightly pointed, sat flat against the skull and he had no nose, just two slits in the skin. He was snarling at Hamilton, displaying a row of razor-sharp teeth. He was wearing an old overcoat, battered and filthy, and a pair of jeans.

As Mike watched, he heard a ripping sound and saw the back of the coat tear open exposing a long tail topped with an enormous ball of spikes. The tail rose in the air, the end swaying slightly, and Mike thought of a scorpion about to strike.

A tail. The thing had a *tail*.

"What the-"

The tail swung towards him and he jumped out of reach, screaming in surprise.

"The gun!" Linda shouted.

Mike looked dumbly at the weapon in his hand and raised it. The tail swung towards him again, but he was still beyond its arc. As the ball swept past him, he could see blood splattered over its end. Hamilton was no longer screaming, head reduced to a bloody pulp. The man – no, not a man, the *thing* – turned to Mike and roared.

He pulled the trigger, making it scream as the bullets tore into its flesh. Red blood spattered the floor behind it, and it fell backwards, landing in a heap next to Hamilton's corpse. The barrel of the gun rose as Mike continued to shoot, bullets spraying into the air. Silence descended as soon as he stopped.

"What the hell is that?" Linda said. She stood, holding onto a pile of boxes and looking at the creature. Mike shook his head.

"I've never seen anything like it."

Linda went to take a step forward but thought better of it. "We should go. What if there are more of them?"

Mike looked around the vast space inside the warehouse. Darkness seeped from the corners like a disease. He swallowed bile. The air was full of an acrid, sour smell, and he gagged.

Linda glanced at Hamilton and gasped. She'd seen bodies before: junkies with needles still in their arms, people mangled in car wrecks, murder victims and old people, alone, surrounded by ready meal boxes. Nothing could have prepared her for this. His head was a mess: blood, bone and brains where his face should have been. In life, he had been a despicable man, but she'd wanted him in prison, not dead. *No-one should die like that*, she thought.

"Do you think it was the thing we heard on the stairs?"

She shook her head. "That was behind us. This came from in front."

"What the hell are these things? Some experiment gone wrong?"

"I don't care, Mike. I don't care. Can we please just get out of here?"

He nodded and looked at the gun in his hands, wondering how many bullets he had left and wishing there was a counter or something on it like in a video game. He could eject the magazine and count, but the thought of having a gun with no bullets, even for a second terrified him.

They crept down the corridor of pallets, crouched over, single file, Mike in front. Linda kept looking back over her shoulder, but nothing stirred behind them. She was half expecting the monster to jump up and chase them, but the shape didn't move and was soon swallowed by shadows.

They reached the end of the pallets and stopped, surveying the area ahead of them. This was the loading area: a wide-open space where goods would be stored before loading onto lorries; five large doors marked with sequential numbers stood about thirty metres away. The sixth door was open - the one he'd seen earlier; more pallets stacked single height in marked bays and an abandoned pallet truck lay across one bay. Two bodies lay on the floor, neither moving. One had no head and the other had its abdomen ripped open, with guts smeared around the corpse. Linda turned and threw up on the nearest pallet. Vomit splashed on her shoes, but it was the least of her worries.

"Ok, let's go," Mike said, his voice seeming loud in the stillness, even though he had whispered.

They ran across the large space, heading for the open door. Another roar rang out, and Linda cried out involuntarily. The noise spoke to a primal part of her brain, but her legs would not make her run as fast as her head wanted. She stumbled and fell.

Mike turned to help her and dragged her to her feet. He didn't look at her, more through and behind her. His face was pale, sweat glistening on his forehead.

"Don't turn around," he pleaded. "Run, just *run*."

This last word he shouted, and they both sprinted for the door. There was a drop outside the exit – only a few feet, the height of the tailgate for a lorry, and they jumped to the ground. Mike winced as the pain in his ankle flared again, but neither paused. The chilly night air was welcoming after the oppressive atmosphere inside.

Mike risked a glance back, and whatever he saw was enough to increase his pace. "Move!"

Another sound – more familiar and comforting – rose over their panting and footfalls: police sirens. At the far end of the warehouse grounds, two police cars sped into view. Behind them came a large van. All three vehicles screeched to a halt and officers jumped out. The back of the van opened and more police in combat armour streamed into the grounds.

"Armed police!"

"Police!"

"Do not move!"

"Turn around!"

"Hands where we can see them!"

Mike and Linda stopped running, Linda collapsing to the floor, sobbing. Her lungs were screaming for air and she alternated between sobs and gulps of air. Mike dropped the gun and put his hands up. An officer walked slowly towards him in a large circle, keeping the area free for his colleagues to shoot.

"Inside," Mike gasped. "Behind us."

He pointed and saw - just for a moment - silhouettes in the bay door. None of the police listened to him.

"On your knees," the policeman said.

"Please, the warehouse!" Mike heard the pleading in his own voice, the desperation and the terror. "We have to leave."

"On your knees." This time it wasn't a request.

Mike sank to his knees and heard the man unclip his handcuffs. He looked back, and the shapes had gone. He scanned the area with wild eyes, but nothing was moving. Mike relaxed, even as the handcuffs clicked into place around his wrists.

As the police escorted him to the car, he caught Linda's grim expression and tried to smile. She looked exhausted, but also relieved. They were safe, for the moment, anyway. But Mike still had a knot of anxiety in his stomach. He knew what he'd seen: four shapes in the open bay. Three tall, with tails waving behind them and one small, like a boy, out far too late at night and with things that shouldn't exist.

02:44 A.M

Kennedy heard raised voices and paused en route to the control room. He glanced to the right, where the pods lay expectant, waiting to release their precious cargo. Excitement coursed through his veins and it wasn't only the thrill of killing humans earlier. Something just felt right about tonight, and he couldn't wait to tell Father about it. All the other times he had gone out scouting only to find something wrong. Not enough people, or too underfed, or too dirty to sustain them all. Now even the air smelt good: thick with pheromones. Oh, the pheromones. The women earlier did not need to wear clothes (although those they did were scant enough) to broadcast their appeal; it was obvious. He turned left, toward the voices.

Father would be pleased.

Patience had been Kennedy's friend and curse through the centuries. Each time, Father summoned him and sent him to scout, he had departed from his brothers without complaint. Each time, he returned disappointed and frustrated. Each time, Father had been angry, as if the humans' lack of progress was Kennedy's fault.

He took a deep breath, remembering the scent of the girl on the bed, and entered the room.

Father sat at the main panel as always. The chair was moulded to his frame, making him look regal. His hair glistened in the bright lights, and his dark eyes reflected the colours of the panel. In front of him stood three Scouts, revived just yesterday: Callaghan, Brown and Baldwin. One of the Princes stood next to them, but given they both looked identical, Kennedy did not know which it was.

"Kennedy," Father said, his voice silky smooth and full of love. "Welcome back, First of my Scouts. Report."

"What is this?" Kennedy glared at the other Scouts, wondering which of them had dared raise his voice to Father.

Father silenced him with a look. "Report," he repeated.

Kennedy held his stare at the others for a moment, but then bowed his head. "The humans have expanded. We can claim territory that should be ours. They are ready."

"No."

Kennedy recoiled at the word. He was confused: as the First Scout he had been out, seen what the people had done. Why was Father not listening? Compared to him, the other scouts were dumb brutes whose purpose was to protect Father and the Princes.

"The humans have the means to fight back. These three lost Major."

"How?" Kennedy looked at the three warriors, disgust on his face. He realised there was a corpse on the floor. Major. The body had holes in his carcass and much of his head was missing. *What has happened? Where did you go?* He kept the thought to himself. Father was angry – no point in bringing the wrath onto himself.

"They have weapons," Brown said. "A tube which fires projectiles so fast it cuts our skin. One human used it on Major."

"Guns," Kennedy said. "I have seen these before, but they are weak. They should not pierce our hides."

"Major would disagree with you." Father stood, filling the space with his frame despite being shorter than Kennedy. "It would seem the humans have become more powerful since you last woke." Kennedy shrank from his gaze.

"They have advanced quickly if their guns can hurt us," Kennedy said.

"Yes, and we have underestimated their capacity for progress. Nevertheless, they must pay for Major's death."

"Father, the humans are now more numerous. The ones I scouted are fit and healthy. It is time."

"Not yet. We need to know more about these," Father paused, seeming to roll the words around his mind before speaking, "-guns. Kennedy, my sons persuaded their Scouts to escort them outside." He glared at the Prince, but it was with a mixture of pride and anger. "They should not have done, and the Scouts should not have let them."

Kennedy nodded and the others all looked at the floor. It hurt him to hear them called Scouts. Only the Prince dared look at his father, the child's black eyes as barren of emotion as the rest of him.

"Kennedy, there were some who saw tonight. People who eluded us." Father glanced at the others and they shuffled together: safety in numbers. "Find them and stop them from talking."

"Yes, Father."

"The humans will know of our existence soon enough."

Kennedy nodded. "This is our time Father." He didn't mention how tasty the woman had been: it wouldn't be a good idea to let Father know he had broken the secrecy law again.

"Yes, but we must be cautious. Find the people and silence them."

"Yes, Father."

"Take these three with you. They need to atone for their failure." Father paused and looked at the Prince. "No, my son, you stay here."

For a moment, it looked as if the Prince was about to complain, but Father's stern expression dissuaded him.

"Go now, Kennedy. Let us see what we are dealing with."

Kennedy nodded and left the control room. He was halfway down the corridor before he slowed and faced the others. They were walking behind him, dragging their feet. He hissed at them.

"Do not slow me down. Keep up."

Callahan hissed back, then stood to one side. The Prince moved forward, his diminutive frame somehow filling the gap.

"You will take me with you, Kennedy."

"Father said no."

"I said yes." The boy regarded him with his pitch-black eyes, and Kennedy felt his resolve crumbling. "My brother is Outside, with Heath. I need him."

"I cannot promise you will be safe, my Prince."

"You need not worry about me, Kennedy, I can take care of myself."

The three Scouts looked as uncomfortable as Kennedy, but they were all looking at the ground. Cowards. Kennedy nodded. "Try to keep up, my Prince. We have a long way to go."

02:46 A.M

BUZZ. BUZZ. BUZZ.

John Carter sat up swearing and grabbed his phone. Sleep clung to him like the duvet he was wrapped in. He shook his head to try to clear it and force the grogginess from his mind as he unlocked the handset. Anger subsided with reluctance – he was not on call today and had hoped for an uninterrupted night's sleep.

Thirteen missed calls. One call from Linda, twelve from an unknown number. How had he slept through that?

He swore again and dialled voicemail. He couldn't quite believe what he was hearing, so replayed the message.

"John, oh God, John. It's horrible. I'm in custody, but I don't think they've arrested me. There was a boy and a man with a tail, oh Christ, oh shit, a man with a tail and he was eating him and Mike shot him and-"

The message cut off. Carter looked at his phone in disbelief, then brought the call log back up. The unknown number was still there. He rubbed his eyes, still waking up, then pressed the number.

"If there is an emergency or your life is in danger, please hang up and dial 999. Exeter Police Station is currently closed. To speak with an officer, please call back tomorrow between the hours of 8 a.m. and 6 p.m." The message repeated, so he hung up.

If he set off now, he could be in Exeter in under three hours; traffic would be light, if non-existent at this time in the morning. Even thinking about those miles left him cold. His duvet was too warm, too comfortable, too inviting. Linda had been arrested before, so he wasn't too worried despite the tone of the message. Grumbling to himself, Carter went for a shower.

Work could wait whilst he sorted this out. The only proper job he had on at the moment concerned a young kid called Stephen Keeler. He was only sixteen years old and someone had put him in the hospital. Potential brain damage, although it was too early for the doctors to be sure, so it was only GBH for now. Someone would do time for it. *Racist hate crime was alive and well in the city*, he thought as he turned the shower on. It might not be as simple as that however, given Keeler's brother was in charge – allegedly – of the biggest gang in Greenwich. They would build a case with care. Any witnesses would be reluctant to talk to the police, and so Carter's job would be difficult. Just another day as part of the Youth Offending Team for South London.

As the spray worked its magic in waking him up, he ran the phone message through his head. Linda had gone to Exeter chasing some info and some rich bloke who, allegedly, was involved in something shady. People trafficking, she'd said. Now she was babbling about a kid with a tail - or was it a kid and a man with a tail? A tail. He must have misheard it. Must have been jail. A kid and a man in jail. The knot of anxiety in his stomach eased as he turned the shower off. For a moment there, he thought his wife had lost it.

05:03 AM

Paul Kingston couldn't sleep. Part of it was the blow still in his system, and part of it was the blow he'd just received. He brushed aside guilt – shame might be a better word - and scratched his arse as he looked out over the city. He could see the Cathedral and the streets surrounding it, and beyond, the unfamiliar suburbs which surrounded Exeter.

He had no plans to return to London any time soon.

First, he was sure Hamilton would look for him as soon as he discovered what Kingston had done. He was a nasty one, without a doubt. Kingston didn't think Hamilton would need the two million he was now lighter, but Kingston had always been cautious: why risk finding out Hamilton *did* mind and wanted a few fingers from Kingston as payback? Or even Kingston's head on a stick?

The two million was Kingston's way out. A better life.

Second, the rest of the Scorpions would probably object to Kingston legging it. They also weren't known for their patience and understanding. Kingston should know; he'd been one of their leaders for far too long.

He scratched at the scorpion tattoo on the back of his hand. Once a badge of honour, now an irritation. As a younger man— well *boy*, really—as he was only seventeen now, he had been so proud to be part of the gang. When it had been just a few of them, shaking down the people in Greenwich, it had been fun.

It had also been a long time ago.

Now, the Scorpions were one of the largest gangs in London, not just Greenwich. They had members whose names he didn't even know. How can you keep things under control when you can't even name those who worked for you? Any one of them could be a snitch and then what? Kingston did not want to spend his days in jail, no thank you.

So, when Hamilton had given him a case to look after, it had been a simple decision for Kingston to take it for himself. The case had been payment to the Scorpions for running interference whilst Hamilton brought his stuff in. The Scorpions had distracted the police earlier - muggings, robbery, setting up some County lines runners, a couple of cases of arson, that kind of thing, all so Hamilton could wheel his big lorries full of people in.

Kingston didn't have many morals, but he drew the line at slave trading.

It had been easy to run whilst the Scorpions and Hamilton were busy. He hadn't thought about it or planned it, just acted. Of course, the thing with Keeler had played its part. He needed to get away, but no-one would even suspect anything for at least a day, by which time he would be gone.

The Scorpions were already travelling back home, their work in Exeter done. Muggings and arson had proved relatively easy to pull off, especially as they'd only be in the city for about six hours.

Very low risk of getting caught and it would tie the police in knots for hours if not days.

Kingston had the easiest job of all: collect the money from Hamilton. Not Hamilton himself, that would be stupid. Kingston had waited in a café near the station for an hour before Hamilton's goons showed up.

One suitcase. Two million quid.

Too tempting, and the time was right.

The hotel room had only been a couple of hundred, and the prossies had been a couple of hundred more each. But Christ, they had been worth it. They were asleep now, taking up far too much space in the bed. He glanced at them and felt a familiar tug from his groin. Money really did buy you happiness, even if it was two hookers who would literally do anything you asked. Of course, they couldn't do anything about the nausea in his stomach. The nausea he used to get, years back, when he let people down.

He turned back to the view. The sun was just beginning to come up, making the sky a pale, almost white-blue right then. The city had yet to get going, but he spied some movement on the streets below. It looked beautiful, the sort of place he would happily settle down, although there were other, better, cities to hide in. All he needed was a fake passport, and he already had plans in place to get one of those.

Kingston stretched, feeling the bones in his back click. He turned back to the bed. Might as well get his money's worth; perhaps it would ease the guilt.

6:02 AM

Danni awoke with a start. She glared at her computer screen with bleary eyes. Something steamed in front of it, smelling so good it consumed her. A cup of coffee.

Charlie smirked at her. "Don't let the boss catch you asleep at your desk."

"Thanks man." She yawned and felt like she would never stop. "Surveillance films are so dull."

"Nothing then?"

She shook her head. "That street doesn't have any CCTV apart from a couple of traffic cams. Whoever did this didn't turn up on one."

"So he knew where they were?"

"Possibly." She shrugged. "He might have walked there and not been captured. It's possible."

Charlie's face told her exactly what he thought of that.

"It *is*," she said.

"Not likely, though." Charlie sipped his own coffee. "Did you look at neighbouring streets?"

"This isn't my first rodeo, Charlie." She bit her lip. Why was she being harsh to him? Must be tired.

"Nothing?"

"Nothing," she said.

"Well, that *is* impossible." Charlie blew on his coffee, like he'd already forgotten it was drinking temperature.

"Yeah, it's like he came out of thin air or something."

"Keep looking, perhaps you missed something."

"Must have done," she said, although her expression matched Charlie's from moments before. "What are you doing?"

"Have you heard about the warehouse thing?"

"No."

"One of Jason Hamilton's warehouses is being secured as a crime scene. At least four corpses."

"Hamilton?" Danni said. "The property dude?"

"One and the same. He also does importing, electronics from Korea, that sort of thing."

"I did not know that."

"Guess he keeps it quiet. Doesn't fit the image of the property magnate, does it?" Charlie stood, grabbing a set of keys from his desk. "Boss wants someone to give the scene another look as it's unusual."

"Unusual? How?"

"He just said for us to go."

"Us? Charlie, I'm rammed as it is."

"We all are," Charlie said. "The uniforms are busy on a string of muggings yesterday. We had an enormous bunch of burglaries, and someone firebombed a few shops on the outskirts."

"Related?"

"Nah."

Danni agreed. Nobody upgraded from robbery to murder in

one day unless the robbery went wrong. This – whatever *this* might be – was definitely not a bungled robbery.

The phone on his desk started ringing. Charlie ignored it; whatever it was, would wait. Instead he said, "But, well, at least one corpse has been eaten."

Danni was out of her chair and on her way to the elevator before he finished the sentence.

6:03 AM

Carter stood at the desk, waiting patiently whilst the duty sergeant verified his identity. The woman tapped away on her keyboard.

"Mr. Carter, I can't see how you have any reason to be here. Your wife has not been charged."

"Charged? She better not be, unless she was holding a gun when you found her. My wife-"

"I cannot discuss this case with you, as you well know. I can tell you your wife and her accomplice were armed." The woman smiled at him without humour. "Obviously I am only telling you as a courtesy."

He drummed his fingers on the desk. Worry gnawed at him. What exactly had Linda stumbled into? A face from his past came to mind, someone he hadn't thought about in a while. "Hey, does Charlie Monroe still work here?"

"Yes, Detective Sergeant Monroe does."

"Please ring him. We go way back."

"One moment, Mr. Carter." She dialled, with an expression

more suited to chewing wasps, waited for a while and then hung up. "No answer."

"Ok, so who oversees the investigation? Can I speak with them?"

More tapping on the keyboard.

"Charlie, I mean DS Monroe is lead investigator, for now." The 'for now' told Carter the case was growing by the minute. Murder squad would be on their way, if not already here. Charlie's involvement would last another couple of hours, tops.

"So where is he?"

"I can't answer that. He's not at his desk. You can wait or you can go, and I'll tell him you are expecting him to call. We have had a very busy twenty-four hours, so I don't know when that would be."

Carter left without another word. He couldn't be angry with the woman; she was only doing her job. However, Linda dominated his thoughts. She – or that tool Mike – caught with a gun next to some corpses.

That was not good.

A car eased out of the parking lot in front of him, and he spotted Charlie Monroe behind the wheel. He concentrated on the conversation with the woman next to him and didn't see Carter. He'd put on some weight – a lot actually, since Carter had last seen him, and he hadn't exactly been svelte to begin with. Charlie pulled into the street and followed a sign reading *Marsh Barton*. Without thinking, Carter ran to his own car and followed.

6:15 A.M

Kingston left the two prostitutes with a tip they'd earned and instructions to be out of the room by ten. Given he'd paid for the room with a fake credit card, he didn't care if they overstayed their welcome or stole everything not tied down.

He climbed on a motorbike and gunned the engine. The roar appealed to him on a primal level. It was a beast of a bike and whilst the rental cost a fortune – or at least it would have if he'd used genuine ID – he would be sorry to give it back later. For now, he enjoyed blasting through the traffic, weaving in and out as he made his way across town.

This was the riskiest part of his plan. In the superb of Exeter called Heavitree, lived a man who could give him a new identity. Richard Blainey, computer whizz, clever bloke but a complete psycho. He'd left London to 'clear his head' months ago. As far as Kingston knew, he'd failed. He was an addict on just about anything you could become addicted to: smoking, drinking, gambling, drugs. Blainey had the info on Kingston already, so he just had to print it.

He crossed the city using the back streets – not that anyone would recognise the bike, or him in the helmet, but Kingston was always cautious – and soon arrived in Heavitree. He navigated the side streets with ease and stopped outside a large redbrick building. Nothing seemed out of place. No big transit vans full of police or worse.

Kingston sat on the bike, watching the street for another few minutes before finally approaching Blainey's flat. He pressed the button for the ground floor and waited for the intercom to buzz. When it did, Blainey's voice came through, groggy with sleep and anger.

"Do you know the time?"

"Yo, time for pizza, dude. You called it."

Another buzz as the door clicked open. Kingston entered a short hallway. Stairs led up in front of him to a landing bathed in the early morning sunlight. Another flight would lead up from there, but Blainey lived on the ground floor behind a thick, battered door. The door swung open and Blainey gestured him in, turning his back immediately. His dressing gown spun open as he turned, revealing his pock-marked bottom and skinny legs. Red welts covered his skin, and track marks were visible on his thighs.

"Using again, huh?"

"What do you care?"

Fair point, Kingston thought, but he said nothing. He followed Blainey into his flat, which was far neater than the appearance of its owner would suggest. The door opened directly into the open plan living room, and there was a small kitchen at the rear. Two doors led off this, both on the left-hand side, one to the bathroom and the other to Blainey's bedroom. Both doors were shut, but Kingston knew the flat well from previous visits. Spotlights were imbedded in the ceiling also, and Blainey asked his computer to turn the lights down. They dimmed, and he pulled the two heavy curtains apart, letting sunlight stream into the room.

"You got my stuff?" Kingston asked as Blainey sat on the only sofa in the room.

Something felt off.

"Of course," Blainey said with a sniff. His hand was shaking and beads of sweat dotted his forehead. "Got your message, so it's ready to go."

Blainey didn't move.

"Well, I didn't come here for a chat. Where is it?"

Blainey waved a hand at the desk housing the computer. "Over there, man."

Kingston looked at the desk and then back at Blainey, anger and frustration building. Didn't he realise how urgent this was?

"Well, it's not going to get itself now is it?"

Blainey didn't move. His eyes were half closed even as he rolled a large spliff. "Relax, man. You want some?"

Kingston didn't waste his breath replying. Instead, he swatted the drugs out of Blainey's hand. Before he could protest, Kingston had dragged him off the sofa.

"Get your hands-"

"Just get my passport, now, before I kick your ass."

Blainey held up his hands to say 'ok, ok' and then shambled over to his desk. He rummaged in a drawer and pulled out a zip-lock bag. Kingston could see the passport and driving licence and relaxed.

As soon as he handed over the bag, Blainey resumed rolling his spliff. "Hey, some guy was asking about you the other day." He frowned. "No, yesterday. Man, my memory." He shook his head but continued to skin up.

"What guy?"

"Don't know. Said he worked for Hamilton, whoever the hell he is."

Kingston felt his legs go cold, but he tried to not show it. "Yeah? What did you say?"

"The truth, man. Told him I ain't seen you in months." Blainey smiled. "You owe me, I reckon."

Kingston nodded. "That I do. Maybe it's time to quit that crap, huh?"

"Tomorrow. Today is too early, man."

Kingston left him to his drugs.

6:55 AM

Danni was out of the car before it had fully stopped.

"Get rid of them!" She roared at some uniformed officers, pointing at a crowd of people pressing against the police cordon barrier.

"Press," Charlie said. "How do they get here so fast?"

"God knows, but we don't want panic now, do we?"

"That's a bit strong isn't it? We have two murder scenes, which might be more than we usually get, but it's nothing we can't cope with."

Danni kept her counsel as they walked across the tarmac towards the warehouse. Several forensic staff went about their business, carrying samples in sealed bags, dusting parts of the door down and looking grim. Or at least, more grim than usual. Danni had never understood the drive to be a forensics expert. For a start, it looked like the most tedious job in the world. And secondly, all they ever did was mop up. Where was the thrill of the chase?

She flashed her badge at one forensic, but he didn't say a word, just pointed into the building. Charlie and Danni each quickly pulled a white over-suit on, covered their shoes, then entered the warehouse.

It was a few degrees cooler inside and Danni shivered as goosebumps broke out along her arms. There were also fewer people here: just two, photographing a body. Danni blinked as her eyes adjusted to the gloom: a stark contrast to the early sunshine outside. A sudden flash of light made her blink again as the forensic team carried on photographing the corpse.

It was a man, but only just. A ruined head, with most of his face caved in, made him unrecognisable. He was open from the base of his rib cage to his pelvis and most of his insides were missing. No intestines spilling over the floor, no pulp of stomach or liver poking through the hole.

"Christ," she said.

"Yes, quite." This came from the forensic who didn't have a camera. "We have an ID though. Just found his wallet."

Another flash blinded them as the cameraman took another photo. How many did they need?

"Who is it then?" Danni asked.

"Jason Hamilton or Clive Bale, depending on which of these two you believe." He held up two driving licences, then waved the Bale one at Danni. "This was in a zipped-up pocket, so I guess we're looking at Jason Hamilton."

"Hamilton" Danni said. "Is this his warehouse? Has anyone checked yet?"

The forensic man shrugged: don't know, don't care.

"So, where his insides at? Have you lot taken them?" Danni asked.

"Nope. Everything is exactly as we found it."

"So where are they?"

The forensic pointed at the jagged edges surrounding the

wound in Hamilton's stomach. "This is far too rough to be a knife. See how it looks torn? That's consistent with a bite – maybe a serrated knife, maybe not – but more likely a bite."

"So someone's eaten him?" Charlie said.

"It's too early to say for sure, but yes, it looks like it. Also, if you look at the spray of blood here and here," he pointed at the boxes next to them, "I'd say it was postmortem."

Charlie and Danni exchanged uneasy glances.

"Look, I've done loads of scenes in my time, but nothing like this," the forensic guy said. His partner nodded in agreement. "But you two, neither of you look at all phased. Everyone else has lost their breakfast. What's going on?"

"I wish I knew," Charlie muttered.

7:03 AM

Carter flashed his badge. "Can I come through, please?" Two uniformed officers stood by the cordon, there just to deter anyone who wanted a closer look. Like Carter.

The first uniform studied his badge. "You're a long way from home, DS Carter. This isn't London."

"Come on, man, we're all job." He knew he was being too desperate, so he tried a different tack. He handed over his card. "I think it might relate to something I'm working."

The uniform barked a terse laugh. "I doubt it, mate, I really doubt it."

"Why's that?"

"It's a mess in there."

"How so?"

"Beyond my paygrade to tell you, mate." He looked around, scanning for his superiors. "I was first here, weren't I?" His colleague nodded. "First in after the others hauled that couple off."

Carter felt sick to his stomach at the thought of Mike and Linda being considered a couple.

"Look, DS Charlie Monroe is in charge of this scene, right?"

"Wrong."

"I just saw him arrive, so come on."

The uniform scowled at Carter. "You're in the youth division mate, what do you want with a murder scene? Your gangbangers up to mischief a long way from home?"

Carter pursed his lips at the man's choice of words. They weren't 'gangbangers', just kids who had no one look after them. Children of those who were barely more than that themselves. Drug addicts. Alcoholics. Gamblers or just-don't-give-a-shits. Neglectful parents came in all shapes and sizes.

"That's what I need to discuss with Charlie, I mean DS Monroe."

The uniform turned away spoke into his radio for a few minutes, covering it so Carter couldn't hear. Then: "Looks like he does know you. Through you go."

Carter nodded his thanks and entered the warehouse grounds. The tarmac stretched before him, white markings showing where lorries should park to load or unload. One lorry sat there now, large and white with the name of a haulage contractor painted in huge letters on the side. Carter strode past them, heading for the main warehouse building. As he approached, a familiar face came into view, flanked by a woman who would have been beautiful if she didn't look so pissed off.

"Charlie," Carter called, leading with his hand.

Charlie shook his hand with a grin. "John Carter, well, well. What the hell are you doing here?"

"You know me, Charlie, bimbling along. How are you? Eating well, I see," Carter grinned. "How's Jane?"

Charlie's smile slipped, just for a moment, but it was enough.

"Ahh, I'm sorry, man."

Charlie shrugged. "We've been struggling for a while, but I

think she's seeing someone she works with. Over in all but name, really."

"Shit Charlie, you never said." This came from the gorgeous woman.

Charlie shrugged again. "You never ask about her, so I didn't tell. John, this is my partner Danni Brent."

"Call me Carter, everyone does." They shook hands, but her expression didn't improve.

"So, what brings you here, Carter?" Charlie said, trying to move the subject along.

"You, actually. You're holding Linda."

"Linda? Is she the witness we have?" Charlie directed this at Danni, who looked blank.

"No clue. You dragged me away, remember?"

"What's going on, Charlie? What is this?" Carter gestured at the crime scene. More forensics were arriving now, as were more press.

"I'm not sure, to be honest."

Danni touched his arm. "You shouldn't discuss this Charlie. Come on, man, you know better."

Charlie laughed at her. "Me and Carter graduated together. He's sound."

Danni shook her head, exasperated. Charlie ignored her.

"There's a few kids at a house in town. Dead. Few bodies here, same MO. We're looking for a link."

"We're less than a mile from the nick, right? Where's the house?"

"Over on Russell Way."

Carter frowned. He had no idea where he was talking about. "When did your bodies drop?"

"Sometime around midnight."

"This is Marsh Barton, right?" Carter asked. He'd seen signs on the way in, and now they were in the middle of a huge industrial estate. Lots of car sales forecourts and the usual chain stores had given way to warehouses the further into the estate he'd gone. "How far from the house?"

"Not far," Danni said, not looking impressed. "Someone could easily get from the middle of there to out here in an hour. I reckon you could walk it. Look, we can deal with this – we don't need no hotshot murder guy from the smoke."

"I'm not with murder squad." Carter tried not to smirk at her choice of words. The smoke? *Christ*.

"So what are you?" Danni crossed her arms.

"I'm with the youth division, gangs mostly."

"Then this is slightly less than fuck all to do with you."

"Easy, Danni, he's trying to help," Charlie said, rolling his eyes.

"Really?"

"Do your bodies have evidence of trauma on them?" Carter waited for Danni to say something, but she kept her face in a scowl. "Yes? Some blood? So, you've got a person or persons crossing Exeter, through several residential streets, covered in blood but no-one called it in – not even anonymously. Really?" His mimicking of her deepened the scowl.

"No-one said they were covered in blood," Danni said.

"You didn't say they weren't either." Carter nodded at the various forensics' vans. "This many techs for a couple of bodies doesn't stack right. My wife told me someone had been eaten. You want to say more?"

Danni glanced at Charlie. "We haven't interviewed your wife yet."

"Well, is she a suspect or not?" Carter asked. "I really, really hope not."

Charlie laid a hand on Carter's shoulder. "Come on, buddy,

we've been up all night. We've got limited uniform support and this is bad. Cut us some slack."

Carter nodded. "Let me see my wife, Charlie."

"Sure," Charlie smiled at his old friend. "You want in on the interview?"

"What the hell, Charlie?" A moment ago, Carter hadn't thought it possible, but now Danni looked pissed off.

"He can be there as a support for his wife. It's not a problem, Danni."

Her face said she thought otherwise. "I'm not sure about this, Charlie. What if it involves her?"

"You think she ate someone?" Charlie somehow kept a straight face. "Come on, we're wasting time. You drive here, Carter?"

"Yeah, my car is over there." He pointed beyond the growing group of reporters.

"Ok, follow us back to the station."

7:04 A.M

Kennedy sat in the shadows of the trees at the edge of the Cathedral grounds. The building sparkled in the morning sun, although he could see a brown shimmer in the air. *They are ruining this place*, he thought. Many of these buildings had not been here the last time he visited, although the Cathedral had been. Its presence was comforting, especially given how much else had changed.

The taste of humans had not.

Small numbers of people were emerging onto the streets. Some were clad in impractical clothing which displayed a lot of flesh, and his heart raced. Some cast a glance his way but turned away just as quickly. His clothes were dirty and tightly bound rags kept his tail tied to his torso, making him look like a hunchback. He longed to free it and tear through the humans. With his tail, teeth and claws he would make quick work of them all. He forced the feeling down.

Father would not approve.

Kennedy would face the full force of Father's wrath should he kill any human other than the witnesses, especially as he had the Prince with him. It was important they found and executed the witnesses before they could speak. Afterwards, he would try to track down the other Prince, although he still had no idea how. The curiosity of children would be the end of them all.

"It is too bright," Baldwin said. He was the oldest of the other three Scouts, nearly six hundred years since his birthing. Callaghan grunted in agreement – all he ever did since Father removed his voice box for some transgression Kennedy was unaware of.

"We need to get thicker clothes," Brown said. His capacity for stating the obvious never failed to annoy Kennedy. Thicker clothes would help disguise more of their form, but nothing would stand scrutiny.

"You have the scent of the humans," the Prince said. "Why are we wasting time here? Father's instructions were to kill them."

Kennedy shook his head. Maybe the *impatience* of children would kill them all. "We must know more, my Prince." He tried to put the required amount of deference into his voice. "The humans are better than we thought."

"The humans are weak," Baldwin said.

"Tell Major."

"He was too young, too rash."

"He is younger still," Kennedy jabbed a finger at Brown. "We need to get closer, have a better idea of what we are dealing with."

Baldwin scowled, baring his teeth, but then he nodded, deferring to the older Scout.

"We can get closer." He pointed at the bracelet on his wrist. It was a source of pride as he was the only Scout allowed to wear one. Covered with ornate symbols which glowed with a faint blue light, the symbols meant nothing to Kennedy, but he knew the order in which to press them to make it work. "Come with me and try not to give in to your desires." Kennedy looked at Callaghan as he spoke. Callaghan snarled at him, and Kennedy grinned in return.

"What are we waiting for?" The Prince said.

Kennedy pulled his hood up, feeling the tightness of the over-coat over his tail. They all linked hands and Kennedy touched the bracelet.

7:05 AM

Kingston was back on the street. Half of it was bathed in the early morning sunshine, so he kept to the shady side. He walked close to the cars, using them as cover, keeping his head down. Nevertheless, he scanned the street ahead, looking for anything out of place.

The street was quiet, with no-one moving around. Kingston stopped and looked both up and down the road. Where was everybody? Surely there should be commuters leaving? *It's Sunday morning, dumbass, everyone's in bed.*

Kingston could see his bike, less than a hundred metres away, but for some reason it felt further. Blainey's comment about some guy looking for him had set his nerves on edge. Why were they looking for him? Were they already suspicious of him? That didn't make any sense – he hadn't done anything wrong. Unless Keeler had told them something.

Christ.

What to do? Go back to Blainey? He was probably already high and would be as much use as a condom in a monastery. Nope, no heading back - always move forward, just carefully.

Something hit him in the back and all the air rushed out of his lungs. He stumbled, falling to the ground, and rolling onto his back. A fat man pounced on him, raining blows on his head. Kingston raised his arms to protect his face, waiting for the bigger man to tire. He didn't have to wait long. Kingston swung his fist and caught the man on his ear. He howled in pain and Kingston punched again, this time aiming for his nose with the heel of his wrist. Cartilage crunched on contact and the fat man sat back, holding his nose as blood trickled over his lips and chin.

His ill-fitting suit jacket swung open, revealing a pistol in a holster. Kingston surged forward, pulling the weapon free and aiming it at the man.

"Don't make me shoot you," he warned.

The fat man was rolling on the ground, moaning in pain. "Due broke my dose."

It took Kingston way too long to figure out what the man was saying. *You broke my nose.* "Hamilton send you?"

Kingston scanned the street in front of him. Nobody in sight. Then, at the far end of the road, a kid and his dad strolled into view. Dammit, witnesses. They were still far enough away for Kingston to be long gone before they reached him, but he had to move quickly.

"Paul Kingston."

The voice made him turn from the nearing family. He had been distracted enough to not hear the goons approach. There were three of them, all the same build: bigger than Kingston, same general build as the fat man but lean. All three carried pistols, making no attempt to hide them.

"What are you doing to poor Greg there?"

It took him a moment to realise the fat man was, in fact, Greg. "He attacked me."

The man in the middle smiled. "Yes, he really should have tried harder, looking at the state of him. Nice to see you don't disappoint, Mr Kingston, even for one so young. Drop it please."

"Hamilton send you too?" Kingston said, trying to force bravery into his voice. He let the gun clatter to the ground. He made eye contact with each in turn: Left, Middle, Right. "Let me go. Tell Hamilton you didn't find me, and I can give you ten grand each."

Middle smiled, then laughed. "You've seen too many films." He raised his pistol. "This isn't a negotiation."

Without warning, pressure built in Kingston's ears and he clutched his head. It felt like his brain was being crushed. Left and Right were doing the same, and Middle was wincing. Kingston didn't stop to wonder what was happening. Ignoring the pounding in his head, he grabbed Middle's gun hand and spun, jabbing his elbow back into the man's face. In front of him were the father and son, but both had strange expressions on their faces. Neither looked at all concerned by the situation. The boy had his hands held out, like he was pretending to be Jesus on the cross.

Later, Kingston would not be able to describe *why* he did what he did next. He leapt forward, towards the gun and the boy, but stumbled over Greg and crashed to the ground. His cheek grazed the pavement, but his hands helped prevent further damage. The gun spilled from his grasp, landing just out of reach. Kingston rolled to a stop at the boy's feet, just in time to see a black circle form three yards away from the boy, enclosing the three of them – father, son and Kingston – in its shell.

The circle momentarily blotted out the sun, making Exeter dark for a few seconds. The pressure in Kingston's head dissipated as quickly as it had come. The father looked down at Kingston, and he then realised just how tall the man was. Kingston swallowed his fear as the man started to remove his long coat. What the hell?

A sudden scream dragged Kingston's attention to the boy. The noise was coming from his small frame as he pushed his arms out in front of him, changing the cross pose to something more like the boy was trying to push a massive crate.

The dome moved.

It pushed outwards, accelerating as it went and then it vanished as abruptly as the pressure in his head. All four of Hamilton's men had disappeared. So too had the vehicles Kingston used for cover only minutes before. A car to Kingston's left had its rear passenger doors and boot missing and one to his right had the bonnet and front missing. Walls that cut off the gardens of the wealthy suburbanites had also evaporated. Nothing was left. No dust, no corpses, no piles of rubble.

"Holy shit."

The words seemed completely underwhelming given the circumstances. A car alarm's shrill call was deafening. He turned back to the father and son. The father, well-built and so, so tall, snarled over the sound of the alarm. Kingston couldn't take in any more details about the man as his tail was swinging behind him, with a large ball of spikes at the end.

The boy, who looked normal, apart from pitch black eyes – no white at all – wailed and slapped his hands against his sides. What limited colour he had in his cheeks drained away and he stumbled and fell. The father grabbed him and cried something Kingston didn't have time to process. He was mesmerised by the tail as it swayed behind the man like a demented pendulum.

A tail. A tail. He's got a fucking tail.

Kingston shook his head, then picked up the gun and fired at the father. The bullets slammed into his body, and he released the boy, pushing him away from Kingston. Blood erupted from the big man's chest and Kingston was relieved to see it was red. The father sank to his knees, grunting in pain, then slumped to the ground.

"No!" The boy cried, standing up. He was still pale but looked a lot sturdier on his legs now.

Kingston stood on far less steady legs and fired again at the thing on the ground, until the gun clicked empty. The boy fell on the father, crying loud enough to be heard over the alarm. His cries slowed and faded in intensity until he was still. He's passed out, Kingston realised. He had no idea what he had stumbled into, but he knew one thing: it wasn't good. Kingston turned and fled, sprinting down the street until he reached his bike. His lungs were burning as he kicked the bike to life. He pulled into the street and glanced in the rear-view mirror.

The father was standing now – *How is he standing?* - holding the limp form of the boy in his arms. He started to run towards Kingston, feet slapping the concrete as he closed the gap, even though he was carrying the creepy kid. Kingston gunned the engine and pulled away, trying to put as much distance between him and the craziness of the street as possible. The creature shrank in the rear-view mirror and Kingston felt his breathing return to normal.

"My prince."

Those were the words he had heard, and for some reason that chilled him more than the fact four men had just disappeared into thin air.

7:53 AM

Carter held Linda's hand as she dried fresh tears from her eyes. He had been surprised at how rough she looked: dirty jeans, ripped shirt, eyes red rimmed and puffy from a lack of sleep and too many tears. They were in interview room Two at Exeter Police Station. Danni and Charlie sat opposite, waiting patiently for Linda to continue her incredible story.

"The man ate him," Linda said. "He ripped a chunk out of Hamilton's shoulder and ate it. That's when Mike shot him."

"This is the man with the tail, right?" Danni exchanged a look with Charlie, one Carter was all too familiar with: *Yeah right.* How many times had she sat in an interview room hearing 'it weren't me bruv'?

"I know how it sounds," Linda snapped. "Ask Mike, he'll confirm this."

"They're just doing their jobs, honey."

"They don't believe me. Do you?"

Carter didn't answer. It sounded too ridiculous, and had he

been on the other side of the desk then he would have the same expression on his face as them.

"John, do you believe me?"

"Mrs. Carter," Charlie came to his rescue. "You mentioned a child on the roof. Could you give me more details about him? Another potential witness could help refine the details of your story."

Linda squeezed Carter's hand harder. "The boy was no witness. He was part of it."

The detectives shifted in their seats and exchanged another glance.

"Mike said something came out of the boy, like a black wall or something." She tried to hold Danni's gaze, but couldn't. "Ask Mike, please, ask him."

"We will, Mrs. Carter," Charlie said, standing up. "John, you can stay here. I'll get someone to bring you a cuppa, ok?"

Carter smiled his gratitude as Charlie and Danni left, carrying their manila folders and weary expressions with them.

As soon as they left, Linda pulled away from him. "You don't believe me, do you?"

He opened his mouth to try and say something reassuring, but it was too late, the damage had already been done.

"Nobody believes me!" she shouted. "I know what I saw!"

"I'm trying, Linda, really I-" he shouted back.

"*I* would believe *you*."

Carter said nothing. Her story was straight up crazy, and he would laugh her out of the interview room if he wasn't married to her. Would she, if roles were reversed? He doubted it, even if it would be the story of the century. That was her problem though: too much time working and not enough on family. Something they were both guilty of.

"Say something," she pleaded, tired now, all trace of anger gone.

"Maybe what you saw," he spoke slowly, choosing each word with care, "What you *think* you saw, was a trick of the light."

"It wasn't a trick of the light." She mimicked his voice.

"Maybe it was a chain hanging from the wall behind the guy."

"A chain? With a ball of spikes hanging from it, like a medieval mace?" Her lips were a thin line and the tears had stopped.

Carter held up his hands, the universal gesture for 'enough'. The door opened and a short man with a ridiculous moustache came in awkwardly carrying two cups of tea. He put them on the table, nodded at Carter and left without a word.

"I don't want to fight."

Linda sagged against the table and he could see how exhausted she was. "Neither do I."

"It's just when you spend time with Mike, it gets me-"

"I know." Linda smiled, but this time it was genuine. "But you have nothing to worry about. I've told you before. He's like my big brother."

"Sorry." He sipped the tea, wincing as it burnt his lips. "I was worried about you."

"I know. You only ever shout at me when you're worried."

"It just sounds so ridiculous." He sat next to her and took her hand. *Take a breath, John, she needs you.*

"Don't you think I know that? A man with a tail. A small boy, with no white in his eyes. People getting eaten. It sounds ridiculous because it is. These things don't happen in real life. They certainly don't happen in *Exeter*."

"No," Carter said. "They don't. But you saw it. Anyone else, I'd say they were nuts, but it's you."

She couldn't do anything other than nod.

7:55 AM

Charlie sat opposite Mike Baxter and opened his folder. He deliberately let the photo of the blood and corpses from the warehouse slide onto the table.

"Seriously?" Mike said. "Aren't you a little old for that sort of thing?"

Charlie quickly scooped the photograph up, feeling his face warm.

"You know full well I have nothing to do with this."

"So, the man with the tail killed Hamilton, then ate him, and you shot the man, yes?" Danni said.

Mike nodded and sighed. "I know how it sounds, alright? The thing took a bite and I shot it. You've seen the body."

"Actually, we haven't," Charlie said. "The only bodies in the warehouse were Hamilton and another man, currently unidentified. You couldn't shed any light on that now, could you?"

Confusion creased Mike's face. "No, that's not right. The thing should be next to Hamilton." Mike drew a circle in the air around his shoulder. "Hamilton should be missing a chunk like this from his shoulder."

"Nope. Hamilton's corpse wasn't pretty, but there was no-one else there. Definitely no lizard man. So where did it go?"

"I don't know." Mike didn't like the smirk on Charlie's face, or the exasperated look on Danni's.

"Well, that would be the mystery now wouldn't it?" Charlie said.

Mike looked at each of them in turn. "I am telling the truth."

"Could you start again please, Mr. Baxter?" Danni said. She smiled at him and he relaxed slightly.

"We, uh, Linda Carter and I, went to the warehouse earlier last night. We were tracking John Hamilton."

"He owns a lot of property in and around Exeter, including this warehouse. Some more stuff up country." She looked at her notes. "East London predominantly."

"Yeah. That's him."

"Why? What's he done?"

"We had information he had made some of his money by smuggling people into the country, running a personal slavery business."

"Really?" Danni raised an eyebrow.

"Really," Mike said. "We needed to film it though, get hard evidence."

"For your network, I assume, not us," Charlie said.

"Well that's irrelevant now, isn't it? People are dead."

"So you say, Mr. Baxter, so you say."

"You don't really think I had anything to do with this?"

Charlie wasn't sure whether Mike was directing the question at him or speaking to himself.

"Right now, we're not sure what to believe, Mr. Baxter," Danni said. "Both you and Mrs. Carter have made some pretty wild claims tonight. Did you take anything before going out? You know we can test for just about anything."

"Be my guest," Mike snarled. "I haven't even had so much as a beer in the last couple of days."

Danni tapped the folder, sliding her chair back and standing. "Come on, Charlie, let him sweat for a couple of hours, then we'll talk more."

"Are you charging me with something?" Mike felt a sinking feeling overwhelm him. If they arrested him, then he was in a lot of trouble. No-one was going to believe his defence. Nausea settled in the pit of his stomach. Fight or flight?

"Not yet," Danni said.

"Then I'm leaving." Mike stood up. *Flight.*

"Please don't do that, Mr. Baxter." Charlie held up his arms as if to say *calm down.*

"You have my address. Now, get out of my way."

"Let him go," Charlie said to Danni who stepped to one side. "You're making a mistake here, Mike. We're not the bad guys."

"Whatever," Mike said and left.

8:00 AM

Kennedy had been watching the entrance for some time. The others were waiting, as requested, behind a large building opposite.

A small sign hung on the wall above the door, and another sat on the small patch of grass outside. Both had the word *Police* on them, and humans in blue uniforms walked in and out, some moving faster than others.

The humans all seemed to be carrying a long tube and as far as he could tell, there were no holes, so he deduced they weren't guns. He still felt trepidation. Major had been rash and was now dead. Kennedy had no desire to join him.

This was where the scent trail had led them. All he had to do now was figure out how to get in the building. He took a deep breath, calming himself. Running through his options. If he returned to the others, then they would get a share of the glory.

He crossed the road, ignoring the blaring noise coming from the human vehicles and headed straight for the main entrance.

8:01 AM

Mike walked through the building, heading straight for the exit. He could hear Danni calling his name, but ignored her. How could someone so pretty be such a pain in the arse? Why weren't they being more sympathetic? Why didn't they believe him?

Easy: the tale was ludicrous, and without evidence of course the cops were going to laugh at him. Without evidence, *everyone* would ridicule him. Without evidence, he was out of a job.

He pushed open the door and squinted in the sunlight: how long had he been in there? Two car horns blared, but he ignored them; road rage didn't warrant his attention, even on a Sunday. Steps led down to the street, and he jumped down them, blinking to try and help his eyes adjust. As he blinked, he bumped shoulders with a tall man. He was hunched over, a large lump on his back. *Poor sod*, Mike thought. He bounced off the hunchback, like walking into a wall.

"Sorry," he muttered. Last thing he wanted to do was annoy some local thug attending a licence meeting. Two things struck

Mike immediately: firstly, the man stank, a deep sulphuric smell like a sewer, and secondly-

"Oh shit," he said.

The man smiled at him, revealing rows and rows of sharp pointed teeth. Mike heard the ripping sound, but now in daylight and with more information, he knew what it was. The man was wearing an overcoat and it tore open, freeing its tail.

Tail.

Topped with a large ball of spikes.

It came at him now, darting forward like an attack from a scorpion. Mike jumped back and tripped on the steps behind him. The stumble saved his life. The tail flew over his head, narrowly missing him. The man snarled at Mike, baring rows of hideous teeth again.

"Mr. Baxter!"

He looked up and saw Danni standing there. Her mouth dropped open when she saw the man with the tail and all those sharp teeth. Her mouth opened and closed a few times before she recovered.

"Stop! You are under arrest!"

Seriously? Jesus Christ, Mike thought and scrambled to his feet. "Not now, not now! Run!"

He started to move up the steps just as Charlie came through the doors. He had a uniformed officer behind him. Mike heard a *swoosh* and he ducked again. Something flew over his head, but it wasn't the tail; it was one of the spikes.

The spike hit the officer in the cheek, embedding itself so deeply only part of it was showing. The officer cried out and held his face, screaming as blood poured between his fingers.

Danni had a baton in her hand, and she extended it to its full length. She charged at the man, swinging the baton at his legs.

Charlie fumbled at the fallen officer's belt, trying to free an aerosol can.

"Get inside, get inside!" Mike screeched, not caring how desperate he sounded.

The baton connected with the creature's leg and it howled in pain. Danni swung again, but it lashed out, catching her head. She fell back, tumbling into the road in front of the police station. The baton spilled out of her hands, rolling into the gutter. Charlie moved towards him, bringing the canister up. He pressed the button on the top and a stream of liquid fanned out, hitting the creature in the eyes. It screamed again, hands moving to protect its eyes and face. Too late. The CS spray had done its job.

"Get help!" Charlie roared, turning back to Mike.

Mike watched in horror as the thing's tail swung again, catching Charlie in the middle of his back. Charlie groaned as the force pushed his considerable bulk into the air, off his feet for a second before he landed with a thump.

The uniformed man was still screaming, and the blood pouring from his face showed no sign of abating. Around the spike, the flesh was peeling away from the bone. Black lines traced a map of blood vessels covering the man's face, running down his neck and disappearing beneath his clothes.

Mike scrambled back up the steps and pushed the door to the police station open.

"Help!" He screamed at the top of his lungs. Then, remembering countless police thrillers he'd seen: "Officers down, officers down!"

The officer behind the desk looked up from her paperwork, took in his panicked expression, and pressed a button under the counter. The door behind her sprang open and four more uniformed officers ran out. They looked confused momentarily as the waiting area seemed quiet.

"Outside, quickly!" Mike yelled. "He's here, he's here! He's going to kill them all!"

The officers sprinted for the external door, batons at the ready.

"You're going to need guns," Mike said, his words bouncing off the closing door.

8:03 AM

Danni rolled as soon as she landed, breathing hard. The air was rotten with the stench of the creature, worse than any body odour she had ever experienced before; the smell was almost sulphuric. Her side ached from the force of the landing, but, as far as she could tell, nothing was broken. She saw her baton lying in the gutter and retrieved it, leaping to her feet before turning back to face the creature.

And it *was* a creature. Baxter and Linda Carter had been telling the truth. The thing was ugly and made from nightmares: bald head, covered in thick scars which shone in the sunshine; gaunt face full of sinewy muscle and teeth designed for tearing flesh; grey, unhealthy skin drawn taught over thick muscles on its chest and arms. It towered over the men surrounding it. Behind it, moving hypnotically, was a thick, scale-covered tail topped with a ball of spikes which glistened with a wet sheen.

Blood.

Charlie lay on the ground, unmoving, whilst one of the officers screamed. Blood poured from the man's wounds and he was trying in vain to keep his face attached to his skull. Most of his cheek had melted away, revealing bone and shreds of muscle.

Don't get hit by the spike, whatever happens.

Four more officers ran out of the police station, batons in hand. The creature had a face full of PAVA spray so it should be rolling on the pavement, but if anything, the spray had made it furious. It lunged at the first officer through the door, catching him with an uppercut that lifted the poor man off his feet and forced him back into the second man. Both men stumbled back into the doorway, collapsing to the ground with cries of pain.

The third officer swung her baton and it smashed into the creature's head with a loud crack. As its head snapped back, she followed up with another swing. Both the officer and the creature were roaring as it caught the baton mid swing. It followed through with its other hand, intending to slap her. Danni saw why a moment too late.

Claws rake the woman's face, separating flesh from bone as they sliced through her cheek. As the skin peeled away from her face, she started to scream, and the creature jabbed her neck with his fingertips, severing vocal cords and cutting the scream short. She collapsed, gurgling and choking on her own blood.

The creature then spun, bringing its tail around. The fourth officer caught the ball of spikes full in the face with enough force to lift him off his feet and send him crashing into the wall of the police station. As he landed, Danni saw his face was caved in; he was totally unrecognisable as a *man*, let alone someone she worked with.

Danni forced herself forward, swinging the baton repeatedly landing several blows on the back of the thing's head. The first strike staggered him, the second made him roar and the third dropped him to his knees.

"Yes!" she screamed. She hit him again, but he blocked the

baton with the back of his arm. He stood, but slowly this time. The blows had clearly hurt. Turning to face her, he snarled, revealing rows of razor sharp, pointed teeth. His breath stank of rotting flesh.

"My turn," he said. He spoke in clipped tones, like the old presenters on Radio 4.

"Bring it," Danni said with far more bravery than she felt. The screams of the men dying made her legs feel like jelly. When she had first become a police officer, a baton had made her feel powerful, ready for anything. Now it was woefully inadequate.

The creature leapt at her; hands outstretched with the vicious claws fully extended. Danni took in every small detail: the blood dripping from the claws, the dirty, pointed teeth and the tail swinging behind him as he leapt. At the last possible second, she dove to the side, rolling as soon as she hit tarmac. She grunted, scrambling back to her feet just as the thing was turning towards her.

Danni ran.

She ran straight towards the car park of the station. It was around the side of the building, barely fifty metres away but it might as well have been on Mars. She pumped her jelly legs, sure any second now they would give way.

From behind her came a roar and the windows rattled in their frames.

She could hear his feet pounding the pavement as he gave chase, and she was sure of one thing: he was faster than her.

"No!" Danni shrieked, trying – *willing* – her legs to carry her faster. They wouldn't. She felt the breath of the creature on her neck, smelling the horrible stench of the thing.

"Armed police!"

She heard the shout and stumbled, falling to the ground. Shots rang out, thudding over her head. She rolled onto her back, still moving on her hands and feet as she scrambled away. Bullets tore into the thing and she heard him shout in pain, but he kept coming. More shots rang out and then the thing exploded.

Three small blue spheres – each no bigger than an orange – flew out from where the creature had been standing. They flew backwards, away from the armed officers and then shot into the ground. She heard a bang as the spheres punctured the ground, leaving three small holes in the tarmac. Around them, cracks spread like spider webs.

"You ok?"

It took her a moment to realise the question was directed at her. The armed officer's face was full of concern.

"Charlie. The others," she said, and passed out.

Kingston leant on the metal railings and watched the river make its inexorable way through the countryside. He was still sweating, but his breathing was back to normal at least. The bike was parked behind him, in a layby. It had not taken him long to leave the city.

He tried to make sense of the morning's events, but he couldn't; it was just too crazy. That man – if it had been a man – had a tail. It had looked like a scorpion tail, but with many spikes at the end, rather than one horrible point. He was beyond ugly too, with no hair, slits where his nose should be and a face full of scars. Kingston shuddered.

The boy was something else altogether. That blank expression. The pitch-black eyes. He had exuded menace, which was ridiculous as he couldn't have been more than ten. Kingston had been tough at that age, but only compared to other ten-year olds. This boy had given the impression he could have kicked Kingston's head in without breaking sweat.

His eyes.

Kingston shuddered again. The boy's eyes had been completely black, all pupil, no white bits. What did that mean for his vision? Also, the boy stunk. Not of body odour, which wasn't a bad enough description to use for the stench coming from the boy and his father.

The black circle had been created by the boy, of that he was certain, however crazy it sounded. It had started about a metre or so away from the boy and had then expanded. Everything it had touched had been destroyed. The cars, the walls of the garden and the men. Hamilton's men gone, just gone. What the hell was that? If Kingston had been just a little further away from the boy, he would have died too.

The boy had collapsed soon after. So did that mean firing the black wall had made him tired? Had it killed him? Somehow Kingston doubted it. The man had walked away carrying the boy. Also ridiculous: the dude had five or six bullets in him.

They were still out there.

So, what now?

Kingston felt he should warn someone there was something inexplicable in Exeter. Should he tell the police? Break the habit of a lifetime and talk to the 5-0? He shook his head. No way. For a start they wouldn't believe him and secondly, they could well arrest him. What if CCTV showed him shooting the big dude? What if it didn't show his tail? Then he'd be looking at a long stretch for GBH and owning an illegal handgun.

If not the Police, then who? Kingston fished into the back pocket of his jeans and pulled out the card of the gang specialist copper. The one who had said to call him, any time, if he wanted out of his gang life. Perfect. He wasn't local to Exeter so Kingston could make this call without feeling like a snitch.

This wasn't quite what the copper had in mind, but Kingston decided a phone call would not be out of order. The Scorpions would never forgive him for talking to a cop. He turned the card over and over in his hands. The events of the morning were not normal, and he didn't plan on seeing any of the Scorpions ever again, so why would he care about what they thought? He looked at the name on the front of the card and made a decision.

He would ring John Carter, then he would get the hell out of Exeter.

8:10 A.M

"Stay here." Carter kissed Linda on the cheek.

"Don't leave me," she said. "Please, John." She put down the yoghurt pot she'd been eating from and looked at him with desperate eyes. Ridiculous-Tache had brought them the yoghurt a few minutes ago. It wasn't enough, but it was better than nothing.

"Something major is happening out there and they might need my help."

"*I* need your help."

"I'll be back in two minutes." He smiled and left before she could say anything else. He felt a small knot of anxiety in his stomach, knowing he was letting her down, but unable – and unwilling - to ignore the commotion outside.

The corridor outside the interview room was long and narrow. Two policemen ran past him, neither paying him any attention. He followed them down a flight of stairs, out into the reception area and straight into a nightmare.

The small room was packed with people, all shouting and

moving with urgency. Some ran outside, armed with batons and pepper spray. Four men and two women were lying on the ground and two of them were obviously dead. One of them had half of his face missing, raw tissue and bone visible. One of the women's throat was open, jagged slices of flesh ripped apart, leaking her blood over her clothes. Carter turned away, feeling bile rise. He'd seen corpses before, but not like this.

The other woman was Danni. She was pale and her eyes were closed but her chest was rising and falling, so at least she was in better shape than the person next to her.

"John!" A hand grabbed his shoulder and made him start.

"Mike, what the hell is going on here?" Despite everything, he felt relief at seeing the reporter in one piece.

"It was him, John. The man. He attacked." Mike gestured in a wide arc with his arm. His meaning was clear: look what he did.

"This was just one man?"

Mike nodded. "They shot him and he exploded." He pointed at a team of three armed officers in full body armour. They were deep in discussion with another man, presumably their boss.

"Mike, what the hell happened to this guy?" Carter jabbed a finger at the corpse without looking at him. He really didn't want to risk his meagre breakfast coming back up.

"He got hit with a spike from the man's tail. It melted his face."

"Wait, what?" Carter couldn't hide his surprise.

"We were telling the truth, John." Mike's mouth was a thin line. "Now *everyone* believes us."

"The man who attacked you and Linda did *this*?"

"Keep up, John. That's what I've been saying." Mike couldn't keep the impatience from his voice. His eyes looked like they were about to pop out of their sockets and his forehead was covered in sweat. "Look, we've got to get out of here, there could be more of them."

That got Carter's attention.

"At the warehouse, I saw something just as the police came. More of these things, John. There are *definitely* more."

"Damn."

Carter ran over to the armed response team. The commander barely hid his distaste.

"Bit busy here, so jog on, sunshine."

"I'm DS John Carter, so lose the look." Carter flashed his badge and the commander's face changed instantly.

"Apologies, it's been a hell of a morning. I can't get my head around what just happened." He took his cap off and ran his hand through thinning hair, taking a moment to collect himself. "I'm Biggs. It's, I mean, holy shit, what just happened?"

"How many more weapons you got here?" Carter had no time for hand holding, even if he agreed with the commander.

His eyes narrowed, his suspicious, supercilious look returning. "Why?"

"The thing that attacked you this morning, I don't think it was acting alone. There could be more. Possibly a lot more."

"Seriously?" Biggs was paler now.

"I don't know who you need to call, but you need to do it and you need all your teams here. Now."

Biggs turned to his squad, two men and a woman. "Samuel," he barked at the woman. "Get the crate open, dole out the kit."

"Sir." The woman ran through the secure doors to the rest of the station.

Biggs turned to the next man. "Get me a list of everyone who has done firearms training, even if they failed." The man went a different way to Samuel.

"Thank you," Carter said.

"No one else is dying here today," Biggs said. "These things come back, we'll be ready for them."

Carter left him there, issuing orders to the rest of the team. He had a feeling Biggs was in for a long day. Even when this immediate threat was over, the paperwork and scrutiny of his actions would take months.

"Carter." Charlie was sitting on a desk near the corpses. He was rubbing his head and a medic was holding an ice pack on his back.

"You ok?"

"I've been better." Charlie waved the medic away and stood with a grimace. "I got hit with its tail and man, it hurt." He snorted. "Can't believe I just said that, and nobody laughed. I got lucky though, look at him. He took a spike to his head."

Charlie felt every moment of the day press down on him then. He rubbed his chest, feeling short of breath for a couple of seconds. The feeling passed, but not the deep sadness he felt at looking at his colleagues. The nearest was Jude Veitch, a young man who'd only been on the force for about a year. Charlie didn't really know him beyond nodding in passing, but the bloke had always been smiling.

Carter forced himself to examine the corpse, studying the wounds. Sections of skin had melted down to the bone and his eyes looked as if they'd boiled in his skull. Where skin remained, it was laced with deep black lines.

"Acid? Poison? Some mixture of the two?"

"Always the detective, John. You're wasted in gangs, you know that?"

Carter said nothing. He didn't see much point in revisiting the old argument, or the need to point out kids were everyone's future and so we really should be taking better care of them. Intervention with gang members was vital to give them and their families a future free from violence, as well as something more important: hope.

"Where's Linda?"

"Still in the interview room," Carter said. "Guess I should go tell her she's not nuts."

8:11 AM

The Prince watched the humans running around outside the police station. Their movements and interactions fascinated him. So loud, swarming over the land as if it were theirs. He felt anger growing, and with it, an accompanying thrill.

Two of them were carrying the metal weapons which had dispatched Kennedy. Black and shiny, the things radiated power. Guns, Kennedy had called them. He had been correct: the humans were getting stronger.

"We should return," Callaghan said. His voice wavered as the Prince glared at him until he was silent. Callaghan swallowed loudly and bowed his head.

"No," the Prince said. "We must act now, before they get stronger. Get the others."

8:15 AM

Danni sat up with a cry. Wild-eyed, it took her a moment to get her bearings, and another to get her breathing even close to under control. A man dressed in a green uniform wiped her head with an antiseptic wipe.

"Take it easy," he said. "You might have concussion."

Danni blinked. "Did you see?"

Paramedic. He was a paramedic and her breathing eased further.

"See what?" He slipped the wipe into a bag filled with them. "You don't seem to be bleeding. You're one of the lucky ones."

"Did you see a body?"

"Yeah, there's a few dead. Sorry." He mumbled the last and went to take her pulse. She waved him away.

"Leave me alone."

"You passed out."

"Yeah, but-"

"No buts. Just stay still for a moment. Can you tell me your name?"

"DS Danni Brent."

He held his finger up. "Can you touch my finger, then your nose as quickly as possible please, Danni?"

Danni did it with a sigh.

"That's good. Can you tell me where we are?"

"Exeter nick. For God's sake, I have work to do." She stood up, pushing his hand away. "Someone else here needs you more than me."

"Alright, alright. Listen, my name's Clive. Just shout if you feel sick or dizzy."

Danni strode away from him, trying not to look at the corpse with a missing face. She scanned the room and saw Charlie leaning on a counter near the main entrance.

"Hey," he said with a genuine smile. "Good to see you up and about."

She gingerly touched her forehead and ran a hand through her hair. No blood, just like the paramedic said. "You ok?"

"Yeah, going to have a nice bruise later, but I don't think I've broken anything."

"That's good, that's good."

"Hell of a morning."

"What now?"

"I think we're about to get a lot more resources," Charlie said. He didn't look altogether happy about the news. "Somehow we've got to contain this from the press. If they find out there are monsters here, we're in big trouble. There'll be panic in the streets of Exeter." He sang the last line, but Danni just looked blank.

"What was that?"

"The Smiths?" Danni's expression didn't change. "Come on, seriously?"

"Jesus, Charlie." Danni shook her head. "They killed him

though. SCO19. They shot the guy. He exploded." She shuddered at the memory. "I saw it."

"Yeah, one down for sure, but think about what the reporters said. They killed one at the warehouse and now there's another one dead here. There could be more of them."

"The reporters didn't say anything about the spheres."

It was Charlie's turn to look blank, so she filled him in.

"We need to check with the reporters."

"Yeah, but what are *they*?"

Charlie shrugged. "No clue. Maybe we need the army."

"The army in Exeter? Thought you didn't want panic?" She rested a hand on the counter, suddenly feeling exhausted. "What about CTSFO?"

"The boss is 'thinking about it,' apparently."

Danni gestured at the carnage. "What's there to think about?"

"Good point. One thing is for sure, this is going to be taken off us soon. Whatever we're going to do it needs to be fast. If we can find out where these things are coming from, maybe we can stop them."

8:16 AM

Carter and Mike burst into the interview room and both started talking at once. Linda jumped as they entered and held up her hands to quell the noise.

"Slow down."

Carter filled her in and she nodded, lips thin.

"I told you." She stabbed a finger at him. "If you'd listened-"

"Let's not do this," Carter said.

She seethed at him for a few moments more, then: "So what now?"

"Well, we're sitting on a pretty big exclusive right now," Mike said.

"You're unbelievable," Carter said. "There are at least four dead out there, maybe more by now. This is about more than a story."

"We sell this right, we're set for life," Mike continued. He focussed his attention on Linda, an earnest smile on his face and she found herself nodding.

Carter's phone rang, preventing him from ripping into both of them. Number unknown. He answered anyway, trying to keep his anger in check. "John Carter."

"Yo, it's Kingston."

"Who?"

"Kingston, man. You know."

"Well, well. This is not a call I was expecting."

"Nah, man, me neither. Listen I got some info for you."

"This really isn't a good time."

"No shit, man, no shit. This is important, man."

"Really, Paul, I'll call you back on this number."

"This a burner phone, I ain't talking to no police on my regular. You think I'm stupid?" There was a pause on the other end of the line, then: "I ain't snitching man, this something else."

Carter frowned. Kingston wasn't turning someone in, then what did he want?

"Go on."

"This geezer attacked some fellas I know. Killed them all."

"Paul, this really isn't a good time. Call 999."

"The dude had a tail, man. I swear to God and on me mother's life."

His legs went cold and the phone felt heavy in his hands. Linda looked up sharply at him, but he turned away from her. If Kingston had seen these things in London, then-

"Where are you?"

"Right now? West Country shithole. Exeter."

Relief flooded through him. Hopefully, this was still local – whatever *this* was.

"I'm in Exeter too. I need to meet you. This is serious, Paul."

"You in Exeter? Well, that is a straight up surprise. I ain't coming to no station."

"Ok, I'll come to you."

"Nah, man, train station. Central. You know it?"

"I can find it."

"You got ten minutes, then I'm gone."

8:17 AM

The deep dark of the tunnel exploded into light as three spheres smashed into each other. When the glare faded, Kennedy stood growling. His eyes adjusted but something felt wrong. Raising his hand in front of his face, he saw it was missing the small finger. Kennedy grunted and wiggled the remaining ones. There was no pain; it was more like the finger had never been there at all. He cried out in frustration, the howl echoing down the tunnel.

He entered the travel tube and headed Home. Kennedy passed the entrance for the Horde but ignored it and made straight for the throne room. Father sat in his chair, transfixed with the screens. It had seemed such a long time ago the humans had started broad-casting, and now Father was addicted. He rarely moved from his chair, but was still as lithe and lean as he had always been.

"Father," Kennedy rasped holding up his hand, displaying the non-existent finger.

Father looked at his hand and shook his head. "Your band is losing power. You cannot rely on it."

"How can it be?"

"The bands are not all powerful, Kennedy. Every time you use it, you deplete the charge." He waved a hand, dismissing Kennedy's concerns.

Kennedy bowed his head.

"Where is my son?"

Kennedy didn't dare raise his head.

"He went with you, Kennedy, yet you are here, and he is not."

It did not surprise Kennedy that Father knew the Prince had disobeyed him.

"I was attacked by the humans, Father," Kennedy lied, still not looking up. Father did not need to know the truth. "They forced me to escape."

"You should have stayed."

"Yes, Father." Kennedy kept his eyes on the floor. He didn't explain the band's self-preservation switch had fired, as it would imply Father didn't already *know*. With luck and enough contrition, he might yet escape this without another scar on his head.

"The others will need your help to keep my sons safe."

"The others-"

"Are not as experienced as you. They do not have a band like you. They cannot protect him like you can." Father put his hand on Kennedy's chin. He had moved without making a sound, the first time out of the chair in as long as Kennedy could remember. He felt an electric charge run through him at Father's touch.

"Return to them. I will never forgive anyone who brings harm to my sons. Keep them safe."

8:20 AM

Carter jogged through the streets of Exeter. He'd driven from the station, making good time through the quiet streets, and parked as near to Central Train Station as he could. Several bleary-eyed people in last night's clothes strolled past him, hangovers meaning they weren't moving quickly.

Carter ran through everything he knew about Kingston, which didn't take long. Kingston was high up in the Scorpions, possibly in charge, possibly not. No convictions, but lots of suspicion. No qualifications as he had just stopped going to school when he was thirteen. Parents absent, lost to drugs. Lived with family members until they all tired of him. Lived on the streets for a short time, then joined the Scorpions. Fairly standard tale of being young with no chance in London these days.

Basically, the lad had already taken his first steps to career criminal, so why had he called Carter? If the Scorpions found out, then Kingston would be thrown out, probably beaten, with a high chance of being killed. Why was he in Exeter now? Coincidence?

Kingston said the man who attacked him had a tail. Had he

seen the same creature as Linda? Was it the same one shot outside the station a few minutes ago? Carter hadn't seen the creature's body, either in the station or in the street. Why not? Where had the body gone? There was much about this whole incident that didn't make sense.

Were monsters really running amok in Exeter?

Carter shook his head. *Now* who was being crazy? He crossed the road and entered the Central station. Tourist signs pointed the way to the High Street, Cathedral and the Quay. Carter ignored them, scanning the thin crowd of faces.

Someone tapped him on the shoulder, making him start.

"Ain't no 5-0 sneaking up on me," Kingston said, but he was smiling, clearly pleased with himself at getting the jump on Carter. "You were cutting it fine. You had thirty more then I was gone."

"It's a trek from the nick," Carter said with a shrug. "You didn't call me just to shoot the breeze, Paul. Tell me about the guy with a tail."

Kingston narrowed his eyes and looked all around him. Sweat beaded on his brow, glistening against his dark skin. A group of kids swept past, all simultaneously on their phones and talking too loudly to each other. Excited at a day out in the big city.

"Relax," Carter said. "No-one is paying us any attention."

"Some cheap cans around here," Kingston said, as two women strode past, lost in a world of music. A man walked by, wearing a huge pair of over-ear Bose headphones. "That dude got some serious beats."

"Talk to me, Paul, and not about fucking headphones."

"Kingston. No one calls me Paul."

Carter inclined his head, trying to stay calm.

"These guys attacked me this morning. Just flat out came at me. I defended myself, like I'm allowed, and then this dude turns up with his son."

"Yeah, right. I'm sure it would hold up in court," Carter said. He was holding himself deliberately still, not letting his face register his contempt at Kingston's choice of words. "Go on."

"Dude has a tail. But the kid, man, some kind of crazy, right there."

"Come on, Kingston, get to the point." The world had disappeared as his entire focus was on the young man. Linda had mentioned a kid. Oh God.

"The kid, right, he throws back his hands like this," Kingston put his hands out in the cross. He slapped a passer-by in the face. The man stopped and turned towards Kingston.

"What the hell, man?"

"Come at me, bro," Kingston said, stepping towards the man and squaring up to him. The man held his hands up and walked away, muttering to himself.

"Yeah, walk away, man, walk away." Kingston smirked at Carter. "Coward, am I right?"

"You were saying," Carter said, finding it increasingly difficult to hide his impatience.

"Yeah, yeah. The kid makes like he's on the cross, y'know, like some weird Jesus shit and this circle thing flies out from around him." Kingston used his arms to show the circle's starting point. "It destroyed everything in its path, man, like obliterated it."

"Shit, what?"

"You heard me. The guys attacking me, they were gone man, totally gone. Not even a body left. Cars too, just gone."

"You sure about this?"

Kingston nodded. "Of course I am. Wouldn't lie to an officer of the law."

By Carter's count, it was at least three lies so far. "You need to come with me and make a statement."

"No way, man. I told you I'm ain't going to no police station."

"Kingston, something serious is happening here and we need all the info we can get."

"Wait a minute," Kingston said. "You didn't even blink when I mentioned a tail." He took a step back from Carter. "You knew. You knew about the guy with the tail. Screw this, man, I'm out of here."

"Where are you going?"

"As far away from here as I can get. Like you said, something bad going down. I'm done."

"I could arrest you, you know," Carter said.

"What for? I ain't done nothing wrong."

"Suspicion of the murder of *some dudes.*"

Kingston shook his head, disappointment clear on his face. "I thought you were one of the good guys. I'm out of here."

8:21 AM

The Prince woke and sat up without making a sound. Heath had propped himself against a tall stone wall next to him. Grey houses lined both sides of the road they were on, but it was quiet. A sudden movement caught his eye and he saw a cat slinking towards them. It stopped when it saw him and hissed, hackles raised on its back. The Prince snarled at it, baring his teeth and the cat ran, disappearing under a car.

Heath looked to be in a bad way, with blood drying on his chest. He should have healed by now. The human bullets were still inside him, preventing the wounds from closing. "You are hurt."

"As long as you are safe, my Prince." The big man nodded, weariness etched into his features. He winced and held his side and when he removed his hand it came away bloody. A wound he hadn't seen before. Another of the cursed human's shots.

"I don't understand. The humans can't hurt us," Heath said.

"We have slept too long," the Prince said. "Father has grown complacent."

If Heath was bothered by the sacrilegious comment, he was in too much pain to show it. Despite being shot several times, Heath had managed to carry the Prince and tried to follow the man. It had been to no avail. He had been long gone before Heath reached the bottom of a long hill where his legs gave out. They had lain here ever since, and Heath had no idea how much time had passed. He touched his wounds, which were starting to close, but too much blood had been spilled.

"I think I can walk again," Heath said, with more certainty than he felt. The sense of duty, the need to get the Prince Home over-rode any discomfort.

"Good. My brother will be anxious for my return." The Prince regarded Heath with his black eyes. "You do not need to carry me anymore. We should head back and get you some help."

Heath nodded and stood on unsteady legs. The Prince inclined his head, but Heath nodded again, this time with more surety. "I can walk," he said. He pulled his coat around him, its volume hiding his tail, but giving him the appearance of a hunchback.

Heath was in no condition to get back up the steep hill, so they headed down where the road swept around a bend. The Prince knew, from the maps he'd memorised, if they walked along there, the road was flat but ran parallel to their destination, so they could join it later when Heath was feeling stronger.

Slowly, they started to walk around the bend, where a sign indicated the station was five hundred yards away.

8:24 AM

Kingston walked quickly, relishing the quiet here – so unlike London. Some people walked the streets, but nowhere near the constant throng of home. He headed away from Central Station. A sign pointed the way to St. David's, where he could get a train back to London. How stupid is this place that Central doesn't go to London? With the signs pointing the way, he didn't have to concentrate on his route. Instead, he tried to focus on his plan.

Get on a train long enough to fool Carter into thinking he was leaving. Get off at the last moment, then return to get his bike. Once he had the bike, then he was gone, out of Exeter, never to return. With his new passport and case of money, he could head straight to a port. Plymouth would do. Again, he felt a twinge of guilt at the thought of leaving people behind, or at least one specific person.

Leaving did worry him slightly. The city was all he knew, so wherever he went it would be different. He fancied New York as the Scorpions would never find him there. Maybe Stockholm.

Those Danish birds were supposed to be well fit. He could put the confusion of the last few months behind him.

Carter was following him with all the subtlety of a slap to the face. The streets were too quiet for anyone to follow inconspicuously. Kingston soon arrived at the station.

"Kingston!"

He sighed. "You a persistent mother, I'll give you that."

"Come on, help us."

"No way, man, not happening. You on your own."

"*You* rang *me*. You want to help," Carter pleaded. "Deep down, you want to do the right thing."

"Yeah, but me, I'm shallower than an empty paddling pool, know what I'm saying?" Kingston grinned at Carter. "See you around, officer."

He was turning away from Carter when something caught his eye. He frowned. *No, it can't be.* In the distance, on the other side of the street, a boy and a man walked slowly down the road. The man was hunched over and that was the reason they were walking slowly. He had one arm around the boy's slim shoulders and the other clutched his side. Kingston felt his legs go cold as fear lurched through his body.

"Carter, that's your man."

"What?" Carter followed Kingston's point.

"That dude. There. The Esmerelda looking tool. He's the one who attacked me."

Carter studied the two figures. He'd had a quip ready to correct Kingston, but it died on his lips. The man was large, but his hunch-back made just how big hard to discern. He was wearing a long overcoat which looked filthy even at this distance. Black trousers and battered trainers completed the look. He had a hood pulled tight over his head, obscuring his features, and he could easily have been mistaken for homeless.

The boy had black hair and very pale skin. He was wearing a t-shirt and jeans, but again both were filthy. The boy walked with a curious posture – extremely erect, almost regal. Carter had seen this level of arrogance before, just not in someone so young or, in fact, so dirty. The boy was staring at everything, watching the cars go by and then up at the buildings. He seemed in awe of it all.

"Where are they going?"

"Not nowhere fast," Kingston said.

Carter stepped into the road and jogged across the street. He was behind them but kept his distance.

"You need this."

Carter looked at Kingston, surprised he had followed him. Kingston was holding a pistol and he tried to give it to Carter.

"What the hell are you doing with a Glock?"

"I'm a careful man."

"You're still a kid really."

"Old enough to acquire myself a Glock."

"Old enough to know better than to give me an illegal firearm."

"Your funeral man, they dangerous."

"Don't look much to me," Carter said, but in his head, he was picturing the police officers lying dead or dying in Exeter Station.

He ignored the offered handgun and kept following the man and boy. They were walking so slowly it was difficult to keep a decent distance. The man stopped and leant on a car, breathing heavily. Carter ducked into a doorway.

"You're crap at this spy stuff, you know?"

Carter grabbed Kingston and pulled him into the doorway. "What are you doing?"

"I don't want to see you get killed. Take the gun." He tried to give the weapon to Carter again.

"Now you want to help me?" Carter smirked but kept his eyes away from the black sheen of the weapon. Guns made him nervous. He leaned out of the doorway only to see no trace of the man and boy.

"Dammit!" He started to jog up the long street. Houses on the left had gardens too small to really be considered gardens or to be worth having, Carter increased his pace, swearing again and again. He passed an alleyway on his left and was halfway across before a fist smashed into the side of his head. Carter cried out and stumbled into the road. He managed to spin, and the second blow glanced off his shoulder.

The man was snarling at him. Behind him, the boy was watching with a blank expression. They must have hidden in the shadows of the alley and Carter cursed his own impatience. Up close, Carter realised he was all muscle and he knew how to use it. The man closed the gap between them, moving with the fluidity of a cat despite his wounds. Carter knew he had seriously underestimated him.

"Kill him," the boy said in a voice lacking emotion.

Carter punched the man, the blow connecting with his chin. It was like punching a brick wall. Pain shot up Carter's arm and for a moment he thought he'd broken his wrist. The man lifted his arm, and Carter stepped forward, grappling with him. The smell emanating from the man made Carter gag, but he knew he couldn't let go. Blood dripped from a patch on his side, but it didn't seem to be slowing him down.

The man grinned, his lips pulling back revealing rows of razor-sharp teeth.

"Carter, let go!"

He heard the shout and didn't think about it. Carter slammed his fist into the bloody patch, making the thing howl in pain. It created the opening he needed, and he pushed the thing away before diving to the ground. Kingston fired three times; each shot an explosion of noise in the quiet back street. Bullets tore into the creature, making him scream. The boy's expression remained blank as he watched his companion advance on Kingston. Carter heard something rip, but ignored it, instead crawling towards Kingston. Anything to be away from the boy. As the tatters of the coat fell to the pavement, the creature stood upright, his tail swinging freely behind him. At the end of the tail, a ball of spikes swayed like a snake ready to strike.

"Holy shit!" Carter cried.

Kingston fired again, another burst of three bullets. The first tore through the ball of spikes, spraying thick blood into the road behind; the second went wild, pinging into the wall behind the man and kicking up a spray of brick and concrete but the third hit the man between the eyes. A small hole appeared in the middle of his forehead, but the back of his head exploded, sending blood, brain and bone raining to the ground. The thing fell backwards, landing amongst its own gore, unmoving.

Carter stood, just as the boy roared "No!"

The boy held his arms out, perpendicular to his sides.

"Run," Kingston cried, sprinting past Carter. Pressure began to build, and Carter winced. Then, he started running after Kingston. The pressure became a whine, a noise vocalising the coming discomfort. Carter risked a look back over his shoulder and what he saw made him increase his pace.

A black wall was heading straight at him. It blocked everything behind it. He couldn't see past or through it at all. He jumped forward as the wall caught up with him. He hit the ground hard, but spun shuffling backwards on his feet and hands. All the breath was knocked out of him and he gasped, trying to force air into his lungs.

The black wall stopped just before him. It stood centimetres away from him, humming quietly. The complete blackness of it was mesmerising. Carter could not see anything in the blackness: no reflection at all. Vertigo washed over him as he lost all perspective of where he was. He reached out his hand, moving to touch it.

"Don't", Kingston said from behind him. His voice was enough to break the spell. Carter dropped his hand. The wall disappeared, taking the hum and pressure with it. Carter blinked at the sudden brightness in the street and then swore.

The cars he had run past were no longer there. Short walls earmarking property divides had also gone with not even a pile of rubble to show they had ever been there. The buildings remained intact, but two had lost the pebble-dash exterior and now showed poor, ancient brickwork.

The boy glared at them both, his face contorted with fury, but then he cried out and collapsed. Kingston walked towards him, registering the pavement beneath his feet was intact, but not thinking about it. He gazed down at the boy, who looked like he was sleeping.

"Screw you," Kingston whispered and shot him in the head.

8:30 AM

Kennedy scrubbed his face and then pulled some fresh clothes on. Scavenged over many years, the clothes were ill fitting but brought him comfort. He pulled the coat over his tail, bending over to accommodate it. As soon as he was done, he returned to the throne room and bowed at Father.

"I will find them," he said.

Father nodded, but then howled like he was in pain. He slumped over his console, breathing heavily. He was always a pale man, but now he was devoid of all colour. His whole body convulsed and shook.

"Father?" Kennedy took a step forward, fear gnawing at his limbs. He had never seen Father like this.

Father threw back his head and roared. He leapt to his feet and punched the screen nearest him. Sparks showered the room as the glass shattered. The picture shrivelled to nothing. Father turned towards Kennedy, anger contorting his features, and raised his fists.

Kennedy took a step backwards, raising his arm to protect his head.

"They killed him," Father roared. "They killed my first."

Kennedy thought better of speaking. The symbiotic relationship they all shared was nothing compared to Father and his offspring. It was as if they were joined mentally. If Father said the boy was dead, then it was true, however unlikely. Truly, the humans were getting more powerful.

"I will make them pay, Father. I will paint the streets with their blood."

"We both will," Father said. "I am coming with you."

"But Father-"

"Do not question me!" Father slapped Kennedy, making him cower.

Father's lithe form was suddenly inches away from Kennedy. His black eyes shone brightly, filling Kennedy with fervour.

"Take me to where the humans hurt you. My Prince died near there and those responsible will not be far."

"Yes, Father."

8:31 AM

Danni rummaged through her desk drawer and found a cereal bar. She took a large mouthful and sighed contentedly.

"Yes!"

"I don't know how you can eat those things," Charlie said.

"These're lovely, what's wrong with you?" she mumbled, mouth full of the second bite. "Honey and oats, brilliant. Keep me going all day."

"It's like eating sweetened cardboard."

"Oh, I wouldn't know."

Charlie shook his head at her. "I could murder a bacon sandwich."

"Yep, murder is the right word to use there."

"Could we have a preach-free day please?"

"Sure, as long as you are comfortable knowing an animal lived and died in suffering just so you could smother it in ketchup and bread."

"Brown sauce," Charlie muttered.

"What?"

"Never mind." He looked at the maps again. Where had these things come from? A circle around the house the murdered kids had been in and a different circle around the warehouse intersected twice –one under the Exe, the other in Topsham. Neither seemed likely places for monsters to hide, although Topsham on a Saturday night would be a possibility.

Maybe they were wrong, and the monsters could run or fly or, hell, even teleport. That would mean they could be anywhere of course. Charlie shook his head. Teleporting monsters. What was he thinking? Still, three blue spheres erupted from the thing, that's what he'd been told. What the hell were the spheres?

He drummed his fingers on the desk. His chest was still sore, but at least it no longer hurt to breathe. There would be a hell of a bruise there later, but no-one other than him would see it. He doubted anyone would ever see his naked body again. Now the adrenaline had left his system, he was tired, but also wired. He was finding it hard to concentrate on the maps. His mind kept flashing back to the monster hitting him again and again. Each time it seemed to be harder and harder.

"Stop the damn tapping," Danni said.

"I can't help it."

"I know, but it's not helping. Go for a walk or something."

"I'm not going out there," he said quickly. Too quickly. The concern on her face made him cringe.

"We have to find these things, Charlie."

"I know, it's just-" He left the sentence hanging, unable to finish it. The fear he felt at meeting the monsters again was overwhelming.

"Me too," Danni said, not unkindly. "Me too."

They returned to studying the paperwork in front of them. The silence between them was uncomfortable and heavy.

"Listen, earlier, I thought-"

Danni held up her hand. "I thought we were all going to die, Charlie. All of us. But we got him, we got the bastard and now we have to find his friends."

"How do you know we got him?" Charlie said.

"He exploded. Three blue spheres came out of him. I told you this."

"Have we got any footage?"

"Front of house is permanently covered so of course we have." She clicked her mouse a few times, and the CCTV footage from the entrance to the station came up. She rewound the footage until she found what she was looking for. Time stamp was 8:03 am. Charlie leant on the desk behind her and watched over her shoulder.

"What am I looking for?"

"I don't know. Teleporting monsters, or something." He shrugged at her. What was he looking for? Maybe he should just call it a day and go home.

Danni advanced the recording a half-second at a time. "Here we go," she said.

The footage showed the bullets hitting the monster and him exploding. Three spheres appeared.

"Go back," Charlie said.

She did twice before she saw it.

"Holy shit."

The bullets hit into the monster, but rather than do anything like fall backwards or even try to get out of the way, the monster took the hits. A bracelet on his wrist glowed and the spheres appeared in his place. The monster disappeared milliseconds before the spheres appeared.

"What does this mean?" Danni whispered. She rewound it and focussed on the bracelet. Her first impression had been wrong: the bracelet itself didn't glow. Indecipherable symbols on it lit up in the instant before the spheres appeared.

"Teleporting monsters," Charlie muttered.

"Are you serious? What the hell does *that* mean?"

"We're out of our depth. This is-," he paused and rubbed his hand through rapidly thinning hair. "I don't know what this is."

"We need to tell the boss," Danni said.

"Even with this footage, she'll think we're nuts."

"Maybe, but hell, Charlie, this is beyond us."

She recorded the section of footage and transferred it to a USB key.

"Let's go," she said.

8:32 AM

Carter dusted himself down as he stood. Grit from the road covered his jeans and he could feel more in his hair. He glanced over at Kingston, who was still aiming at the boy. Carter wrapped his hand around Kingston's and forced him to lower his arm. His hand was shaking as he slipped the gun into the top of his jeans and pulled his t-shirt over it. The young man was extremely pale and tears welled in his eyes.

"He's dead," Carter said.

"I ain't ever killed nobody before." Kingston was still trembling.

"It was him or us."

"You sure about that?"

The boy was lying in a slowly increasing pool of blood. A dark hole sat in the middle of his forehead, and Carter didn't need to look to know the back of his head was missing.

"Yeah, pretty sure." Carter started to approach the corpse, walking slowly. The street was far too quiet. "Where did the guy go?"

The only body in the street was the boy – there was no sign of the man who had been with him. Another mystery to go with the vanished cars and walls. The black wall thing was clearly massively destructive.

Kingston hadn't moved. He shook his head and wiped the tears away, then retched and threw up. His bile splashed onto the boy's corpse.

"You ok?"

Kingston wiped his mouth with the back of his hand. "Better out than in, right?"

"You don't need to do that," Carter said. "The tough guy thing. I don't buy it."

"Whatever, man."

Carter handed him some chewing gum. "Where did the big guy go?"

"Gone, like those others from this morning." Kingston winced as he chewed. Clearly the chewing gum wasn't cutting it.

"Christ." Carter thought about how close he'd come to touching the black wall and shuddered. If he'd made contact, would he have crumbled to dust? Disintegrated? Lost his hand?

"What the hell happened here?"

A new voice. A man in a tracksuit was running towards them, kitbag banging on his leg. Behind him a small and similarly dressed group were following, all coming from the gym opposite the station end of the road. Most of them were frowning and two were already on their phones, taking photos.

"Police," Carter shouted, flashing his warrant card at the gathering crowd. "Please stay back. This is a crime scene. For your own safety, stay back by that car." He pointed at an intact car at the edge of the circle of destruction. "Please put your phones away." Who wants to see this in their feeds?

With his free hand, he took his mobile phone out and dialled the number for Exeter Police Station. Request for urgent assistance filed, he hung up.

"More officers are on the way," he shouted. "This area needs to be secured. Please return to your home or wherever you want to go. There is nothing more to see here."

The crowd started muttering amongst themselves, and a few of them walked away. The majority stayed huddled by the car.

"Carter, I got to go man." Kingston was frowning at the lead man in the tracksuit.

"That guy got a badge?" The gym bunny pointed at Kingston. "Only I didn't see it. How do I know you are real cops?"

Carter strode towards the man, pulling his warrant card out again. "I am DS John Carter, sir, now please step back, you are contaminating this crime scene."

"I want to see his ID. Yours could be fake." The man jutted his jaw out and Carter resisted the urge to punch him.

"He is a witness. He's coming with me."

"He's no witness. Look at him. Did he kill the kid?"

Carter put his hand on the man's chest. "Sir, I have asked you nicely, now I'm telling. Step back or I will arrest you for obstructing-"

"Arrest me? With him standing there?"

"Sir-"

"Get your hands off me."

Carter sighed, then spun the man and pushed his arm up his back. The man cried out, but Carter kept the pressure on. "I really don't want to do this, sir."

"You're hurting me!"

"Are you calm now?"

Carter was aware of the grumblings from the crowd. Two police cars pulled into the top of the street and screeched to a halt.

Officers jumped out and started ordering the crowd back. Carter let the man go.

"Disappear," he said, "before I arrest you for inciting racial hatred."

"You can't do that," the man said, unzipping his tracksuit top. "I did no such thing."

"There is a boy dead in the street there. What did you see?"

"I didn't see anything. I heard a bang and come out to see this bloke standing over a dead kid."

"That's great. So you didn't actually see the kid get killed, right?"

"Well-"

"It's a yes or no kind of question."

The man shook his head.

"So, you saw a black man and started complaining. Classy. Two and two does not equal five. He's coming with me, so you can just wait here. I'm sure the uniforms will take your statement."

Carter took Kingston's arm and turned his back on the man before he could say another word. More police cars were now arriving.

"Let's go," Carter said.

Kingston fixed the man a stare that would have soured milk. "Dick," he muttered.

"Yeah, for once I agree, but it's not safe for you here."

"Don't know if you noticed, Carter, but I don't think it's safe anywhere today."

They walked past the cordon of police cars, with Carter flashing his badge again. He explained Kingston was a witness and he was going to escort him to Exeter station. They headed away from the crowd, towards where he'd parked earlier.

"I ain't going to no police station, I told you already." Kingston's bravado was starting to return.

"Want to stay out here with this crowd, who are pretty sure you killed the kid?" Carter smiled with thin lips. "Of course, you actually did, so I could let that slip out."

"You a wrong 'un, Carter."

"It's not the first time I've heard that," Carter said with a more genuine smile. He opened the door to his car. "Come on, it's not far. Or would you prefer me to cuff you?"

8:40 AM

"Seriously?"

Danni paled and shook her head.

"You want me to believe this thing is not dead?" Inspector Reeves was a big woman and was currently using all six foot four inches of her frame to intimidate Danni. It was working, and she hated herself for it.

"Ma'am, we have proof. It's on this." She handed her the memory stick and was ashamed to see her hand tremble a little.

"I really don't have time for this."

"Ma'am, if he's still alive, we need to make time," Charlie said. "He took out four of us without breaking sweat. He's the prime candidate in the murders of three teenagers-"

"Let me stop you there, Monroe. I am knee deep in a crisis we are ill equipped to deal with. I have a crime spree across the city which is only now beginning to ease. In addition, there have been several murders and the public are, justifiably, jittery. Any second now, the bigwigs from London are going to come in and steam-roll everything we have done so far on this case. I have four partners to visit to tell them their loved ones are not coming home today. I can do without this."

"What shall we do, ma'am?"

"Right now, Monroe, I don't care. I need to get CTSFO in the air, now."

Reeves stomped away barking at her assistant to get the Counter-Terrorism unit airborne. Fifteen minutes until they were in the air then another fifteen of flight time. Charlie looked at his watch. Thirty minutes from now made it 9:10 am, and that was a maximum. He nodded to himself. This was completely doable: stay safe for thirty minutes and then all of this was someone else's problem.

"She's an arsehole," Danni said.

"See, what I like about you Danni, is you are still surprised by that."

8:41 AM

The Prince sat, staring at the wall, not moving. He'd been sitting still for over ten minutes. Callaghan was beginning to get worried.

"We are ready, my Prince," he said for the third time but still garnered no response from the immobile boy.

"Something's happened," Brown said.

Callaghan and Baldwin both scowled at him. Baldwin was watching the entrance to the police station, the shadow of the wall shielding him from the other side of the street. The fabric of his heavy overcoat strained to contain his tail, and his expression was one of impatience.

A cordon had been set up around the entrance to the police station. Two humans stood in the doorway, holding their guns and constantly scanning the street ahead. Behind them, the building gave away no secrets, hiding the humans away from Baldwin's prying eyes. An occasional car rattled past, but the street was quiet.

The guns were the weapons Kennedy had warned them against, but where was he now? Had he been captured? They had come closer to the station to try and answer the question but were none the wiser. Baldwin had assumed Kennedy was somewhere inside the building, surrounded by the dead of their enemy.

"They are no match for us," Baldwin said. "I am done waiting."

"Then where is Kennedy?" Brown asked.

The Prince opened his eyes and Brown recoiled in surprise.

"My brother is dead."

All three bowed their heads instantly. They knew better than to ask how the Prince had garnered this information.

"The humans must die," the Prince snarled, face contorting with rage. It was an emotion Baldwin had believed him incapable of. The Prince stood and crossed the road. As he moved, he held his arms out perpendicular to his body. Pressure began to build.

"Move back," Baldwin cried and the three of them scuttled back down the road, heading away from the Prince. "Be ready!"

"Hey!" One of the armed officers shouted. "Stop right there!" He raised his weapon, but then clutched his head as the pressure built further. A high-pitched whine pierced the air, worse than ever before.

Blackness erupted from the Prince and rushed outwards in a hemisphere of destruction. Cars crumpled in an instant, obliterated by the indestructible wall. Two screams rang out before ending as abruptly. The wall raced towards the three of them, and then stopped scant centimetres away. Baldwin stood wide-eyed and rigid, his entire field of vision filling with the deadly, perfect darkness.

Then the wall was gone, taking the pressure and whine with it. The two officers had disappeared, along with the glass doors of the building. Stone crumbled to the ground now that its support had evaporated.

"Move!" Baldwin cried.

The Prince staggered in the middle of the road. He had continued to move forward as the Wall fired out – a sign of his growing strength. Breathing heavily and swaying, he collapsed, sinking to his knees with an anguished cry. Baldwin and the others covered the distance quickly, reaching the Prince barely a second after he collapsed.

Shocked faces were gathering in the ruined doorway as the humans came to see what had happened.

"Kill them," the Prince said, panting hard. "Kill them all."

8:43 AM

Danni and Charlie walked downstairs into the waiting room. Four body bags lay on the floor and the paramedic who had helped Danni was filling in paperwork next to them. He looked exhausted, just how Danni felt. A sudden pressure built in her head, making her wince and she frowned, rubbing her temples. Next to her Charlie was doing the same. It seemed to be getting dark now, the light fading rapidly.

A black wall slammed into the doors and obliterated them. No explosion, no shattering glass or loud bang. The wall smashed a few feet into the waiting room and sat shimmering in front of them. Someone screamed, and the wall disappeared.

"What the hell just happened?" Danni said.

The front of the station was ruined. Where there had been secure doors was now an empty space, as if someone had removed the front of the building. One of the body bags had disappeared, with no remains left behind to suggest it had ever been there in the first place.

Charlie staggered forward, fear ripping a path through his

nervous system, making his legs feel like jelly. He stepped into the street, just in time to see a small boy fall to his knees. Three men were running towards the boy, presumably to help. All of them ran with a curious gait, caused by them all being almost doubled over. Each of the men had a large hunchback. The boy was kneeling in a circle of emptiness. No cars. No people. Just the kid.

Something clicked in Charlie's mind.

Linda Carter had mentioned a kid in her statement.

A creepy kid.

"They're back!" Charlie roared. "Get weapons, call for back up, get the army! Christ, they're back!" Twenty-seven minutes until CTSF could arrive. They needed to be here sooner.

Two of the men continued past the fallen boy and Charlie turned away, heading back into the building as fast as he could. It was like running through treacle. People were beginning to respond and the noise level was rising. The armed response team he had seen earlier was moving to the ruined doorway, weapons at the ready. One, the woman, smiled at him as she passed.

"We got this covered," she said.

"I hope so," Charlie muttered. He read her name badge: TFO K. Samuel. "Well, Samuel, avoid the tail and watch out for spikes."

"Don't worry, they won't get close."

She jogged to catch up with her friend, boots clomping on the ground. She was carrying so much equipment Charlie was impressed. No way could he carry that and still run. Danni caught up to him.

"What do we do?" Her voice was steady, but her eyes told a different story.

"Stay out of their way, let SCO19 take this." He nodded at the two officers in the dust and rubble of the doorway.

"How many are there?"

"Three, I think." He remembered the boy, kneeling in the epicentre of nothing. "Maybe four."

"Then we need to help," she said. "Just one of them nearly took us all out."

"Yeah, but we didn't know what we were dealing with then. Look at them, they're ready."

One of the officers was kneeling, the other- Samuel - standing. Both had MP5 machine guns trained on the street.

"Armed police, halt!" Samuel barked. "Stop or we will open fire."

Charlie had to admire her training. It was obvious to him the men were not stopping and he would have just opened fire as soon as he'd seen them. The third man had left the boy and was sprinting to catch up with the others.

"Take their legs!" Samuel shouted the order and opened fire. Her colleague joined in, bullets spraying out of their weapons. The first man howled as the bullets tore into his legs. He somehow kept upright long enough to absorb more of the fire before his legs gave out and he crumpled to the ground with a grunt.

"There's a kid out there!" the male SCO19 yelled.

"Hold your fire!" Samuel called.

"No, don't," Charlie said, but it came out as a horrified whisper. He could see the two remaining creatures closing the distance to the station. They were moving with a speed that belied their size.

The creatures both leapt, covering five metres in a single bound. At the same time, their coats ripped, revealing their monstrous tails. Samuel's colleague turned his weapon to the nearest creature and opened fire. Bullets thudded into its chest as it swung its tail.

The ball of spikes hit the officer full in the face, lifting him off his feet and throwing him across the room. He hit the wall behind Mike and slumped to the floor. Something sharp and triangular jutted out of his face: spikes. Around the wound, flesh was already peeling away from the bone, slowly at first but then more rapidly. The man didn't scream at all, which meant he was already dead.

Charlie stopped his retreat. Everyone in this part of the station was in danger. Danni was right – they needed to help. He could see the dead man's MP5 in his lap and his Glock still in its holster. Many of the people in the lobby were running away from the monsters and Charlie fought his way through them until he reached the corpse. He pulled the MP5 free and spun back to face the two creatures.

The one which had been shot was kneeling on the floor, clutching its chest whilst the other tore through the fleeing humans. Charlie counted at least three people on the floor not including the SCO19 man.

Charlie pushed back against the flow, but two people fell in front of him, both screaming in terror. The creature slapped one with a clawed hand and blood poured out of the scratches on the man's face. He turned to the other person, just as Charlie opened fire.

The creature fell back, sliding across the floor as the bullets hit it repeatedly. Charlie pulled the uninjured woman to her feet.

"Take him and get him somewhere safe!" Charlie roared. The woman nodded, eyes dazed, but helped the bleeding man to his feet. He was holding his face, hoping pressure alone would keep his cheek attached. The skin wasn't melting, so the man would probably be ok – horrifically scarred, but alive.

The creature stopped sliding and tried to get to its feet but failed. The kneeling one looked at his fallen friend and roared. It bared its teeth, getting back to its feet.

"No! Go to the Prince," the thing on the floor said.

The creature spoke.

The monster said actual, real words.

It didn't seem right for the thing to be able to speak, but Charlie couldn't explain why. It just seemed one more crazy thing on a day filled with madness. The confusion gave the creature the split second it needed.

The creature turned and ran back outside.

8:46 AM

Danni saw Charlie shoot the thing but couldn't move. Fear had rooted her to the spot. When the shooting started, she had dived behind the counter and only now had the confidence to peer over the top. She saw the corpses before Charlie shot the creature. Danni had to resist cheering as the thing fell.

Then the thing had spoken.

English.

The other creature was now running down the street. Danni stood and watched it go. It was running towards the boy in the street. The thought of a child being at the mercy of the creature galvanised her. She stood and started to go after him.

"Danni!"

She turned towards Charlie who threw a Glock towards her.

"Take it!" Charlie shouted. He had the MP5 trained on the creature on the ground.

She nodded as she caught the pistol. The other SCO19 officer – Samuel – fell into step beside her, MP5 ready.

"Take him out!" Charlie called after her. "Don't let him get away."

Danni ran into the street, squinting as the bright sunlight clawed at her eyes. The creature was nearly at the stricken boy now. Ten metres away. The boy was struggling to get to his feet, staggering as he rose. Five metres.

"Stop!" she shouted. Two metres. "Police! Armed police! On your knees, now!"

The creature ignored her, so Samuel opened fire. Bullets smashed into his back with a few going wild around him. It staggered forward, stumbling under the onslaught of bullets. Blood splashed onto the tarmac as it keeled over and lay on the ground with arms outstretched.

"No!" The boy roared.

She saw a car coming closer at the top of the street. Oh God, not more civilians, not now. Before she could do anything, pressure started to build in her head, like being in a plane at take-off but a hundred times worse. A high-pitched whine pierced her ears and she winced, gripping her head. This was like before, when the black wall had hit the front of the station. Danni sank to her knees, moaning and out of the corner of her eye saw Samuel do the same

The boy was standing over the dead creature, raising his arms and making the shape of a cross.

8:47 AM

Carter saw the woman shoot the running creature; the carnage at the front of the station and the boy raising his arms. Kingston clutched his head as the pressure began to build again and he started moaning. Carter didn't stop to think, although all he wanted to do was collapse and hold his head.

He pressed the accelerator to the floor and the car surged forward.

8:48 AM

Samuel forced herself to move. She grabbed the back of Danni's jacket and dragged her away from the boy. They hobbled back to the pavement, leaving the boy alone with the corpse of the creature at his feet.

She felt – rather than heard – footsteps of someone approaching but couldn't do anything about it. If it was another creature they were done for. Her head was banging now, and she let Danni go before collapsing herself.

Charlie was crawling towards them, pain etched all over his face. He was pointing back at the building, but Samuel couldn't move. All her focus was on the boy.

A car hit him, smashing his tiny frame into the air, catapulting him over the vehicle as it skidded to a halt. Black tyre marks stretched down the street and they could all smell burning rubber. The pressure and whine stopped instantly.

The boy landed with a thump, his leg twisted awkwardly beneath his body. He screamed in agony and tried in vain to get to his feet. Two men got out of the car: Carter and a black teenager. The black man was holding a gun and as Samuel watched, helpless, he unloaded the weapon into the kid.

8:49 AM

Father staggered suddenly, crying out as if in pain, and holding on to the wall in support. Kennedy watched aghast as Father sobbed, his chest rising and falling violently as he cried.

Kennedy had never seen anything like it. This was even worse than in the Throne Room.

"Father," he started, but he was cut off by another moan.

"My son," Father sobbed. Kennedy said nothing, realising now what Father had felt instantly: the other Prince was also dead.

Father stood straight and surveyed the area in front of him, blinking heavily. They were in a quiet street away from the main parts of the city centre. A sign to his right read *Library* and it was surrounded by other, non-descript buildings. No humans walked this street. It was as if they could sense Father and Kennedy and stayed away. Kennedy, at least, was grateful.

Father's brow creased in concentration, eyes narrowing.

Kennedy backed away slowly. He did not want to face Father's wrath now. He almost felt pity for the humans. Father raised his arms, and Kennedy swallowed hard.

He felt pressure start to build in his head and closed his eyes when the whine started.

8:50 AM

Carter got out of the car as soon as it stopped. The bonnet was crumpled, probably beyond repair and, judging by the burning smell, he also needed four new tyres. Now that the car had stopped, and the whine ceased, a heavy silence fell on the street.

A loud bang shattered the eerie silence. Then another and another as Kingston emptied the weapon into the boy. Bullets rained into his body, blowing large holes into the tiny frame until, at last, the gun clicked empty. Kingston was screaming as he fired, tears streaming down his face.

"Jesus, Kingston."

Carter heard footsteps running and turned to see Charlie sprinting towards them. When he saw the expression on Charlie's face, he held up his hands.

"Wait Charlie, wait!"

Charlie ignored him and rugby tackled Kingston. His considerable bulk caught Kingston in the back and they both tumbled to the ground. The gun spun out of Kingston's hand, clattering away across the asphalt. Charlie grabbed a firm hold of Kingston's wrist and forced his arm up his back.

"Don't," he said, as Kingston started to struggle.

"I didn't do nothing, man!"

"Charlie, let him go," Carter cried. "He's with me."

Charlie pushed Kingston's arm further up his back.

"That was no kid." Carter touched Charlie gently on the shoulder. "Come on, Charlie, let him go and I'll explain."

Charlie let him go with some reluctance and Kingston scooped the gun up as he stood. He held it loosely by his side.

"The kid was one of them." Carter nodded at the boy on the ground. "Did you hear the whine? Feel pressure in your head? It was him."

"The *kid?*"

"That hurt," Kingston said, rubbing his arm.

"They just attacked us again, four of them," Charlie said. "They killed some more of ours, but we got them. This time we got them."

"What the hell is this?" Carter looked down at the boy. "This is one messed up family."

"Are there more?" Kingston looked around him, scanning the road ahead and behind. His eyes settled on Danni, but she ignored him and walked back to the station with Samuel.

"We don't know," Charlie said, after Carter introduced them. "Come on, I'd feel better inside."

It was hard to argue, and they made their way back to the police station. They were a few metres away from the entrance when Charlie suddenly clamped his hands over his ears and screamed. Carter stared at him before he felt it too: pressure building like it had with the kid earlier.

But not quite.

This was worse. Far, far worse.

He sank to his knees, holding his head as if it would stop the pressure building. Out of the corner of his eye, he could see Kingston rolling on the ground, mouth open in a silent cry. No, he thought, not silent, but just inaudible over the whine. The high-pitched whine came next, building to a level sufficient to send dogs mad.

Nausea built with the pressure and he knew he was screaming. Just when he thought his head would actually explode, like that dumb old film, the pressure was gone.

Blood trickled from his nose and he wiped it away with the back of his hand. He blinked rapidly, eyes full of water. It was dark, so he rubbed his eyes again. Blinking again he looked up.

The sun had gone. Dark shadows stretched as far as he could see.

"Oh… my… god…"

Carter glanced over at Charlie, who was staring up at the sky. A large wall of black stretched as far as he could see, disappearing behind the buildings in the distance. When he focused on the buildings, he realised the black wall cut *through* them. He spun and the wall spun with him.

No. It didn't spin with him; the wall was circular. It completely enclosed the area he could see. A dark, malevolent dome. It shimmered and twinkled on the inside, creating an eerie kind of light, like dusk on a winter's night. He shivered.

"What the hell is this?" Kingston asked, his voice full of tension.

"I have no idea."

In the distance, an orange glow started to fill the sky. The lights had come on across the area they could see. Carter glanced at his watch; not even nine o'clock in the morning yet. Distant thuds echoed around the buildings, as the ones touched by the dome started to collapse.

Then, as he watched, the black wall started to move outwards, and the distant thuds became loud bangs.

8:55 A.M

Father let his arms fall to his side for a moment, breathing hard. Then, with a growl, he flung them apart like he was pushing something away from him. Kennedy grimaced as the wall moved outwards, destroying everything in its path.

When it was done, Father collapsed, drool spilling out of his open mouth. Kennedy ran to him, catching him before he hit the ground and lowering him gently.

Father grunted and gasped, then coughed. "Take me back. I must rest. The barrier will hold well enough whilst I rest."

"What should I do?"

"Wake the others."

Kennedy was confused. All the Scouts were out in Exeter, with the Princes. Although, as the Princes were dead, then it was highly probable his brothers were too.

"Everyone," Father said. "Tonight, you will feast well"

"Yes, Father."

Father nodded, happy his favourite lieutenant was at hand to follow his instruction. "Kennedy, the black man."

Kennedy waited, hoping for more. There were many black humans.

"He lives, the black man lives until he sees me, do you understand?"

Kennedy tried not to let his confusion show - he really tried.

"He killed my sons. He will suffer at my hand and no-one else's."

"Father, which black man? There are many."

"He has a scorpion drawn on the back of his hand."

8:56 A.M

The black wall moved. One moment it was a still monument to lost light and the next it was moving away from the centre of Exeter. It destroyed everything in its path, reducing once proud buildings to piles of rubble in an instant. Any living thing caught in its wake was vaporised, with not enough time to ring home to declare love to significant others, nor even enough time to realise what was happening.

As soon as the black wall touched something, it was destroyed.

The helicopter carrying the highly trained CTSFO team collided with the wall, its appearance too sudden to give the pilot time to alter course. The helicopter disappeared as it hit the barrier, everything and everyone disintegrating on contact.

Eventually, after a short but destructive path across the land, it stopped on the outskirts of Exeter, making a perfect dome which cut the ancient city off from the rest of the world.

8:57 A.M

Linda and Mike sat in the interview room, waiting. Their cups of coffee were long empty, and Linda was beginning to get a back-ache from the uncomfortable chair. She stood up suddenly, metal legs screeching on the floor.

Mike shook his head and stared at her with bleary eyes. He rubbed his face and groaned.

"I can't believe you were falling asleep." Her ears were still ringing, and she was all too aware she was speaking too loudly.

"Sorry, been a long night," Mike muttered.

"What was that whining noise anyway?"

"What whining noise?"

"Oh for God's sake, Mike." Linda stamped her foot in frustration, knowing it made her look like a petulant child. "Something's happened," she said, "and I'm going to find out what."

"They told us to wait here," Mike said.

"When did you turn into such a yes man?"

With a sigh, Mike stood, still rubbing his eyes. He followed her out of the room, but much more slowly.

Linda marched down the corridor, looking into the other interview rooms as she went. All the doors were open which shouldn't be allowed, should it? She frowned. Something wasn't right here. In addition, all the rooms were empty, and that made her go cold: in a city the size of Exeter, surely someone was always being interviewed for something?

At the end of the corridor was another door and this led into a large open plan office. Everyone in the office – although they were not numerous - stood near the windows, staring out at something. Strip lights filled the room with harsh artificial light and Linda realised it was dark outside. She looked at her watch.

8:56.

"What the hell?" She crossed to the window and joined the others in staring. A large black wall stretched as far as she could see, curving around to disappear behind the side of the building. She spun and looked at the other windows on the far side of the office and started to moan.

The wall completely circled them, and reached high over the tops of the buildings, blotting out the sun. *It's a dome,* she realised, *like someone had put a massive black bowl on top of Exeter.*

She could see the cathedral in the distance and the various high-rise buildings making up the shopping centre in the middle of Exeter. Beyond was a huge pile of rubble: the rest of the city had been completely destroyed. The wall itself was giving off a strange half-light, shrouding everything in shadows.

"Oh my God," Mike said.

"Where's John?" Linda whispered. "Mike, we have to find John!"

"I'm here."

She turned and relief flooded through her. Carter was with the other cops, Charlie and Danni, and a black kid who couldn't be more than seventeen. She hugged him hard, not caring how dishevelled he looked. He winced, reminded of aching muscles, but returned the hug just as fiercely.

"I thought you were dead."

"It was close," he admitted. "Kingston saved me." He gestured at the black kid, who had the grace to look sheepish.

"I didn't do nothing, man."

"Yeah, so by definition you did something," Carter smiled. Kingston frowned, his entire expression saying 'huh?'

"What's going on?" Mike asked. "What the hell is this black thing?"

"I wish I knew," Carter said, finally letting Linda go.

"We're trapped," Mike said. His eyes were wide, pupil's black pits that threatened to swallow his face.

"It would appear so." Danni frowned at the black wall in the distance. "I don't want to go near the thing."

Carter had to agree with her: something about the wall snapped at the back of his mind. A knot of anxiety formed in his stomach whenever he looked at it and he could feel cold sweat pooling at the base of his spine.

"Look at the city." Linda's voice barely rose above a whisper. "What's happened to the city?"

"The wall. Everything it touches." Kingston put his hands together then pulled them apart, making an explosion noise.

"What about the people?" Linda said.

"What people?" Mike said. He was now sitting at one of the desks.

"Them," Linda gestured at the windows, pointing at the city. "How many people are dead?"

Silence greeted the remark. It was as if none of them had even thought about it until then. Maybe they hadn't wanted to think through the ramifications of the destruction. How many people had died when the wall expanded? How many people were panicking now? How many were already looting? Carter swallowed hard. What was the saying? Civilisation is only two meals away from ending.

"We need to get patrols out on the streets, keep people calm, stop looting, that kind of thing," Danni muttered.

"I'm sure it's in hand," Carter said. "You guys have your ERR, right?"

Danni and Charlie exchanged an uneasy look.

"Yeah, but it rolls down from up country," Charlie said. "Helicopters and support come from London or Southampton."

"Really?" Carter said and they both nodded. "Well, shit."

"What's an ERR?" Linda asked.

"Emergency response and recovery," Danni said. "It's mainly meant for terrorism and disasters, not whatever the hell this is."

"So, we're cut off and help isn't coming." Kingston looked at them all in turn. "That's if I'm understanding all your jargon and shit."

Mike hit the desk hard enough to get everyone in the room's attention. "We shouldn't be here. What the hell is going on? We're surrounded by a black wall that has already destroyed half the city. Thousands of people are dead. Thousands. Oh, God, I feel sick."

A wastepaper bin was near his feet and he picked it up before retching noisily into it. Linda went to him, put her hand on his back and made soothing noises. Carter shook his head and looked away, much to Kingston's amusement.

Charlie watched the city and the wall, ignoring everyone. Smoke was rising in at least three different locations and he shuddered at the sight. His thoughts were filled with pictures of his soon to be ex-wife, dead in a pile of rubble or obliterated into nothing, not even a pile of dust.

He felt a sudden surge of emotion. No chance for a last-minute reconciliation - although if he were honest with himself, the chance was long gone. The days of sitting around, making each other laugh whilst drinking far too much wine, had disappeared faster than his waistline. He wouldn't be able to say sorry now, or even wish her well. Life was a precious, fragile thing and hers was almost certainly now over. She lived in Heavitree and it looked as though the wall had flattened the whole area.

"So, what now?" Charlie said when Carter joined him. He wiped his eyes, hoping his old friend hadn't noticed the wetness there. If he did, he didn't mention it.

"I have no idea. Get out there and get the public safe I guess."

"Keep *them* safe? Carter, what about *us*?"

"I know."

"What is this?" he gestured at the wall. "Where did it come from?"

"The kid made something like this," Carter said. "Earlier. This is like a bigger version."

"Do you think there are more of the creepy kids out there?"

"Christ knows," Carter said. "To be honest, I just want to stay here and hug my wife until the cavalry arrives."

They stood in silence staring at the wall of black, both lost in their own thoughts. Its oppressiveness was not weakened by familiarity. If anything, he was feeling worse. He glanced at his watch. 8:56. The seconds hand wasn't moving. He shook it for a moment, but nothing happened. The station clock on the wall showed the same time, second hand not moving. Charlie rubbed his stomach to try and calm the unease there.

"Christ, I feel awful," he muttered.

"Me too," Carter said.

"Yeah." Danni handed them a bottle of water each. "Something about the wall is just *wrong*."

"Apart from the fact it's there, you mean?" Carter shrugged. Any sort of sense or logic about the day had rapidly disappeared.

"You know what I mean. I don't like looking at it."

Carter agreed. "Yeah, I know what you mean."

Danni put a hand on the window, relishing the cold feel of the glass on her palm. A new plume of smoke started rising in the distance and she shuddered at the thought of what was happening on the streets. She felt impotent, but also – and with more than a pang of guilt – safe. It was better to be here, surrounded by her colleagues, in a large secure building – even with the smashed front – than out there.

Instantly, she felt ashamed of herself. This was not why she became a police officer, to stay safe whilst others were in danger. Of course, the real reason she had joined up seemed stupid now. Good pension, varied work, chance to meet some hot women.

"We need to get out there," she said.

Charlie watched her with narrow eyes. "You're a detective, not a bobby. Let them do their jobs." As he spoke, cars were rolling out of the station with lights flashing and sirens howling. "They will follow the protocols and arrange safe places for those that can't get home. We can't do anything."

"We'll be an extra pair of hands."

"We'll be in the way."

"Seriously, Charlie?"

"She's right, mate," Carter said.

"You go with her then."

"You're not going anywhere, John Carter!" Linda cried from across the room.

"I need to help," he said, shrugging. He went to her and hugged her again. She resisted for a moment, but then hugged him back.

"I'll come," Kingston said.

"Really?" Carter couldn't hide the shock in his voice. The kid was full of surprises.

"Yeah, man, being with all you 5-0 types is making me nervous."

Carter nodded. Maybe Kingston wasn't the selfish gang banger he made himself out to be. Plus, the lad had saved Carter at least twice from those freaky kids, so he couldn't be all bad.

"I'm going to regret this," Charlie said with a rueful smile.

"You're all crazy." Mike crossed his arms, looking more like a petulant child than hardened, cynical reporter. "I'm staying here."

"Good. You two can stick together." Carter nodded at Linda.

"Well, let's roll." Danni led the way out of the office.

"Does she always speak like that?" Carter asked.

"Yeah."

"Christ."

He kissed and hugged Linda then said, "Look after yourself, ok? I'll be back before you know it."

She gave him a tentative smile. "Don't do anything stupid."

"I won't," he hesitated. "Keep an eye on Mike. I'm not sure he's coping too well."

Mike was hugging himself and rocking back and forth on the chair.

"I don't think I am either," she said.

"You're stronger than him." He kissed her again, and then jogged to catch the others up.

8:58 A.M

Kennedy was carrying Father by the time they returned to the entrance. Father was heavy but Kennedy still carried him with ease. They passed through tunnels just under the surface of the streets, with Father slipping in and out of consciousness. Kennedy reached the control room and then he carefully put Father in his chair, surrounded as always by the large bank of monitors and machines. Working quickly, Kennedy attached two wires to Father's arms. Two plugs had been inserted there long ago to make the process quick and easy. One of the wires pumped Father's blood into the machines and the other returned it, presumably clean of whatever toxins made him pass out.

The effects were instantaneous.

Father gasped and sat bolt upright in his chair. He breathed heavily for a moment and took in his surroundings.

"Thank you, old friend."

Kennedy swallowed his excitement. Father had called him a friend!

"Did you wake them?"

"Not yet, Father. I wanted to make sure you were safe first."

Father nodded, weariness returning far too quickly. "Do it now, Kennedy. The Barrier exhausts me and it will not last indefinitely. We must be prepared for when it falls."

"Yes, Father."

"Take as many as you can with you. The humans must die." Father gasped again. "But not the black one. The Scorpion. He is mine. Do not let anyone forget."

"Yes, Father."

"Go now, Kennedy."

Kennedy bowed and went deeper into their home. He passed rack after rack after rack of tall cylindrical pods, each of which contained one of his brothers.

Well not quite *brothers* exactly. Cousins would be a better word. Father created them all, but he didn't do it equally. Kennedy and the other Scouts had powers that went beyond their strength. The tails and acid were not gifts bestowed on just anyone. The majority of Father's children did not possess them.

Kennedy moved with speed through the tunnels, moving deeper and deeper into the breeding room. Every hundred metres he stopped to activate the panels which would awaken his cousins from sleep.

They had nearly been awoken twice before. First time had been just as a disease nearly killed every human. The Horde had watched as their food store was reduced daily and had retreated to sleep until the crisis passed. If the Humans were wiped out, there would be other sources of food for the Horde. Father had made them all sleep for over five hundred years, until waking them nearly two hundred years ago. Kennedy remembered it vividly: the summer had been warm and the city was prosperous with a growing population. But many of the humans fell ill again and this time the disease threatened to spread to the Horde. This disease was not as awesome as the first, but the risk to the Horde was deemed too great.

Kennedy and his brothers had watched the city become crippled by the disease and thought it a wasted opportunity. Nevertheless, Father had ordered them to sleep and the brothers were not brave enough to argue.

Kennedy had woken once a decade to check on the progress of the humans since then. It had been an honour to be the chief Scout for his people. Kennedy hadn't been able to resist taking the odd human here and there over the years; he had seen it as just reward for his endeavour.

But now, the Awakening was finally at hand. So many centuries had passed before Father finally deemed them ready. Kennedy had thought them ready at least twice in the last hundred years, but Father had disliked the bombs. He wanted to co-exist with the humans, not fight them.

It had been over the course of the last century they'd learned to speak the language of the humans. Father had monitored something he called 'radio waves' and then he'd discovered the pictures the humans broadcast. Father picked up the language easily and, of course, what Father knew, so did they all.

One by one the Scouts were named by Father, who seemed to be drawing inspiration from the human names he heard in the broadcasts. Kennedy didn't know anything about that. He found the messages and images unfathomable. As far as he could see, the humans were inferior to the Scouts in every way, but he had to bow to Father's greater knowledge and understanding.

Still, Kennedy hit the activation panels, and heard the groans and cries of his waking cousins. There were lots of them now. Once he completed the loop, he started again. He felt the telepathic tingle of Father's instructions trickling through to them all. It was weaker than usual, a sign he was still struggling with the effort of producing the Barrier. The message was easy to understand all the same.

Find the humans and kill them.

Kill them all.

But not this one. A picture of a young black man seared itself into Kennedy's memory. He was holding a gun, aiming at Kennedy and with a start he realised he was reliving one of the Prince's last moments. This was the man Father wanted brought back alive, his image broadcast to the Horde.

Kennedy shuddered. He didn't want to know what Father had planned.

He turned back to face the crowds of his cousins. Some were still shaking as they emerged from their cocoons, features still soft. As he watched, their skin tightened, stretching taught over muscle. Each was shorter than him, standing at six feet, but their broad frames and muscle-bound upper bodies gave the impression of greater size. Thin but powerful legs held them erect, but none of these had been blessed with a tail. That was a privilege only given to the Scouts. They did have long nails and sharp teeth to match their cousins, and they were also completely bald.

He thought they looked magnificent.

Kennedy waited for a few moments, until the Horde was silent. Father had given permission for them to break the rules, which meant he'd given up – at least temporarily – on any thought of living alongside the humans.

"Follow me," he said. "We will eat well."

PART II

1

THEY MADE their way through the station, weaving through bewildered looking people. Civilians had started to arrive at the station, looking for answers. They all wore similar expressions: wild eyes, sweating and tense posture. Carter tried to push past them but there were too many. He wasn't sure what they expected to find. A huge black wall obliterates half of a city was not on any ERR plans. Over a hundred-thousand people lived in Exeter and a huge number of those were now dead. He shuddered, burying ever present nausea.

"This way," Danni said and led them down a back stairwell, paint flaking on the walls. The stairs led to a heavy-duty door which in turn opened to the car park for the station. They walked out into the eerie twilight caused by the wall. Three cars and a large van sat in the car park: all other vehicles had already gone. A car was pulling out into the street and Carter watched it head down into Exeter.

The car screeched down the road, dark smoke billowing from its exhaust. It was nearly out of sight when it exploded.

In less than a second, bits of the car shot into the air as the vehicle disintegrated. A tyre rolled away from the wreckage. Three small blue spheres flew out of the wreckage, their stark colour contrasting with the black smoke coming from the ruined vehicle. Indistinct figures seemed to dance in the smoke. The spheres circled each other for another second and then collided with a bang.

One of the creatures stood where the spheres had been. He was pointing towards the station, shouting as his tail swung behind him.

"Shit," Carter said.

Through the smoke, shapes started to become more solid. Humanoid in basic shape and without tails. Thin, but heavily muscled. Hordes of things poured through the smoke, a large mob of them moving towards Carter and the others. They were all screaming and shouting as they started to run towards the police station.

Carter froze, mouth open as the things ran towards them. Too many to count. They were less than a hundred metres away.

"Christ," he said. "We're fucked."

2

"Run!" Carter yelled. Nobody needed telling twice. The creatures screeched and hollered as they advanced. Kingston made it through the opening, followed closely by Carter. Danni paused, waiting for Carlie to catch up.

Thankfully, the entrance was now empty, civilians and police alike having moved deeper into the station. They sprinted past corpses and ran upstairs, heading to the main central office.

As he entered the stairwell, Charlie slammed the doors shut and forced the locks into their housings. Sweating and breathing hard, he made his way up the stairs on weak legs. He heard a thud from behind him, then another as the bangs reverberated up the stairwell. The creatures were already at the door. Wincing, he rubbed his chest and wiped his brow. His hand came away slick with sweat and he tried to control his breathing even as the pain in his chest subsided.

"Where are we going?" he panted. "They're coming in, no matter what!"

"Just get in here, Charlie!" Danni cried.

"They're coming," Carter said to the assembled officers in the room. Linda and Mike were at the rear, near the interview rooms. Mike was visibly shaking. Carter tried to smile at Linda but found he couldn't.

He looked around the open plan office and felt his heart sink even further. Ten desks were dotted around the room, with metal racks full of deep trays near them. Each tray was labelled with a name: personal storage space. Carter rattled the rack nearest him, but it was bolted to the floor and didn't move. At least there were only two doors into the room, the one he had just come through and the one at the rear of the room, near Linda.

"What are we going to do?" Kingston whispered.

"You still got the Glock?"

"Of course." *One clip left,* he thought.

"Get ready to use it."

Kingston swallowed hard as several uniformed officers came forward holding their batons. They were clutching them tightly with white knuckles. Carter had to admire their bravery but wondered if it was just stupidity.

"Barricade the doors," he shouted. "Grab anything to use as a weapon."

Two officers pushed a table over to the doorway, upending it to block the space. Samuel ran to the front and kneeled by it, MP5 trained on the stairwell with a steadiness Carter envied. Another man stood next to her, aiming his own weapon.

"What about the other stairs?" Charlie was still red-faced and breathing hard. Every couple of seconds, he rubbed his chest and winced.

"With me," Danni said, pointing at Kingston who had drawn his Glock. She took a baton from a nearby desk.

"Who are you ordering around, sugar tits?"

Danni gave him a hard look. "You. You're the one who's armed."

"No way, sweet cheeks, first chance I get I'm outta here." Kingston jutted his chin out, but it only made him look younger.

"Good luck, but I think you noticed how many of those freaks are out there." She pointed at the windows. "How the hell you going to get out of here without getting got?"

"Getting got? What the hell?" He looked at Carter. "She for real?"

"You coming or not?" Danni demanded.

"Kingston, I need you to go with her otherwise we're not getting out of here," Carter said.

Kingston glared at him for a moment before kissing his teeth and following Danni. Carter jogged after the younger man.

"Your husband is spending more time with that black kid than with you," Mike said. Linda ignored him and watched Carter's retreating back.

Another bang echoed from the stairwell, followed by the sound of wood splintering and glass shattering. A cacophony of roars and cries made her blood run cold.

"Oh Christ," Linda whispered. "They're here."

3

As soon as the car exploded, the three spheres coalesced with a bang and Kennedy stood in the street. He looked at his hands and wriggled his toes. Everything seemed present and correct. Relief washed over him, and he pointed at the building into which the humans had fled.

"In there!" he roared. "Remember the one Father wants. Kill the rest."

His cousins charged towards the police station, a wave of snarls, claws and teeth. Half of them poured in through the ruined door and Kennedy heard the bangs of the humans' guns. The other half ran around the side of the building, chasing the other four. He waited, weighing up the best option, but then smiled to himself.

Always be direct. The time for sneaking around had passed.

4

"WE NEED MORE WEAPONS," Carter said. He was now at the opposite end of the open plan office, staring down a different stairwell. Past the top of the stairs was another corridor where the interview rooms were. He'd seen a couple of people duck into them to hide and he couldn't blame them.

Kingston pointed his Glock at the stairwell. "Nah, man, I'm good." The tremor in his voice belied those words.

Danni clutched her baton, extending it to its full length. It still looked woefully inadequate. "Just don't get spiked," she said.

"Help me." Carter pointed at one of the desks. Danni took one end and helped Carter carry it to the top of the staircase. They tipped it up, papers flying into the opening as the table blocked just over half of the landing. Carter and Danni shifted another table into place, blocking the stairwell completely. It wouldn't hold for long.

"Thanks for your help." Carter scowled at Kingston.

"No problem."

Screams erupted from downstairs and Carter peered over the

top of the desks. Blood splashed against the wall at the foot of the stairs, red fingers leaving traces on the grey paint. A man's head rolled into view. Just a head. No body. Carter swallowed hard, trying not to stare at the still open eyes.

"Here we go," he said.

5

THE CREATURES FLOODED THE STAIRWELL, shouting and roaring as they ran. Samuel aimed, and opened fire at the same time as her colleague. Bullets rained into the first wave of creatures making legs, chests and heads burst open as metal rained into them.

"Reloading!" Samuel roared. She changed her magazine quickly and aimed down the sights. *So many of them*, she thought, *there's far too many of them*. Despite her nerves, she continued to squeeze the trigger, moving to the next target as soon as the bullet left her weapon.

Soon the bodies were piling up in the stairwell, making it harder for the next wave to come up. It was now easier to pick them off with headshots, creating more of a barricade. The shouts from downstairs subsided and the creatures stopped coming into the stairwell.

"Yes!" her colleague shouted, punching the air.

"Check your magazines," Samuel said, before checking her own. Two, both full. It was nowhere near enough.

"That was pretty easy," he said. "Thought these things were badass."

Samuel ignored him, just like she was trying to ignore the growing pit of anxiety in her gut.

6

"STOP!" Kennedy roared as the bullets rang out. He backed it up with a mental command and the Horde stopped their assault. The humans had cut a sizeable number down, their weapons creating a swathe of destruction through the ranks. His group stood stock still in the lobby. Several dead humans littered the ground, surrounded by a far larger number of dead Horde. One of his group wiped blood from around his mouth but it was the only movement.

"Listen!" he shouted, pointing to the back of the building. "That sound is the humans' weapons. Our brothers and cousins are getting cut down back there. Stop, or you will be next."

His cousins looked at each other uneasily, shifting from foot to foot with unspent energy and frustration.

"We must be more clever than the humans."

Kennedy looked around the room, scowling at the blood on the walls. The desk that used to bar the way in was wrecked, shards of glass littering the ground around it. Sharp splinters of wood protruded from the panels like teeth. Kennedy's eyes drifted to the ceiling and he smiled.

7

"WHERE ARE THEY?" Danni muttered. "Did they all come in the other way?" The stairwell in front of her remained devoid of life – human or otherwise. Only the severed head continued to stare at them with vacant eyes.

"I doubt it," Carter said. "There were lots of them. I'd have split my forces."

"We don't know if they're actually intelligent," Danni said.

"Nah man, they clever enough." Kingston's eyes flicked back and forth, scanning the stairwell and his leg bounced up and down. "They can talk and everything."

"Talking is no measure of intelligence," Danni gave him a pointed look.

"I plenty clever enough, lady," Kingston grinned. "I's got me a gun."

Charlie came over to them, jangling some keys. "These are for the van downstairs. We could get maybe fifteen, twenty of us in."

Carter surveyed the room. "There's more than twenty of us here."

"Yeah," Charlie said. "There's also a tunnel which goes from here to the Courthouse across the road."

"A tunnel?"

"Yeah," Charlie made a face. "But it's downstairs, through the back and down into the cellar. The doors are secure, they won't get through."

"If we can get there," Danni said.

"Maybe if we get the van going, it'll distract them long enough for the rest to get to the tunnel." Charlie shrugged. "Maybe."

"Not a bad idea," Danni said.

Carter had to agree. "Who goes to the van? What do you want to do, draw lots?"

"I don't know, but it's an idea."

"I'm a civvie," Kingston pointed out. "Do I get to go first?"

Carter scowled. They were police: their first duty was the protection of the public. Moving the civilians to a more secure location had to be first priority.

"What's your plan?" Carter said.

"The SO's have blocked the other stairwell with bodies and the things are not coming that way. Maybe we can get out by going there. Maybe the creatures think it's death to come up the stairwell and so it'll be safe to go down it." He met Carter's eyes and took a few deep breaths. "Maybe they've all gone."

"That's a lot of maybes," Carter muttered.

"There are more guns over in Heavitree," Danni said.

"Where's that?"

"Less than half a mile away." She pointed over her shoulder. "We need them."

"Then they're gone." Carter was harsher than he intended. He couldn't waste time thinking about what they might have been able to get from an armoury. There were far more pressing concerns.

Charlie nodded. He seemed to have, finally, stopped sweating. "It was in the path of the wall."

"That's us screwed," Danni said. She was rubbing her hands on her clothes, then making fists with them and repeating the action.

Carter surveyed the room. Tired, worried, frightened people huddled in small groups around the room. Screens that should have been glowing were black and silent. Piles of paper sat untouched. The smell of cordite hung heavy in the air.

"Let's get moving," Carter said. "The longer we stay here, the more they will figure out how to get in."

"Agreed," Danni nodded. "So who goes for the van?"

"Let's load up as many as we can. The rest can go on foot, covered by those guys." He pointed at the SO19 officers, who were still watching the stairwell. "Down to the tunnel and into the secure bit of the Courthouse."

"That's crazy," Mike came up behind them, with Linda. "We're in a police station for god's sake. Surely there's nowhere in Exeter more secure than here?"

"Get back, Mike," Carter said.

"No way. You don't get to tell me what to do."

"Mike, I'm not ordering you around. You want to stay here, that's fine by me, but you need to arm yourself."

Mike paled.

"These things have already given up on that staircase. Any second now they are going to figure out another way in here. Probably up *this* staircase." Carter indicated over the makeshift barricade and realised with a wince he was pointing at the severed head in the stairwell.

"I'm going to get SO19 over here." Danni stood but she only took a few steps before the floor exploded.

The centre of the office floor heaved up, spraying splinters, plaster and dust into the room. Two people were blown apart in the initial blast. Someone was lying on the floor and screaming near the hole. Both legs were severed at the knee. Three small blue spheres headed the eruption. They stopped for a moment in the air, hovering malevolently above the damage. Then, they shot forward, straight into a group of huddled police officers. Each sphere slid through a different person like a knife but left gaping holes in each of their torsos rather than neat incisions. All three fell to the floor, dead. The spheres buzzed around the room, hitting another group and again killing three. Finally, they headed straight for the SO19 team.

Samuel leapt to the side, narrowly avoiding the spheres. The other was not so lucky. The spheres hit him in his chest, arm and face. Blood splashed over the walls behind him as he crumpled to the floor, gaping holes now where there had once been flesh. The spheres collided with each other, and one of the creatures stood in their place, catching the man's weapon before it hit the floor.

The creature swung its tail and launched spikes across the room. Most of them missed, smacking into walls with audible thuds but two people were in the way. One man took the spike in his stomach, his hands instantly covering the wound, even as the flesh started to melt. The second spike hit a woman in the shoulder, and she collapsed, also clutching the wound. Their screams combined to make a cacophonous noise which gurgled wetly to a stop.

The creature looked down at the gun, turning it over in his hands, a look of awe on its face.

As soon as the floor exploded, Danni jumped, rolling clear of the debris. She pushed herself up, and without thinking, charged at the creature with her baton raised. She screamed, but before she could reach it, bullets started to hit the thing, spinning it towards the stairwell. The spheres erupted again, heading straight up and breaking through the ceiling and roof, the weapon clattering to the floor.

Samuel lowered her weapon, with shock clear on her face. She glanced at her fallen colleague and blanched. At least ten people were now dead, and the thing had only been in the room for a few seconds.

"Run!" Danni yelled.

Samuel snapped back to the now, burying her fear with her training. Forget monsters, think about the public, keep them safe. She swallowed and shouted, "With me!"

She headed for the main staircase, weapon leading the way. A magazine and a half left. Christ. Survivors – far fewer of them now – ran after her, their terror over-riding any immobility.

"Let's go," Carter yelled. He pushed Mike back into the room with a shove harder than it needed to be. Mike stumbled towards Danni, grabbing her to keep himself steady. Kingston headed for the other side of the hole, Glock aimed into the room without really pointing at anything. Charlie moved next, staying close to Kingston.

"Get down!" Danni yelled as the spheres started to fall back towards them. As they crashed through the roof, they hovered for a moment and then continued in an arc around the room, unperturbed by the damage they wrought. Their path took them towards Danni, who screamed and rolled again at the last moment. Blue light flashed over her head and something wet splattered to the ground behind her like sudden heavy rain.

She looked up as the spheres continued their trajectory around the room, and then she realised she was looking through a hole in Mike's torso. All three had hit him in close formation, blowing apart the centre of his body. He crumpled to the floor without making a sound.

"Mike!" Linda screamed. Carter held her down as she tried to crawl to the corpse. Fresh tears rolled down her face, leaving clean trace lines in the grime.

Danni felt something hard underneath her and reached for it just as the floor beside her exploded. The spheres passed through the floor again, widening the hole and raining debris into the room below. She gasped in relief, but then heard a groan over the noise in the station.

The floor beneath her gave way, and she fell into darkness.

8

SAMUEL LED the way down the stairs. Four civilians and two police officers she didn't know were with her. Both officers carried extended batons and were trying to look brave. They were failing, but Samuel didn't hold that against them.

As a child, one of her chores had been walking the dog. For most of the year it was fine, and it had been a great way to round off the school day. Except in the dead of winter. Then, it was dark before she finished the walk. Most nights she was fine, but sometimes her imagination would kick in and she saw shapes – men, usually – lurking behind trees, ready to jump out at her. They weren't there of course, but she always managed to scare herself just the same. That's how this staircase felt. When she thought her fear couldn't get any worse, she reached the bottom of a dark hallway filled with the corpses of dead creatures far more horrific than anything her mind could conjure.

Samuel scrambled over the pile of bodies. Her boots squelched through severed tissue and slipped on wet bone. The smell was horrendous – both from the stench of the dead creatures and the evacuated bowels of the human corpses. She was breathing hard by the time she reached reception.

"This way," she whispered, pointing through the secure doors to her right.

"No way." The first officer shook his head. "I'm getting in the van."

"We don't know what's out there," she said.

"Yeah and we don't know what's through there either," the man snarled.

"Stay here then," Samuel gritted her teeth. "I'll go look."

She nudged the double doors open. A dull thud came from the distance, monotonous and repetitive, like someone with no skill hitting a drum. No creepy men down here, just monsters with claws and teeth and an insatiable hunger for human flesh. Willing herself on, she crept into the corridor, easing the door shut behind her.

Halfway down, she turned left through a thicker door leading to another stairwell. Here she paused. It stank in the stairwell – not of bodies but something else. Something rotten.

Creatures.

She peered over the top step, staying as flat as she could. The creatures were banging on the secure doors to the tunnel between the station and the courthouse. The door was holding for now, but there were too many creatures at the bottom of the stairs to count so the door would fail – probably sooner than later.

A well-placed grenade would take them all out, but she didn't have one. Her CS gas might not do anything except alert them to her presence. With reluctance, she turned away, heading back to tell the others the tunnel was a no go.

9

"Danni!" Charlie roared when he saw her disappear. More of the floor gave way and a desk tumbled into the gaping hole. He ran to the edge of the hole and peered into the gloom. The floor shifted and creaked as he moved.

"Careful, not too close," Carter said.

"There she is!"

Charlie pointed through the clearing smoke and dust. Danni was lying motionless and face down on the floor below. He couldn't tell if she was breathing.

"Let's go!" Carter tugged on Charlie's arm.

Linda stood behind him, face pale, but her expression was alert, not panicked. She was no longer crying, but the tracks were visible in the grime on her face. She couldn't take her eyes off Mike's body and the wet hole where his chest had been. She thought of all the times he had propositioned her and all the times she'd turned him down. It had never put him off. He'd been persistent without ever being nasty or pushy. Just persistent. She'd been tempted a few times, when things had been rough with John, but had never gone through with it. He'd been more of a brother figure for her – a work colleague, but a friend also. Now he was dead. She swallowed fresh tears; mourning would have to wait.

"I have to get her," Charlie said.

"You don't know if she's alive." Carter knew it was cold to say it out loud, but he didn't regret it. Other people were counting on them now and they had to get as many people as possible out of the building.

"I'm not leaving without her." Charlie stuck his jaw out, defiant.

Carter shook his head. Back in college, Charlie had a reputation for being something of a lady's man. Looking at him now, those days were long gone. Did he even realise?

"Christ, Charlie. It's your funeral."

Carter and Linda made for the stairs, and after a moment more of staring into the hole, Charlie followed. They clambered over the dead creatures blocking the stairwell, recoiling at the stench. Flesh squished and occasionally bone crunched under their footsteps. Carter was reminded of climbing sand dunes as a kid, his feet sometimes sinking in. He would give anything for this to be a mound of sand. As they cleared the pile of creatures, Carter pushed to the front.

Now what?

10

THE SURVIVORS WERE HUDDLED in the entrance hall, no-one willing to push open the door to the car park. Next to the stairs, a more solid door led through to the entrance of the station, where Danni currently lay.

"You got the Glock?"

Kingston nodded, showing him the weapon.

"How many bullets?"

"Ten in there, ten more in my spare clip."

Carter didn't want to know where the spare clip had come from, but right then he was glad.

"John!" Linda pointed at the door through to the ground floor of the station, where Charlie was about to open it.

"Don't."

"You can't stop me." Charlie crossed his arms.

"We don't know what's on the other side of the door. There could be more of them."

"Danni's out there."

"Charlie-"

Charlie wiped a tear from his eye. "Please, John, help me."

Carter grimaced. "Ok, ok, but let's be quick."

He looked back to the faces in the stairwell and grimaced. Two officers handed over their batons with shaking hands.

"Where's the tunnel?" Carter asked one.

"Through there, turn right, follow the corridor," the man said, pointing at a different set of doors. His voice wavered as he spoke, but Carter didn't blame him. They were all scared. "The SCO went that way."

As if on cue, Samuel reappeared through the indicated door. She shook her head. "Loads of them."

"Get to the van," he said to Linda. "If we're not back in two minutes, get the hell out of here."

She opened her mouth to protest, but he silenced her with a kiss, drawing her close to him and holding her.

"Go with Kingston. I'll be right with you."

11

CARTER EASED the door open and they squeezed through, Charlie's stomach brushing the door. The room was a mess. It had been bad earlier, following the initial attack, but now it was ruined. Corpses littered the ground, most of them missing limbs. Some of them bore clear bite marks and were covered in post-mortem wounds. The furniture in the room was in pieces, glass shards laying on the ground, chairs reduced to frames, both metal and wood desks shattered. Blood decorated the walls, replacing the neutral décor.

Danni was lying near the centre of the room on top of two corpses. Around her lay the detritus of the ceiling, and next to her body was an MP5 machine gun. Nothing moved in the room, except for a trickle of dust and rubble from the floor above.

Carter crept forward, baton at the ready. He put each foot down carefully, wincing whenever glass crunched or rubble moved. Still nothing moved in the lobby. Every sound – however slight – made his heart race. After what seemed an age, he reached Danni, Charlie close behind him. Carter reached to check her pulse just as she rolled and sat up with a cry.

"Shh," he put his finger to his lips. "Come on, we're getting you out of here."

"What happened?" Her voice was too loud, so Carter shushed her again. He stood, listening for the sounds of the creatures. Samuel had said they were deeper in the station, but it didn't mean they *all* were.

"You fell. Those sphere things-"

"The reporter," she said. From deep in the station they heard a loud bang and then something which could have been a triumphant roar.

"Mike's dead." Carter was surprised at the emotion in his voice. Baxter had never been his favourite person.

"Christ, I'm sorry, Carter."

"I didn't really know him. He was my wife's work mate." Carter had always thought the man was trying to steal his wife, even though she always said he wasn't. They were colleagues, she insisted, nothing more. He was like a brother, she said. Yeah, right – Carter had seen the way he'd looked at her.

"Where are *they*?" Danni got to her feet gingerly.

"They found the tunnel," Carter said. "They all seem to be back there."

"I thought you were dead," Charlie sobbed. He looked embarrassed at the sudden outburst of emotion.

"I'm a bit banged up, but I'm ok." Danni patted his arm. "Cheers, though."

Charlie smiled at her and Carter thought for one horrible, awkward, moment he would try and kiss the young woman.

"Come on, let's go before those things come back."

12

SAMUEL OPENED the door to the yard first and stepped outside whilst peering down the barrel of her gun. Kingston went next, the Glock giving him an air of authority he didn't feel. He had been given the keys to the van – despite his youth, he looked the calmest - which hadn't made him feel any better. Linda followed them, and then the rest of the survivors.

The air was filled with distant shouts and screams. Bangs, thuds and explosions had replaced the usual background hum of a modern city. Linda felt her legs go weak as she realised just how widespread the carnage was now.

"Go to the van," said Samuel. "I'll cover you."

Kingston stepped into the yard and jogged over to the van. Clicking the central locking, he put his hand on the door handle but then heard a noise from his right. He looked over his shoulder, staring at the entrance to the street.

"Move now!" Samuel cried and opened fire. Kingston yanked the door open and jumped in the van. The others ran across the yard and the creatures struck. Two of them ran towards the group from the top of the car park, just to be cut down by fire from the MP5. More of them arrived at the gates, pouring through. How many *were* there?

Samuel moved as she fired, covering the rest of the group. Creatures fell as she fired, but not in the quantities they had in the stairwell. The things were moving side to side as they ran, making themselves harder targets.

They were learning.

Linda reached the back of the van first, tearing the doors open and jumping inside. It was the size of a minibus with enough seats for twelve in the back. At the rear was an equipment locker, but its gate swung open, banging in its frame. Someone had cleared out all the gear from the van – someone who had been in a hurry. She screamed in a mixture of frustration and fear. Two other people made it to the van, moving inside.

Samuel was firing as she ran, but there was no way she could stop the tide of creatures. She stopped firing and sprinted for the van, jumping into the back of the wagon. Linda pulled her inside, and she readied her weapon again.

Kingston had the keys in the ignition and started the engine. For one long, horrible moment, he thought nothing would happen and then the engine burst to life. He pushed the accelerator down with his foot and the tyres squealed on the tarmac. To his right, the creatures were feasting on the dead and more of them were pouring back into the station, chasing the humans who had fled back into the building.

"Go, now!" Samuel roared. She was already down to her last magazine.

Kingston released the handbrake and the van lurched forward. Creatures scattered as he drove, but he still hit a few of them. One spun over the bonnet, cracking the windscreen before he fell, and the van lurched as it was crushed under the wheels. More were hit by the wings, each collision crumpling part of the bodywork. Kingston heard gunfire but didn't dare take his eyes from the road immediately in front. He'd never driven anything this big before and it felt sluggish, especially compared to his bike. This was not some hotwired car.

Suddenly the crunching and thudding stopped, and they were out of the yard. Kingston spun the wheel as hard as he could, and the van turned into the street. In the wing mirror he could see fallen creatures, some of them not moving. More creatures ran into the street, following the van, and others still stopped to help the fallen ones.

The gunfire stopped, and he looked in the rear-view mirror to see why. Samuel was staring out the back of the van but wasn't shooting. Why the hell not? He returned his attention to the road, just in time to see Carter's abandoned car in his way.

"Shit!"

He yanked the wheel to the left and van careened, tipping onto two wheels. For a second he grinned - just like GTA baby - and then they were falling. He braced himself as the van slid along the road, windows shattering and metal crumpling. Screams came from behind him as they slid and the passengers fell, hitting the wall of the van. After what felt like an age, the van skidded to a halt.

Kingston released his seatbelt and fell to the ground. He stood on shaky legs, realising he was standing on shattered glass when it crunched under his feet. The passenger door seemed impossibly high above him. He brushed his hand over his hair and glass rained onto the ground. Cuts and grazes covered his hands and face.

"They're coming!"

A high-pitched squeal from the back of the van. Kingston glanced back and saw his passengers getting to their feet, although slowly. Linda was first and she went to help a man up but stopped when she saw the angle of his neck.

A woman tried to stand but cried out in agony. Her arm was hanging loose and at a strange angle, with her pale face showing exactly how much pain she was in. Beyond, the first of the creatures came into view, less than twenty metres away and closing fast.

"Out! Out! Out!" cried Samuel. She pulled the woman's good arm, pushing her out the back of the van. In shock, the woman ran the wrong way, towards the police station. Towards the creatures. She tried to turn as soon as she realised her terrible mistake, but stumbled and a creature pounced, silencing her with its second bite.

Linda staggered down the street, away from the creatures and tried to wipe blood from her face. Her head was cut under the hairline and she felt sick from being thrown around the inside of the van. The world was fuzzy and blurred around the edges.

Kingston tried to push himself up to reach the passenger door, but he couldn't push hard enough to open it. He couldn't climb out through the back – he just didn't have time, or room so he tried to push open the door again, but it was just too heavy from his angle.

"Come on!" Samuel yelled. She turned immediately and fired at the approaching creatures without aiming. Some bullets thudded into the creatures, felling them. More took their place in an instant.

Ten metres now.

"Run!"

The shout came from outside the van. Linda, this time. Kingston heard her start running, footsteps muffled by the walls of the van. He saw her pass, just as Samuel looked at him, eyes wild. Kingston nodded at her, his heart sinking.

"Sorry." She pointed at her weapon. "I'm out."

"Go," Kingston said, his voice steady despite the terror coursing through him. With a final look of pure frustration, Samuel set off after Linda. He was trapped and now alone. Maybe the things wouldn't see him. He pulled his legs up to his chin, making himself as small as possible like he used to when his father came home from the pub. A long time ago. The Glock was still stuck in the waist of his jeans and he retrieved it now. Its weight was reassuring. The creatures were nearly at the van. He sank down into the seat, hiding behind it. Clutching the Glock tightly, he tried to slow his breathing. The noise from the creatures was getting louder and the smell was increasing in intensity.

Why had he told the tough lady with the gun to go? *Because then she'd be waiting to die now too, dumbass.*

"Here we go," he muttered.

13

CARTER STOPPED in the ruined doorway and held his hand up. The creatures were running past the doorway, heading towards the car park. He watched as the van smashed a hole through the Horde and resisted the urge to cheer as it sped into the street. When it tipped over, he watched in horror as it slid across the ground, before it was eventually halted by a lamppost.

He saw Linda stumble away, heading further down the street. Creatures started to run back past the doorway, paying him no attention, but running straight for the fleeing humans. Finally, Samuel appeared. She seemed to be talking to someone in the van, but then she was running too, soon catching up to Linda.

He turned back to Charlie and Danni. "How fast can you run?"

"I'm pretty banged up, but I got gas." Danni's pale face hinted at the fact she might be lying.

"You?"

"Fast enough," Charlie said, definitely lying.

"Ok, so they've gone, after the others. I say we follow and pick off any stragglers. We can catch up with Linda and the other survivors then." He held up the MP5 he had picked up from next to Danni. "Yours?"

She nodded and took it from him. "Thanks."

"Why did they leave?" Charlie said.

"I think they were setting a trap for us." Danni had a bit more colour in her cheeks – not much, but enough.

"Not them. Our lot. Why did they leave?"

"It doesn't look like they had a choice." Carter pointed down the street. "Jesus, how many of these things are there?"

The Horde had reached the van now and continued past it. Four of the creatures stopped, sniffing around the van. One of them reached into the back and pulled a man out. He didn't complain as they started to tear large chunks of his flesh from his body and stuffing them into their mouths.

Already dead, Carter thought, battling a surge of nausea. He tried not to think about that happening to Linda. She was fast, he knew that from their youth, and still kept in shape. *Keep running, babe.*

One of the creatures stopped feasting long enough to stare into the van. It clambered slowly into the rear of the vehicle, clearly moving slowly to not disturb something further inside.

"We go," he said. "*Now!*"

14

THE SEAT WAS NOT big enough to cover Kingston, however much he tried to shrink into it. He watched the Horde stream past and grinned to himself. Maybe this was going to turn out okay after all.

Without the creatures distracting him, he tried to work out how to get out of the van. He knew the door was too heavy to push from below, so he turned to the windscreen. It was a spider-web of cracks and judging by the slight bow round the cracks, it looked like one good hit would shatter it all. That would create too much noise, though, and the creatures were still outside, not far away. He just had to sit tight for a few more minutes, then he would be home free. He drummed his fingers on his chest, whilst his leg jittered underneath him. This was going to be a long few minutes. He chewed his lip and slapped his chest, tapping a light rhythm there. Just sit still, that's all you've got to do. He made his hands stop, but his leg was harder to control. First thing he was going to do was find the canteen in the police station and hole up in there until help arrived. He nearly started whistling but caught himself just in time. Yeah, go find some food, some caffeine and maybe some chocolate. Cops were bound to have a supply of chocolate. The size of Charlie, he probably had a shop's worth. It would keep him going until help came.

If help arrived.

He sank back against the seat, trying – without success – to get more comfortable. The aches and cuts in his body started to protest now that the adrenaline was fading. He breathed out heavily as more creatures streamed past the van. Man, this was taking forever. He drummed his fingers on his knees and then on the steering wheel, relishing the noise for a moment and then-

What the hell was he doing?

The creatures continued past and he let out a breath he hadn't realised he was holding. Kingston smiled to himself. *What a donut.*

A hand clamped onto his shoulder. Kingston screamed as long nails dug into his flesh, drawing blood. He dropped the Glock as pain coursed through him. With his other arm, he swung his fist and it connected with the creature's face just as it leant in to bite him. He punched again before the teeth made contact and the creature howled. It let him go long enough for Kingston to push himself away from the seat. He rolled into the gap under the console, feeling the pedals dig into his back. The Glock was by his feet, just out of his reach. He stretched, feeling his fingers brush the metal.

The creature tore at the chair, pulling chunks of it off and throwing the foam behind it. It snarled at Kingston, baring its long sharp teeth. His hand closed around the grip and he brought the Glock up to the creature's screaming face.

"Yeah, whatever," Kingston said and shot the thing between the eyes. As it slumped to the floor, Kingston swore at himself.

Two more creatures were now coming into the van, the shots and screams alerting them to his presence. Kingston fired again but the first creature ducked, and the shot pinged into the seat behind.

He was dead if he stayed put. Kingston scrambled out from under the console and fired at the windscreen. Nothing happened except for a click from the gun. Kingston screamed in frustration and punched the windscreen with the butt. Nothing happened. He hit it again. Still nothing. *Fuuuuck.* He kicked it and the windscreen cracked, even as pain shot up his leg. He kicked again and again, ignoring the pain as the cracks grew and the glass splintered then shattered.

He rolled into the road, glass crunching underneath him. Standing quickly, he tried to get his bearings but all he could focus on was the snarl of the creatures. They were already out of the rear of the ruined van, already moving towards him.

Run, he told himself, but his legs weren't working. He was trembling all over. He risked a glance over his shoulder and saw the Horde that had passed him had turned around. They were coming back.

Should've stayed in school, he thought. *Got an education. Gone to College. Anything but join a gang and spiral into a life of crime.* What the hell was he doing? All his actions as a member of The Scorpions seemed irrelevant and, above all, petty now, although he wouldn't have met Stephen. How different would things have been?

Exhausted, he waited for the creatures to take him.

15

Two creatures emerged from the back of the van, their focus directed towards the figure crawling away. Carter swung his baton as hard as he could and the first creature fell to the floor, his head snapping more than ninety degrees. Carter then swung at the other, but it moved out of the way and the baton whistled by, millimetres from its chin. It swung its claws at Carter, raking his face and drawing blood, making him grunt in pain. Carter cried out and aimed the baton again. This time it connected, just as Charlie arrived, swinging his own baton and they alternated hitting the creature until its head caved in, spraying them with gore.

"Gross," Danni said.

"Yeah," Charlie said, before kicking the other creature as hard as he could. He kept kicking it, each swing of the leg punctuated with a word. "Fucking. Stupid. Smelly. Shithead. Cock. Mother-"

"Charlie!"

He stopped, breathing hard then spat on the corpse.

"Hey!"

They all turned to the voice and saw Kingston getting to his feet. He looked terrible: face cut, blood seeping out of various wounds, glass frosting his hair. His shoulders were slumped, and he stumbled towards them.

"They're coming back." He pointed behind him. In the distance, the Horde had stopped en-masse and then turned back towards the station. Screams and shouts rang out as they started to run back up the street.

"Oh, shit," Danni said. "We've got to run."

Charlie groaned. "I'm not sure how much more running I can do."

"Run? I'm so tired," Kingston tried to stand up straight, square his shoulders. He grunted. "Everything hurts."

"We need to hide," Charlie said.

"Move then, we don't have much time!" Carter spoke through gritted teeth.

The screams and shouts increased in volume as the creatures closed the distance between them.

16

THREE SPHERES COALESCED in the tunnel and Kennedy snapped back into existence. He quickly checked himself over but couldn't find anything missing. The band had worked properly – this time, at least.

He made his way through the tunnels with a growing sense of frustration. The humans had been theirs for the taking, but as he'd split into the spheres for the second time, a message had come through and he was back home, heading for Father. Why had he interfered now?

Kennedy headed straight to the Throne room, ignoring the pod of eight Horde heading the other way, towards the surface. Mother was busy. As he approached Father, the anger subsided, and he tried not to think about how much his hands were shaking. What had he done? Was Father displeased?

"What took you so long? Report."

"The humans have weapons, Father, and they are more terrible than we first thought." Had he called him back for a situation report? Kennedy's hands closed into fists, but he forced himself to calm down and reopen his hands before Father thought it a threat.

"The Horde are many."

"Yes, Father, but the weapons can hurt *many* quickly."

Father slammed his hand on the metal counter in front of him. The noise echoed down the corridors behind Kennedy. He cried out and sank to his chair. The background hum Kennedy was already used to ceased for a moment, but then restarted.

What was that? Kennedy thought, but Father was speaking, and he dragged Kennedy's attention back to him.

"I want a land for us, Kennedy. A place out of these cursed tunnels. Somewhere we can grow and expand. I did not want to hurt more humans than was necessary for this goal, but they insist on hurting *us*."

Kennedy didn't speak for a moment: it would be churlish, and possibly fatal, to suggest the wall would be seen as an act of aggression and that Father's last instruction had been to kill them all. Eventually he said, "I have located the man."

Father regarded him with a baleful stare. "Then why is he not with you?"

Kennedy kept his mouth shut, biting his tongue.

"Go, Kennedy. Return with the man who killed my sons."

17

THE WALL FLICKERED. For a moment, Exeter was once again bathed in the glorious sunshine the rest of Britain was enjoying. Sun beat down, lighting up the mounds of ruins, the shattered homes and roads, giving hope to survivors just for a second and illustrating just how many corpses littered the ground. The central part of the city remained, an island oasis of intact buildings surrounded by a desert of ruins.

Pressure built and Exeter was surrounded by an impenetrable black wall once more.

18

"SLOW DOWN," Linda gasped. Her chest was heaving and sweat made her shirt stick to her back. She looked back over her shoulder and saw the creatures still coming, although there seemed to be less of them now.

"They'll catch us," Samuel said and then, "This way."

Samuel grabbed Linda's arm, leading her down a path between two houses. They were on an estate. Red brick buildings rose on all sides around them, small blocks of flats, each no more than three storeys high. Many of the ground floor windows were smashed and doors hung off their hinges. Front yards were littered with corpses and body parts – a fact that made Samuel's stomach lurch again. She tried not to notice some of the bodies had bite marks on them.

"They're eating everyone," Linda said. "Oh, Jesus Christ, what is this? What is happening to us?"

Samuel shook her head and then put her fingers to her lips. "Quiet. We don't want them to find us. There could be more."

Linda looked around, her eyes wide. "There can't be more. They're all at the police station."

"Not necessarily," Samuel gestured at the bodies on the ground. "This whole estate looks like it's dead. That's a lot of manpower. No way those things did all this before attacking us."

A heavy silence fell between them, punctuated by Linda's deep breaths. Every time she thought she had it under control, her eyes would flick to a dismembered corpse and the tightness would return, forcing her to gulp air down. She needed a distraction.

"I'm Linda," she said. "What do I call you?"

"Most people here call me Samuel; some call me Katie." She gave a wry smile. "My friends call me Kree, but that's a long story."

"We need to find somewhere to hide."

"Copy that." Samuel's gaze also lingered on the dead.

"Up there," Linda said. She pointed at a staircase running up the side of one of the houses. She led the way, gagging at the stench of urine and rubbish. Once the corpses started to rot and smell, the stairway would be nigh on unpassable.

The building was longer than she had first thought. Three front doors could be seen on the first floor. All three were brightly coloured: red, green and black in that order. The windows on this floor were not broken. Had the creatures missed the stairs? Linda let out a breath.

Samuel tapped Linda's shoulder and pointed along the passage. A waist high wall ran the length of the floor. They crept along below it. Samuel risked a look over it. The grassy area between the flats was still covered with half-eaten bodies. Nothing had moved in the time they had run up the stairs. No sign of any creatures.

Linda pushed at the red door, but it didn't move. She hadn't expected it to, but now she knocked on it with a soft tap. Nothing, no response at all. She pressed her ear against the wood but heard nothing. Maybe the person who lived there was out at work. Maybe they were lying on the ground below.

She moved on to the green door and gently pushed it. Again, it didn't move. Again, she tapped and was about to move on when a faint voice called, "Go away!" She reached up and opened the letter box. It revealed a short hallway with two doors on either side and a further door at the end. This last was ajar and she could see a kitchen. A pale face peered around the doorway, then shot back out of view.

"Please, let us in," Linda called. "We're tired."

No sound came from the kitchen.

"Please," Linda said again.

"Out the way." Samuel pushed Linda to one side, ignoring her protests. Then, she put her shoulder to the door. She banged it again and on the third attempt, the door opened with a screech and a splinter of wood.

"What are you doing?" Linda asked.

"Like you said, we need to rest."

"We could have gone to an empty flat for that."

Samuel pushed the door open and stepped inside the flat, pulling Linda in behind her and then she pushed the door closed, where it clicked against the frame, but the lock refused to engage. The flat was full of the sobs of a woman coming from the kitchen.

Linda pushed open the door on the left and saw a small living room, dominated by a television too large for the room. A pizza box and a beer can lay in the middle of the floor, in front of a small two-seater sofa. Pictures on the wall showed a pretty woman with a small boy.

"Katie, we should go," Linda said. The boy had a sweet smile and he was holding a lamb that looked like it was trying to get free of his grip.

"I'm a police officer," Samuel called. "We're not here to harm you."

"Go away!"

"We just need somewhere to rest," Samuel continued. She was easing her way along the short corridor. Her hand reached for the kitchen door but then it was yanked open and a small woman leapt out, swinging her arm. Something glinted in the pale light and it took Samuel a moment to realise it was a knife. She caught the woman's arm before the knife made contact and pushed her back into the kitchen. The woman stumbled back and hit the kitchen table, dropping the knife. Samuel leapt forward and kicked the knife away before she could reach it. The knife skittered across the floor and came to rest at the feet of a small boy.

"I'm not here to hurt you!" Samuel roared. She pointed at the badge in her chest.

"Katie, for Christ's sake," Linda called and stepped in front of her. She held her hands up and tried to smile at the woman, who was both shorter and not as pretty as the photos suggested. Bags under her eyes and the set of her mouth were the hallmarks of a difficult life, even before today.

"We're sorry," Linda said. "We just need to rest. There aren't any creatures following us."

"Get out of my house," the woman hissed. The boy started crying, the knife still at his feet.

"Please," Linda said. "Please just let us rest."

"Get out!" The woman screeched and then burst into tears. The boy ran to her, crushing her with a hug. They nearly toppled over, but she just managed to keep them both upright. "Please leave us."

Linda looked at the floor, wishing she could be anywhere else right then. The boy's tears were like a sledgehammer to her heart. "I'm sorry," she tried to say, but it came out as a croak. She cleared her throat and tried again.

"Sorry?" The woman laughed, a bitter, hollow sound. "You break into my home and you're sorry? You put me and my boy in danger and you're *sorry*? Get out!"

"Please," Samuel said. "We just need to rest."

"Mum, I'm scared."

Linda could see he was trying very hard to control his tears, and the sledgehammer swung again. "We should leave."

"I'm exhausted," Samuel said. "We need to stop, just for a bit." She looked at the woman and tried to smile.

"Get out!" The woman screamed.

Linda nodded and pulled Samuel towards the door. "I'm so sorry," Linda said. She picked up the knife and offered it to the woman. "Keep him safe."

Samuel closed the door behind them and sank to the floor. Cold seeped into her bones through her clothes. "What did I just do?"

"You tried to help us," Linda said. She smiled at the other woman, but it was tinged with sadness. "Not the right way."

"I know. I'm just so tired."

Linda said nothing. There was no need. Instead, she peered over the wall and ducked straight back down. All the colour had drained from her face.

"What?" Even as Samuel asked the question, she knew the answer.

"Creatures."

19

CARTER LED the charge down the street, feet pounding hard on the tarmac. He ran past the entrance to the station without slowing. No point going back there. Even now, he could hear fresh screams from inside. Opposite the station, the courthouse looked inviting, but with barred windows and secure doors there would be no easy way in. The creatures were too close to allow the time to smash the door down.

At the end of the block, on the left-hand side but with a small side-road separating them, he could see a car park and a large shop set back from the road. The furthest end from him was ruined, a large mound of rubble spewing into the car park, burying some cars. The wall had started here, cutting the end of the building off and making some of the rest collapse. Twenty or so of the cars were unburied, but two were cut cleanly in half.

"There," Carter said, pointing at the shop. "Stay low."

"Waitrose," Kingston smirked. "I ain't ever been in one of those. Guess I'm going up in the world, hanging out with you middle class folk."

They both ducked down behind a car and waited for Danni and Charlie to catch up.

"Where are they?" Carter asked as Danni slid in next to him. She was breathing heavily, but not as hard as Charlie.

"Back there, about two hundred metres away."

Carter risked a look over the top of the car. The creatures were coming up the street, but much more slowly now. A group of eight peeled away and filed into the police station. Another eight headed to the Courthouse, but they stayed on the strip of grass in front of it. That left around thirty of them still heading along the street.

"If we move now, they might not see where we go," he whispered. Intact windows lined the wall leading to the rubble, but he couldn't see a way in. The mound was around ten feet high, but there was a gap at the top.

Carter set off through the car park. Staying crouched, he moved from car to car. He peered around the car and saw two of the creatures standing about thirty feet away, both sniffing the air. He held up his hand and the others all stopped. Carter took in Charlie's red face and pressed his fingers to his lips, then held up two fingers.

He risked another look, but the creatures hadn't moved. Where were the others? Were they creeping around behind them? Getting close enough to pounce? Nothing else was moving in the car park, and he couldn't see any more creatures. Breathing slowly, he looked again.

They were so close: the rubble pile and monsters were equidistant from him. He could sprint for it, get over the pile and into the store, but then the creatures would just follow. What would be the point? Also, no way was Charlie making it over the debris before they caught him.

Carter touched his face and winced. The cut was warm where

the creature's claws had raked him, but at least it wasn't bleeding anymore.

Danni touched his arm and pointed. The creatures ran to the side of the building, followed closely by more which emerged from between the cars and then disappeared, blocked by the building. Screams soon rang out.

"Move!" he hissed and stood.

A huge group of creatures rounded the corner, nearer to the rubble than Carter. They would not make it to the store before the creatures saw them.

20

LINDA WAS BREATHING HARD, close to hyperventilating. Samuel peered over the wall again and ducked down so quickly she almost hit the wall. She, too, was short of breath.

"There's about twenty of them," she whispered, leaning close so Linda could hear. "They're clearly looking for survivors. It won't be long before they come up here."

When she'd looked, the creatures had been prowling around the grass area in front of the flats. The creatures had been the thinner type, without the tails. Whilst they still looked menacing, they did not appear as tough as the larger monster. Two of the creatures were more than enough to kill them both, so more than twenty was overkill.

She risked another look. The creatures were spread out, sniffing around the flats on the ground floor. A shout went out and a shadow moved on the other side of the green. It was a teenager, making a run for it. The creatures moved quickly, sprinting after the boy.

"Now," Samuel said. "We go right now." She felt sick to the pit of her stomach. Sick because she was using a teenage boy as a distraction; sick because she knew what would happen when the creatures caught up to him; sick because she was glad it was the boy and not her.

They sprinted down the stairs as quickly as they could, taking them two at a time. The piss didn't seem to smell quite as bad this time, and then they were out in the fresher air of the green. They turned right at the bottom of the stairs and ran along the front of the flats hoping the shadows would keep them hidden from the distracted creatures.

Samuel looked over at the creatures and immediately regretted it. They were all kneeling on the floor, ripping the poor teenager apart. Blood and body parts were flying out of the corpse. One of the creatures stood up, roaring and punched another one in the side of the head. Soon the two creatures were fighting whilst the others carried on eating the teenager.

She swallowed bile and kept moving. After another ten metres or so, she couldn't resist a look back over her shoulder. One of the things was standing over the corpse of the other, its face dripping in blood. It was roaring, making the veins on its neck stand out.

Then it looked directly at Samuel.

It stopped roaring, head cocked to one side. Samuel found herself slowing, matching the creatures gaze. The thing narrowed its eyes and raised its arm to point at her.

"Linda, faster!" she screamed as the creatures started to run towards them.

21

CARTER HIT the deck as soon as he saw the creatures. Behind him, the others all ducked between the cars. He could see the things in the wing mirror of the car as they headed through the car park. In moments they would be upon them.

Nothing else for it: he crawled under the car, moving with a strange combination of urgency and caution. As soon as he was under, he scanned the area in front of him. The others had each crawled under a car, except Charlie who had clambered into a broken one.

It would have to do, although if the creatures turned around, they would see him. By the expression on Charlie's face, he knew this too. It was the world's worst game of hide and seek.

Snarls and cries echoed around the building as the creatures swarmed through the car park. Filthy feet, topped with long, sharp claws clicking as they ran, swarmed past without slowing. They didn't look twice at the car Charlie hid in, which was odd but also a relief. It was like they didn't think to look *in* things.

The noise faded as the creatures continued to run, heading to God knows where to do bad things to God knows who. Carter waited a few more minutes, sharing concerned looks with the others, and then they crawled out into an empty car park.

22

LINDA RAN, Samuel close behind. She could hear the shrieks of the things getting closer and closer, the air was full of their cries. The shouts echoed around the flats and she thought of the boy, sitting in his kitchen. What would he make of the noise? How scared must he be?

She saw a narrow gap between the flats and headed for the path, making like she was going to pass it. At the last moment, she turned and ran into the passage. Samuel yelped as she crashed into the wall as she attempted the same turn. Linda turned back, but Samuel was on the floor.

Their eyes met and she shook her head.

Samuel was clutching her ankle and all the colour had gone from her face. Linda started towards her as Samuel tried to stand. She screamed and collapsed.

"No!" Samuel shouted holding up her hand, telling Linda to stop. "No!"

Linda stopped in the narrow alley, staring at the woman. Samuel tried to crawl, entering the top of the alley. Linda could see the tears in the other woman's eyes and felt impotent rage flood through her.

"Run!" Samuel screamed and then a creature leapt on her. Clutching her head with both hands, it twisted, and Linda heard the crack. She stifled a scream, trying desperately not to draw attention to herself as she backed away.

Then the thing started *feasting*. More of the things arrived, and joined in, pulling lumps off Samuel and stuffing the pieces into their mouths. The first creature pulled at the string of intestine, unravelling the pale tube and biting into it. With gore dripping down its chin, it finally looked into the alley.

It was empty.

23

FATHER SAT, watching his screens, alone. Kennedy had gone and would now not return until he had the man who had killed both Princes. He was a good servant and Father knew Kennedy's desire to please would make him successful.

The Clan had lost the Scouts today, but the Horde were many and would prevail. Of this, Father had no doubt. Revenge would be his today, but at what cost? He could replace the Scouts and many of the Horde given enough time, but how much time did he have?

Many of the humans in this city were either dead or soon would be, plenty of food for the under-nourished Horde. They would get stronger and the humans weaker. This alone would help to ensure victory today, but Father needed the human found. The black man. The one who had killed the Princes. Once he was caught, the rest of the plan would fall into place. Once he was caught, the Horde would never go hungry again. Until then, they ate to gain strength.

It was time to send the humans a message.

His rage at the loss of the Princes had accelerated his timeline.

Had he acted in too much haste? Exposing the existence of the Horde to the humans had been huge but necessary. He had to have revenge.

The second part to the plan was more of a calculated risk. Now he needed to get a message Outside to buy Kennedy and the Horde the time they needed for their task. Once the Humans understood what was happening, the Horde would be safer. He had never intended to go to war with the humans, had always envisaged a peaceful co-existence with infrequent sacrifices the humans would give gladly.

Father pressed some buttons on his console, then relaxed his mental grip on the Barrier. The Horde would have to cope without his direct instructions for a few minutes. The low hum in the background stopped suddenly, its absence more ominous than its presence.

He looked straight at one of the screens and started to speak.

"By now, you know we are here. By now, you have realised you are no match for my Horde. My Scouts have watched you for centuries, without quarrel or discovery. Today, everything changed. Humans in this city declared war on my kind. They have killed my people with extreme prejudice, yet I did not retaliate. There are many amongst us who wanted to, but I seek a different solution. We could live side by side.

"Today, in cold blood, my sons were murdered. They were not armed. They posed no threat to any human, yet the same man hunted them down and executed them both." Father paused, surprised at the emotion in his voice. "I have quarantined this city until we find the man responsible. The inhabitants' lives are forfeit until the man is found.

"Once we have him in our care, our priority will be releasing the innocents in this city. Anyone who survives our search for justice will be granted safe passage from our land. The city will remain under our control, forever separate to your civilisation but the survivors will be free to leave. I did not want to resort to this course of action, but I have been forced to be as barbaric as you."

Father transmitted the message, then focussed his mental energy again.

24

THE SHOCK of Mike's death was still omnipresent, driving Linda onwards, running for far longer than she had thought herself capable. Though she'd barely known the woman, Samuel's death galvanised her further and she covered ground quickly.

A hill brought her energy to an end and she stopped at the top, gasping for air. Her legs were burning from exertion and she was shaking. Linda knew she needed food, but more urgently, a drink.

Despite the exhaustion present in every fibre of her being, she pushed onwards. She was in a more upmarket part of the city now, with large red brick buildings standing proud around her. She entered an alley and rested in there once more. Dark shadows shrouded her from the street, and she sank to the ground, relishing the feel of cold stone through her clothes. Her back was slick with sweat and she felt sick. Her legs and arms trembled, and she wasn't sure she could stand again.

An unassuming door broke the neat lines of the stone wall opposite her, with a keypad above the handle. She tried to focus on it but was just too tired. If it was a secure door, then hopefully the people behind it were safe. Her eyes felt heavy and she closed them for a second. Mike's face came to mind immediately, but she tried to focus on John instead. Where was he? Was he even alive? How would she find him now?

A scream forced her upright. Another echoed around the buildings, making it hard to pinpoint. She hung her head. Whoever was screaming wouldn't be for much longer. That was the way of the world today. Shame tugged at her, but what could she do? She wasn't armed and her self-defence classes were built for getting out of tight spots with unwanted male attention, not for dealing with monsters.

No, she had to take care of herself. Stay alive. Find John.

"I'm sorry," she whispered to whomever had screamed. She rested her head on the cold stone wall, letting the tears come but trying hard not to make any noise. Images came to mind, unbidden. Mike staring at her open-mouthed as she'd wandered into his hotel room in just a towel, fresh out of the shower. She knew what he wanted, and it had given her a thrill to see it so clearly on his face.

It was nice to be wanted.

Would she have gone further if she'd known what the next twenty-four hours would bring? Linda didn't want to answer the question, because she was afraid of the answer. How long had it been since John had looked at her like that? How long since he'd actually paid attention to her? It was a cliché to say they'd been married too long, and they were both more married to their jobs than each other, but like most clichés, there was a gem of truth in there.

She knew John could handle himself. He was fit and strong; always had been. It had been one of the first things she'd been attracted to. She kept thinking about him back in the police station with those *things* coming to attack them all. John had taken charge, started telling people what to do. John had always been able to command respect and get people to do what he wanted.

Was it enough to keep him alive though?

Today, of all days, was it enough to survive?

Sunlight flooded the alley and she squinted, shielding her eyes from the sudden bright light.

The blackness was gone.

25

CARTER POINTED at the front of the store and then right. Despite the lack of creatures, he still wanted to keep noise to a minimum. They snaked through the lot, heading for the main road in Exeter. Carter stopped when he saw a creature feasting on a woman in what had once been a pretty dress. The thing was oblivious to him, and he had a moment where he considered rushing it. Sense prevailed; he could do nothing to help the woman and he would only alert the creature to their presence. He left it pulling her intestines out.

They reached the main road, keeping cars between them and the feast. The police station was opposite them, now a dark and oppressive building. They could hear crashes from inside and then a scream.

Carter winced at the noise. He knew what it meant. Anyone still in the station was being hunted. Carter didn't rate their chances of survival; he wasn't convinced of his own.

"What now?" Kingston prodded Carter in the back. Whilst

there were no creatures in sight, he still barely raised his voice above a whisper. "What's your plan?"

"Well, Linda went that way," Carter pointed up the road, past the police station and court building. "So, we go that way too. I have to find her."

"Ok, but what's there? Shouldn't we find somewhere to just hole up?"

"Maybe. You can. Me, I'm going to find my wife."

Bright sunlight blinded them. It was so sudden, the bright light almost hurt. Warmth flooded through them all as blue skies and warm fluffy clouds returned to the skies above Exeter. The background hum was gone too, conspicuous now by its absence. In its place, the distant screams were obvious, an aural testament to the fact they were still in danger.

"Holy shit!" Kingston said. He stood up, punching the air. "Get in!"

The darkness returned. The wall was back and, with it, the low hum they had all nearly got used to. Beyond the hum was another noise: one that had not been there moments before. A thumping noise Carter was all too familiar with.

"Helicopter," he said.

The noise increased in volume and two large helicopters flew over their heads. Camouflage and other military designs covered the underside as the machines passed over head. Over the noise of the engines, a message was being broadcast.

"...STAY somewhere safe. If you are secure, stay where you are. Do not take any unnecessary risks. Stay in your homes. If you are not safe, go to the Cathedral-"

. . .

AND THEN THEY WERE GONE, heading in a large arc around the black wall.

"Ok, let's go," Kingston said. "Let's get to the Cathedral."

"What's the best way?" Carter directed that at Charlie, but it was Danni who answered.

"Straight down this road and through the shopping centre. That's where it is."

"How far?"

"Fifteen minutes, maybe ten if we don't stop."

Carter nodded. "We have ourselves a plan. Let's go."

26

KENNEDY EMERGED INTO SUNLIGHT, which was unexpected. He growled and covered his eyes until they adjusted, but by then the darkness returned and the dome was back in place around Exeter.

He scanned his surroundings, looking for movement. Some of the Horde were waiting for him, ready to escort him to wherever he wanted to go, an honour guard. The fact he was more powerful than all of them combined didn't matter. Eight of them, a sacred number. One of them bowed and held up a clawed hand. In it, he was holding a severed arm, long and thin and fresh.

Kennedy took the offered limb and bit into it. The flesh ripped easily on his teeth and he tore through to the bone. He pulled a strip off and chewed it whilst grinning at the Horde. Too long had he been cautious, hiding in shadows and darkness. Too long had he suppressed his urges for the human flesh.

Today, he would feast.

It was still dark, but he was not hidden. Standing in the middle of the street, shops on either side of him, in plain sight, he marvelled at the sheer audacity of it. Human corpses lay on the ground along the length of the street. The ones who couldn't – or didn't – run fast enough. Even in the dim light, his enhanced eyes could see the meals in which his brothers had already partaken. It filled him with a joy he would never be able to explain to Father.

Kennedy threw the bone to one side, swallowing flesh. A woman, he would guess, based on the tenderness of the meat. His teeth hit something solid and he pulled it out of his mouth. A silver bracelet adorned with two hearts and engraved with the words 'Oliver' and 'Patrick'. The humans did like their little trinkets. He tossed it on top of the pile of discarded bones.

"Brothers," he said, "out here, there is a man who killed the Princes."

Hissing from the Horde. He knew Father had already broadcast the man's face. They all knew who they were looking for. No sense in letting some lowly Horde take the glory for the find.

"Father wants him alive. He has plans for revenge on the human who caused him such pain. You may eat what you want, kill whomever you want, but not this man. He is to be brought to me and I will take him to Father. He has not yet been found, which means he is hiding."

The Horde looked at each other, confused expressions on their faces. Of course, Kennedy realised, they were too new, too freshly batched. They had no concept of the human world. They did not know what the structures around them were. Kennedy doubted they would even have set foot in the buildings unless they'd seen humans in them.

His mind link with the Horde was limited, and nowhere near as strong as Father's. It was good enough for the simple command: search the buildings and alert me when the man is found. He broadcast it now, brow furrowed as he concentrated. With the message sent, he returned his attention to the group in front of him.

"Go," he said. "I will follow."

With a roar, the Horde ran to the nearest store, smashing the glass and rushing into the building. Kennedy looked at the sign and decided John Lewis, whoever he was, was about to have a very bad day.

27

LINDA ALMOST CRIED at the sight of the sun. The sudden warmth filled her with a joy it was impossible to vocalise, and she grinned, even as tears rolled down her cheeks. This can only be good, she thought. With the barrier gone, surely now they would be rescued. Police would storm the city, probably the army too. Doctors and nurses on standby to help the wounded. In time she would be able to write about her experiences. All the majors would pick it up, perhaps even a TV series. It would make her a fortune. She would find John and head back to London, their worries and troubles gone. She could even set up a scholarship and call it the Baxter Memorial Fund for Young Reporters. Some good would come of today after all.

As abruptly as it had gone, pressure threatened to crush her head and then the hum resumed.

"No!" she whispered. Linda sank to her knees and this time the tears were pure frustration and terror. Sobs wracked her whole body as she curled into the foetal position. She couldn't remember ever feeling so helpless. To all her friends she had been so independent. Count on no-one – not even John. Her circle of friends had always been small, which she had always put down to her drive: keep up or get out of the way. Why had she always been like that?

Why had her career taken precedence over everything else? How many friends would be at her funeral, which was looking like arriving much sooner than she expected. She'd always believed herself to be a strong woman, but did it make her weak to take a holiday or even to want a family?

With death looking more and more like the only outcome of the day, her career was looking more and more inconsequential. A child was not a sign of weakness. She shook her head, trying to force some sense into it. Her thoughts were all over the place. She didn't *want* kids. Did she?

A dull noise pierced the background whine of the dome, gaining volume until it thundered overhead. She looked up and saw a sleek black helicopter fly over, skimming the roofs of the buildings. A message followed and her doubt evaporated with it.

She wiped her eyes, stood and started following the signs for the Cathedral.

28

Caution made them slow, but at least it kept them alive. Carter went first, and Danni brought up the rear with the others spread out between them. He took a meandering path, so they were always covered from the road by cars – of which there were many, with their owners either dead at the wheel or long gone.

Every time he reached a junction, he felt his heart beat faster. Every time there was a scream or shout in the distance he wanted to yell in frustration. They saw very few creatures and were ignored by those busy eating their prey.

The worst moment was crossing a large roundabout. He had felt so exposed, weaving through the wrecks and abandoned cars. A cinema was on his right, with its glass entrance hall smashed in. Blood trails came out of the building, like someone had been dragged. A half-eaten body still sat in the doorway.

"What's the problem?" Danni hissed.

Carter shook his head, trying to clear it. The corpse's expression was forever stuck in an anguished cry. It looked like it was caught somewhere between agony and ecstasy and he wondered again if the dead were the only true winners today.

"Come on, man," Danni said. "Let's get the hell out of here."

"Do you want to bounce?" Kingston smirked.

Carter had seen the creatures kill indiscriminately, even uncontrollably like they were overcome with bloodlust. Why did the sitting corpse bother him so much? Was it because, at first glance, it looked like it was just chilling out, waiting for friends who would never show?

"How much further?" He directed the question at Danni.

"Up there." She nodded at the road opposite the cinema, which led up a steady incline. A large bus station was on the right and further up the hill, a sign read *Parking*. "Through the shopping bit, then it's down an alley."

"Ten minutes?"

"At least, at this pace."

Carter nodded. He looked at each of them, trying to ignore how much Charlie was sweating. It was a minor miracle they'd survived this far.

"Time to bounce," Kingston said.

"You're such a dick," Danni replied. Charlie gave her a thumbs up and she returned his smile. Just for a moment, the day didn't feel so bad.

"Nah, don't be like that. I like it. Let's bounce, bounce, bounce."

"Cut it out you two," Carter said.

"Us *two*?" Danni cried.

Kingston blew her a kiss, but at least he stopped saying 'bounce'. He followed Carter and they headed towards the shopping precinct. They made good time, covering the open area quickly. No tell-tale shouts or screams from the creatures; they didn't see any of them, although the familiar corpses and abandoned cars were evidence of their passing.

They stopped at the car park. A road rounded a corner to their left, and the main road led to some traffic lights about a hundred yards ahead.

"Which way?" Carter scanned both streets, but both were deserted. For now.

Danni shrugged. "You can go either way from here. Doesn't make much odds." She pointed to the left. "That way is quieter usually."

"Quieter is good," Carter said.

"Carter, the things seem to be leaving the main roads alone," Danni said. "Look at this, we've barely seen any of them since we left Waitrose. Maybe they've gone exploring the side streets?"

"Shortest way," Charlie was on the verge of hyperventilating. "Let's just go the shortest way."

"Charlie, we'll go the *safest* way," Danni said.

Charlie groaned and wiped the sweat from his brow. "Just give me a minute, I'm not as fit as I used to be."

"Well, no shit, fat man," Kingston smirked.

"Hey!"

"Leave it out, Kingston," Carter snapped. "We don't need to be winding each other up."

"Whatever, man, I'm just calling it as I see it."

Danni walked away from the group. She slid down by a car, grateful to take the weight off her feet, just for a moment. *Men*, she thought. *Even at desperate times like these they still can't help themselves.* They had to dig at each other; had to be the alpha male. It was like being back in Hendon, except the monsters were a little more obvious here.

A sudden noise got her attention. She peered around the car and saw a group of seven – no, eight – monsters emerging from a building further up the hill. They were staring at their surroundings, taking it all in as if they hadn't seen it before. All eight swayed gently as if buffeted by a strong wind. Then, as one, they turned and ran towards the top of the street, heading for the crossroads at the summit. Dormant traffic lights didn't change as they passed.

The creatures had not seen them, and she let out a long breath. Her hands were shaking so she made fists to stop them. Where were they going? What were they up to? They'd been moving with a purpose after those few disorientated seconds. Why was that? Where had they come from?

She looked back at the group. Kingston and Charlie were still arguing, with the latter's face still crimson. She waved to get their attention, but they all ignored her.

"Hey!" she cried, louder than she intended.

Nothing moved. The creatures were out of sight – and earshot.

"They just came out of there," Danni pointed at the one the creatures had emerged from.

"So? Probably just killing more folk."

"What's up?" Carter said. "What's there?"

"Some of the things came out and looked really groggy, but that's the Underground Passages."

"Change of light, then?" Charlie asked.

"I'd have thought it's too dim out here for that," Danni said. "It's not exactly 'hot sun in the middle of the day bright' is it?"

"Maybe it was dark in there?"

"It's dark out here!" Kingston laughed at Charlie.

"What are the Underground Passages?" Carter said.

"Exeter is riddled with tunnels. They were built over five hundred years ago." Charlie perked up, looking like his old self for a moment. "What's really interesting is-"

"Dude, I skipped school for a reason."

"They didn't build them as tunnels," Charlie muttered, looking at his feet.

"Come on," Carter said. "Let's get to the Cathedral. The army will know what's going on, or at least have some weapons. I'm kind of sick of just running from these things."

He didn't vocalise his immediate thought, and thankfully, nor did anyone else. What if the soldiers *didn't* have a clue how to help them? They'd seen one helicopter only.

One.

It wasn't enough to help a city, even one with less than a square mile still standing. He pushed the thought aside. Safety in numbers was their best bet. Carter led them up the side street, skirting around a large multi-storey car park. The dark levels of the car park sent a frisson of fear through him, but no creatures leapt out at them.

In the distance, the spire of the Cathedral loomed over its surroundings, a towering beacon of hope.

29

KENNEDY STOOD in the middle of a crossroads. He was surrounded by buildings, most of which had broken windows and ruined displays. Places for humans with large faces, or where they could get dry quickly and a place to take an animal to listen to music. Yet more places were full of tables so the humans could all eat together. Shops and restaurants. Strange words which didn't explain the function of the building at all.

Kennedy snarled. The humans were truly mystifying.

When the machine had gone overhead, he had sent a call for more Horde members and they were arriving now. Eight of them, clearly new. Their skin was stretched so thin over their bones they almost had their skeletons showing. Mother must be running out of materials. Kennedy nodded to himself. They would have to do until the others returned.

He sent another call for some of the Horde to return to Father with materials for Mother. It would help make the Horde stronger, in time. Kennedy didn't really understand how it worked and part of him didn't want to.

"Come," he said aloud. The Horde followed him as he jogged down the streets, passing the huge stores and restaurants. Dead humans littered the ground, but none of them stopped to feed; Kennedy's will was too strong.

Eventually the maze of shops started to open up and Kennedy stopped. He held up a hand and the Horde shuffled to a stop behind him in two rows of four.

About fifty feet away from Kennedy, a short wall surrounded a green area. Beyond, a large, and admittedly impressive structure towered over the buildings around it. The place looked old, and Kennedy dimly remembered it from a previous visit, although it had not looked quite as impressive then.

The Cathedral.

Where the humans had been told to come.

The flying machine sat on the grass in front of the Cathedral. Surrounding it were several men dressed in identical black uniforms. They were all kneeling, with the weapons capable of decimating the Horde all pointed away from the Cathedral.

Kennedy snarled again. More weapons were not a good sign. He looked down the street and saw two humans making their way towards the armed men. He could see more shops and paths leading into the Cathedral grounds. *There are other ways in,* he thought, *but not yet. Find the young black man first. Let the humans make their little sanctuary*. There were more than enough out in the city itself. They could deal with these humans later.

He moved his group further back into the shadows and headed back into the city, away from the Cathedral.

30

LINDA FOLLOWED the signs for the Cathedral until she could see the old spire ahead. Excitement built and she felt her pace quicken. She forced herself to stop and rest in the doorway of an old house. No sense in rushing now and attracting the creatures. She tried some yoga breathing to calm herself. It took longer to work than normal, but then everything about this was very far from normal.

With her breathing finally under control, she set off again, moving from doorway to doorway. She came to a long, deserted alley and ran down it on tip toes, wincing at the slightest noise she made. It meant she ran in a hunched over shuffle rather than sprint and it was debateable whether it was quicker than just walking.

The end of the alley opened onto a street with shops on the right and a knee-high wall surrounding a green. Beyond the green, the Cathedral stood as impressive, impassive and ancient as ever. Its yellow sandstone walls looked grey in the half-light cast by the Wall.

A movement on her right made her start and she spun towards

it, ready to run. Sitting at a table, with an enormous bowl of salad in front of him, sat a boy of about ten. He smiled at Linda and gave a little wave.

The Cathedral was so close, salvation at hand.

Linda looked up and down the street several times but couldn't see any creatures. A helicopter loomed large on the green, incongruous against the ancient building.

So close.

Linda beckoned to the boy, but he just waved. Linda tried again, but the boy continued eating his salad, watching her with big doleful eyes. Normal eyes. Deep brown, but with whites clearly visible. A normal healthy boy, just eating a salad.

For Christ's sake.

Linda entered the shop, heart beating fast. She was in an Italian restaurant, judging by the pictures of pasta and pizza on the walls. The ovens were clearly not working so the boy had raided the salad bar. Clever.

"Hello," the boy said, shattering the silence. "I'm Ethan." There was a slight Devonian twang to his words.

"Linda." She looked around the restaurant, but it was empty. "We need to go, ok?"

"Are you going to be my mummy now?" Ethan said, throwing a whole baby tomato into his mouth. It burst when he bit into it, a little of the juice dribbling from the corner of his lips. He wiped it with the back of his hand. "My mummy has gone. She was taking me to my arsehole daddy, but the monsters came."

He frowned at the words 'arsehole daddy' like it was something he'd been told but didn't really believe.

"Did-" Linda started but Ethan nodded. His face was blank now and Linda decided not to push it. What would she do with a crying ten-year-old?

"That looks like a nice salad," she said instead.

Ethan nodded. "Mummy likes it when we eat healthy, but Daddy always says no good story starts with a salad." He pushed the bowl to the side.

"Where does your daddy live, sweetheart?"

"Over in Heavitree, just on the edge of Exeter. He likes it there, cos he can get straight on the M5. He's very busy."

Linda was beginning to think perhaps 'arsehole daddy' was a good sobriquet for the man. Was this how it would be if she had kids? Too busy?

"Well, there are people in the Cathedral," Linda said. "Maybe they can help?"

"It's where the black thingy went through."

For a moment, Linda was confused, and she tried not to picture the swathe of destruction the Wall had wrought as it expanded. She tried to keep her face neutral, but, judging by the expression on Ethan's face, she'd failed.

"He's dead, isn't he?"

"We don't know for sure," Linda said. She had a vague recollection of one of her old college friends saying you should never lie to kids. They can sense lies the way a dog can smell fear.

"Well, fudge knuckles," Ethan said. "Can I come with you?"

Tears welled in Linda's eyes and she found herself nodding. "Of course you can, sweetheart. Come on, it's not far."

31

CARTER STOPPED by a statue of a blue boy. He held up his hand bringing them all to a standstill. Danni pointed down the street in front of them. He nodded and set off at a jog, but behind him Charlie groaned. Carter skidded to a stop at the end of another short street.

Opposite him was a large pedestrianised area, with shops lining both sides. Many of the shops had broken windows and displays, with yet more corpses on the ground. The death toll for today was truly horrendous, but he couldn't think about it now: all they could do was focus on getting to safety. None of which was why he had stopped though.

Heading towards them was a group of the creatures. Eight of them, marching in two lines and at the head of the column was the one with the tail. The one who had initiated the attack on the police station. The one who seemed to be the most dangerous of them all.

For now, the creatures hadn't noticed them.

"Move!" Carter hissed, pointing back up the street. He turned and ran back toward the blue statue. The others all turned and ran, all except Charlie.

He was bent double, holding his chest. "I can't-" he gasped. "I can't breathe." Charlie groaned loudly and fell to the ground, still clutching his chest. His breathing was short and ragged, with sweat pouring off his brow. "Help!" he said, closing his eyes.

"What's happening?" Kingston yelled. "S'up with fat man?"

"He's having a heart attack," Danni said. *Not now, Charlie, not now.* They were so close to the Cathedral, so close. Charlie had taught her so much and she had much to be grateful for. She'd watched as he'd gained weight, knowing something was up, but saying nothing.

A roar echoed down the street. The thing with the tail was pointing at them. They'd been seen.

"What do we do now?" Kingston said. "We gotta go!"

Carter knelt next to Charlie, trying to remember his first aid training. Was Charlie out cold? He linked his hands and started to push on his chest.

"We need a defib." Danni spun on the spot but couldn't see anything. No tell-tale yellow box.

"Danni," Kingston nodded his head at the fast-approaching creatures.

"We're not leaving him," she said.

"We can't do anything for him." Kingston's voice was filled with panic.

Carter stopped the compressions. "He's not breathing!"

"Carter, let's go!" Kingston was already moving away from Charlie.

Danni knelt next to Charlie and took over doing compressions. The creatures were less than twenty metres away now, the skinny ones overtaking the one with a tail.

Carter howled in frustration. Charlie wasn't responding and Carter choked out a sob.

"No," he said. Despite all the other deaths today, Charlie was different. He was a mate, for a start. Not a mate he'd seen in a while but still a mate.

The creatures stopped. Five metres away, snarling at them both, they stood waiting. The one with the tail pushed his way through them and pointed. At first, Carter thought the creature was pointing at him, but then he realised the thing was pointing past them.

At Kingston.

"There!"

The thing had a surprising accent, clipped and almost upper class, rather than a guttural roar Carter had been expecting. There was nothing he could do: no weapons other than his fists and after hitting one earlier he wasn't in a hurry to try again.

"Come on then!" he screamed, standing and facing them. The creatures all ran past heading straight for Kingston, who turned and sprinted back up the street. One of them paused long enough to snarl at Carter, but then ran after the rest of its pack.

"What the hell?" Carter didn't stop to think. He'd caught a break, but Charlie was still in trouble. Kingston was hopefully quick enough – and had enough of a head start - to find somewhere to hide. He hauled Charlie up. *Still alive. Jesus, somehow still alive.* Danni slipped under his other arm, sagging under the weight. Carter was already sweating under the exertion as they dragged Charlie towards the Cathedral.

Five hundred metres had never seemed so far.

32

KINGSTON RAN AS HARD as he could. Exhausted, legs and lungs burning, he ran on anyway. Running for your life will do that. He turned down a side street, losing track of the shops as he went.

He emerged from a long, covered passage to find a wide street with a single lane road down the middle of it. More shops lined this street. He saw Boots, Clarks and Waterstones amongst others. He ran alongside the shops, heading slightly uphill until he reached a clothes shop with smashed windows. He jumped in, and then ducked down beneath the displays.

Kingston waited. He was certain the things had not seen him go in there. They had not come out of the passage before he'd entered the shop. He scanned his surroundings but couldn't see anyone – or anything – in the store. Two corpses, both women, lay by the door, with blood trails running through the middle of the store and ending by the bodies. Employees turning up for work just as the world went to shit. They must literally have arrived as the wall went up.

Movement in the street.

Kingston ducked back down. He was behind the cash tills with just a flimsy piece of wood blocking him from view. Hyper aware of all noise, including his heart rate, Kingston held his breath.

Growling.

Snarling.

"Find him!"

The voice was so loud Kingston jumped. He couldn't help himself; it sounded like the person speaking was standing next to him. Next, he heard the crunch of glass as the creatures ran into shops looking for him. He didn't dare look to see if anyone had come into Gap.

He had no weapons, no way of fighting back.

If the creatures found him, he was dead.

He could hear a creature moving around in the store. By the footfall, it was only one creature. Kingston debated rushing the creature and jettisoned the idea almost immediately. What if he was wrong and there were more than one? He'd never fight two without a weapon. What if it was the big one? The one with the tail. Kingston didn't want an acid spike to his face. Of all the ways to go, it was way down the list of wants. What if the creature cried out? Then his friends would come running and that would be the end of that.

Kingston tried to stay as still as possible. He hugged his knees to his chest, tucking himself into a ball. He concentrated on his limbs, clutching them hard. No tapping or shaking this time. He caught a glimpse of his scorpion tattoo and felt guilty about hiding. The Scorpions didn't hide from no-one. The Scorpions would not lie still hoping not to be discovered.

But then, the Scorpions had never come face to face with a blood-thirsty, flesh eating, hard as nails bunch of monsters who were rampaging through a city killing all they came across. There was a good chance even the mighty Scorpions would run and hide.

A snarl sounded close to him. An exaggerated sniff. Another low growl, but then the footsteps faded. Kingston risked a look over the top of the counter and saw the back of a creature as it climbed back out of the window. The door was open right next to it and he bit down a sudden giggle. With a snarl, it turned around just as Kingston ducked back under the counter.

Nothing moved in the shop. Complete silence and Kingston held his breath. So stupid, looking and laughing, so stupid. He stayed as still as he could – just his treacherous leg shaking away despite his best efforts - for what felt like an age, and then he heard the thing's footsteps fade again.

Kingston breathed out, grinning to himself. That had been too close. His hands were shaking, so he made fists like he'd seen Danni do earlier and tried to calm himself down. He peered around the corner of the counter again and saw an empty shop. Or at least, empty of creatures. The two women were still in place, forever dead in their shitty uniforms. He crept over to them and saw a handbag between them. Almost by habit, even though it had been many years since he'd boosted a bag, he looked inside. With a grin, he pulled a packet of cigarettes out and checked it. Twelve left, with the lighter in the pack. He hadn't smoked for a few months now, but he was already salivating at the thought of a victory cigarette when he caught back up with Carter.

Carter. The dude was alright for a copper, and Kingston felt better in his presence. Both Carter and Danni, had an air of confidence and competence about them. Kingston reckoned his best chance of survival was with them and not on his own.

He risked a look outside, trying to stay hidden in the shop doorway. The creatures were far away, heading towards the big bookshop. Kingston stepped into the street and started to retrace his steps, back towards the Cathedral.

33

THEY WERE MOVING FAR TOO SLOWLY under the weight of Charlie. He moaned every few seconds but didn't open his eyes. The stores watched them pass, their broken windows and ruined displays the only witness to their troubles. Carter watched the stores, feeling nervous with every step. God knew how many creatures were hiding in the buildings, how many eyes were on them now.

He expected a creature to jump out at them any second.

He was breathing hard, but they pushed on. Charlie wasn't groaning, which was a small mercy or a bad sign. The only sound was their feet on the concrete as they edged ever closer to the Cathedral.

Eventually, the ancient building came into view, but Carter didn't have time for its majesty. He could see soldiers moving around the perimeter. They were all carrying, and Carter was relieved to see armed soldiers on the streets of Exeter.

"Help!" he called. All attempts at quiet were now gone. If the creatures came now, they would be cut down by the army, and he half wished they would attack again. Two soldiers came running towards them, taking Charlie from them and moving quickly back to the boundary wall.

Relief flooded through him as the weight was removed and he collapsed on the other side of the wall. Danni sank to the grass beside him, wiping sweat from her brow.

"What's your name?" Another soldier said as he arrived.

"John Carter, I'm police." Carter panted, and Danni introduced herself. "Who's in charge here?"

"That would be Captain-" The soldier turned his head as he said the man's name, so Carter missed it. "He's going to want a full debrief from you." He held his arm out to pull Carter to his feet.

Carter waved the man's hand away. "Give me a minute, mate. I haven't stopped running since about six this morning."

"Well, from what we saw on the way in, it ain't safe out here. Just a few more steps and we'll get you inside."

Carter nodded, knowing the man made sense. Muscles protesting, he stood up. He swayed on the spot, exhaustion arriving on the same wave as relief. He didn't need to look at Danni to know she was doing the same.

"You got a drink?"

"Yep," the soldier smiled. "We're brewing up. Come on, I'll sort you out."

They walked across the green and onto a gravel path. Soldiers scanned the buildings around them, keeping weapons ready.

"How many survivors have you found?" Carter said.

"Not many. You're only our second group."

Carter felt his heart sink. Only two groups had made it to the Cathedral. How many people had died today? How many were still huddled in their homes hoping for rescue?

The two soldiers who had taken Charlie came out of the Cathedral and nodded to the man escorting Carter.

"Where's Charlie?" Carter asked. "Is he ok?"

"Nah mate, he's dead," said the younger soldier and they jogged back to their place on the perimeter.

Carter gasped and tears welled in his eyes. He felt as if a large weight had just landed on his chest.

"Sorry," the escort said. "That's Mclean. He's not known for his tact. I'm sorry for your loss."

Carter stood in the doorway of the Cathedral, feeling utterly helpless.

34

KINGSTON CREPT THROUGH THE STREETS, taking great care to stay hidden. The wall created such dim light there were lots of areas which were shrouded in darkness. He only had a vague idea where he was going, but he was trying to retrace his steps.

Now, he stood in front of Fat Face, looking up and down the street for some kind of indication as to which way he should go. Shops both ways. Corpses both ways. No creatures.

The longer he stood out in the street, the more likely it was some of the creatures would find him. Nothing else for it, he chose to keep going along the street. He passed shops tempting him to steal some clothes – a Hollister, Superdry and a decent looking suit shop. Kingston ignored the temptation and pressed on. No point in having cool clothes if you were dead.

A large Debenhams came up on his left. Kingston looked into the doorway. The perfume section was a mess: stands broken, bottles of perfume – both intact and broken – littered the floor, corpses of workers strewn about. He was amazed at how numb to his surroundings he was. Would anything ever shock him again?

A sudden scream rang out from inside the store and then he heard the snarls of the creatures. Kingston didn't wait to see what was happening. He knew the scream by now and knew the sound of the creatures' blood lust.

He ran.

Keeping Debenhams behind him, he sprinted down the street. Feet pounding on pavement, he barely registered the shops he passed. Gradually he became aware of the street widening but he didn't slow down. He emerged next to a bank, out into a wide street with a narrow road running through the centre of it.

He was back on the High Street.

"Oh no," he said aloud. A cry echoed off the buildings, and it was met with answering cries. Kingston looked towards the source of the noise. He could see the clothes store he had hidden in about a hundred metres away. Standing in front of it were three creatures.

They were all pointing at him.

He skidded to a halt, panting.

Another two creatures came out of shops on the far side of the street. Then, the big one, the one with the tail, came out of another store and walked into the middle of the road. He roared, pointing at Kingston.

Kingston had no choice. He ran back the way he came.

35

THE DOOR to the Cathedral swung open and they were ushered in. Carter noticed a glass door set half a metre inside the ancient wooden one. Something for visitors? The wooden door looked sturdy enough, so perhaps the glass one was to save the hinges of the original. Row upon row of seats stretched out before them. The interior was huge. The seats looked comfortable, for a church, and several large stone pillars lined the area, holding up the vaulted, impressive ceiling. Many of the stained-glass windows displayed various religious scenes, although some had coats of arms and others had the names of towns engraved on them.

Also set into the walls were many plaques and at other parts, the words were engraved into the stone itself. Carter didn't bother to read any of them. He was too exhausted and frankly, not interested. The ceiling was impressive, but the sheer amount of stone over his head made him nervous. *Relax*, he told himself, *this place has stood for centuries. It'll last one more day.*

At the far end of the vast space, an altar sat in the middle of a semi-circle created by chairs. Some people sat in these chairs, heads bowed, lips moving silently. To the left of the group was an intricately carved pulpit which would offer the speaker a commanding view of the congregation. Beyond was a stone wall which seemed to cut the room in two. Above the stone wall were the pipes for the organ, but he couldn't see the organ itself.

Inset into the walls were many carvings of bodies: knights, monks, kings or queens. It looked creepy as hell in the grim half-light they were in. Shadows lay deep in the corners of the room, where the half-light didn't penetrate. Carter turned his attention back to the rows of seats.

Groups of people sat in pews in various states of distress. They all looked shell-shocked.

"I thought we were the second group in?" he said.

"Yeah, these people were already here when we got here," the escort shrugged.

Danni sobbed next to him, tears rolling down her face as her shoulders convulsed. "I can't stop crying," she said. "Why can't I stop crying?"

The soldier looked at his feet as Carter put a hand on her shoulder, waited a moment, then pulled her into a hug. She pushed him away.

"I didn't really like him," she said. "I saw the way he used to letch over me. I knew what he wanted, but Christ, no way. Not even if I liked men." She wiped her nose clear of snot with the back of her hand. "I didn't even like him and now he's dead and I can't stop crying." She shook her head and sat in one of the chairs. "Leave me alone," she whispered.

Carter glanced at the soldier, not sure what to do. "Look, who's in charge?"

The man pointed at someone further into the Cathedral and Carter tried to smile at Danni. "Get some rest, I'll come back with some food."

The escort took him over to the man and Carter shook his hand but didn't catch a name. He was a similar height and age to Carter, solidly built with dark hair. His eyes had a haunted expression, like he had seen more than he ever wanted to. Carter knew how he felt.

"You must be exhausted," he said.

Carter nodded. "Yeah, it's been a rough day."

"We'll sort you some food." He nodded at the escort who ran further into the Cathedral. "What can you tell me?"

"What can I tell you?" Carter was aghast. "You mean you don't know what's going on?"

The captain held up his hands to calm him down. "This morning I was on a base in Kent. We were scrambled when the wall went up. We've been waiting outside with no clue as to what was happening in here until the wall came down again."

He looked like he was going to say more but bit his tongue.

"What?" Carter said.

"Three helicopters took off when the wall came down. We're the only ones who made it through."

Carter kept silent.

"What are the creatures?" the captain asked.

"We don't know," Carter said. "The first I saw of them was this morning. I'm a police officer, but I'm not from here. I came because my wife asked me to."

The captain frowned and the lines revealed made Carter revise his age upwards.

"My wife found them in a warehouse. She's a reporter," Carter said. "She was attacked by the things. Local police took her into custody, and I got a phone call. Her story seemed-"

"A little far-fetched?" The captain smiled. "I have some experience. I sympathise."

"Anyway, there seem to be three kinds of them. The biggest

ones have tails, and you don't want to get hit by that. They can also shoot the spikes out of the tail. It has some kind of acid or maybe poison in it."

"Acid?" The captain said. "Really?"

"Yeah. I saw it melt someone's face off."

"Jesus."

"Yeah."

"Ok, anything else? What are the other two kinds?"

"The main kind look a bit like skinny versions of us. Really well muscled though, and their skin is really tight over their bodies. They look pretty disgusting." Carter made a face to show how grim he thought they were.

The captain nodded. "Ok, the third kind?"

Carter paused, taking a deep breath. He ran his hand through his hair, hating the greasy feel of it. "This is the worst bit," he said. "They are children. Pitch black eyes, no white at all. The big things seem to do what they say. They can make something like smaller versions of the wall too. I've seen it."

"Kids?" the captain said. "So the big things are, what, their fathers?"

Carter shrugged. "We've killed two of the kids and loads of the main kind. I've only seen one with a tail since the wall went up and none of the kids."

"Ok," the captain said. "You've given me a lot to think about. Thank you."

"There are others out there," Carter said. "Someone I was with. He ran, when Charlie-" his voice cracked, and he took a moment to get it under control. "My friend ran, making the things follow him. He drew them away." Carter paused, knowing what he was saying was not strictly true. "I'd like to go and look for him. My wife is out there somewhere too. She needs me."

The captain shook his head. "Absolutely not. You need to rest and get some food in you. I have a team ready to look for survivors. Let them do it."

"But-"

"No buts. I have you safe at the moment and I'm not prepared to lose anyone else today."

"I can take care of myself," Carter said.

"I've no doubt you can, but it changes nothing. If I let you go and you get killed out there –"

"I don't imagine you really give a shit."

The captain scowled at him. "Like I said, I know you can take care of yourself. You wouldn't have got this far otherwise. Please, let my men take care of this. Nobody leaves. No exceptions."

The escort came back. "We have some food ready."

"Good," the captain turned his back. Without another word, he went to a small group of armed soldiers and started talking to them in hushed tones.

"I guess we've been dismissed," Carter said to the escort, a young man who didn't look old enough to shave.

"Well," the escort cleared his throat, "it makes sense to stay here. It isn't pretty out there."

Carter laughed, and the young soldier looked embarrassed.

"Look, the captain is a good man. He was promoted from the ranks, which is pretty rare these days."

"What'd he do?" Carter sneered. "Rescue some soldiers who shouldn't even have been in a country?"

"No, he saved a bunch of people in a village in Devon. It was under attack from a bunch of wolves."

"I read about that," Carter said, the sneer melting from his face.

The escort nodded. "That was him. I'm pretty sure he's got our backs, you know what I mean? Come on, let's get some food in you."

Carter followed him through the pews of the Cathedral,

heading further away from the main doors. He looked to the rear of the vast space and saw a woman sitting with her back to them. A child was hugging her tightly, but she didn't seem to mind which was odd as he would recognise the woman anywhere. He called her name.

"John!" Linda cried. She put the boy down and ran to him. The hug took his breath away and he held her tight. Her familiar scent overwhelmed him, obvious even beneath the sweat and grime, and tears welled in his eyes.

"You're alive," he said. It felt woefully inadequate.

She broke the hug and grinned at him. "Is anyone-"

"What happened to the others you were with?" Carter asked, cutting her off, and immediately regretted it. Linda's face, full of joy and love, fell, crumpling into grief.

"They got them all." Linda explained everything she had been through. Carter pulled her into another hug, crushing her with his relief she'd been through so much and come out - relatively - unscathed.

"I found this boy," she said. "Ethan, this is John. He's my husband."

They sat in one of the pews, with Ethan perched next to them. Carter had his arm around Linda, and the boy kept looking at them with a frown on his face.

"There's a lot of bad stuff today. Charlie had a heart attack." Carter snorted. "Unbelievable, right? I bet he wanted to do something about his weight. You know, join a gym tomorrow, that kind of thing. Who'd have thought there'd be monsters in Exeter?"

"I know. It was supposed to be a quick visit. Me and Mike, all we were meant to do was get some footage of Hamilton dealing in illegals." She shook her head. "Nothing is worth this."

"I'm sorry about Mike." Carter was surprised to find he meant it.

"You hated him," Linda said, but her lips were a thin line, curved upwards. Was that a smile?

"Hate is a strong word. He just spent more time with you than I did."

"Jealousy doesn't suit you, John."

"I know. I felt I was losing you."

She didn't respond but rested her head on his shoulder. They sat quietly together for a few moments, until exhaustion caught up and they both drifted off to sleep.

36

KINGSTON SPRINTED through the streets again. He had a vague idea of where he was heading now – a signpost pointed the way to the Cathedral. *It's a big building,* he thought, *I'm bound to find it.*

Behind, the roars of the creatures told him two things: firstly, they had not stopped following; and secondly, they were getting closer. He jumped down a small flight of steps and landed heavily, stumbling as he did. For a horrible, sickening second, he thought he'd twisted his ankle, but the pain proved to be short-lived.

Adrenaline. Better than cocaine. Who knew?

He saw a shape moving ahead and panic gripped him again. The shape was slow moving, oblivious to him. As he approached, he made a decision. He could get past and keep going at full pace. With luck he would be past and clear before the thing realised he was there.

Gritting his teeth, Kingston forced himself to move more quickly. His legs were burning now, and he felt sick. He was sure his body was going to give out on him any second. As a borderline alcoholic, drug-using gang member, his fitness could do with work. *Tomorrow,* he thought, *always tomorrow.*

He surged past the shape and heard it scream. Somehow, some way, he increased his pace and sped past the creature.

His arms were burning and his legs felt like jelly. He buried the pain though. Self-preservation was a powerful instinct. Soon the shops disappeared, and he was in the clear, crossing a narrow road with the Cathedral right in front of him. Footsteps behind were more of a concern. They were loud, so close.

Closer.

"Hey!" Kingston roared. He could see two soldiers sharing a cigarette by the small wall surrounding the grounds of the Cathedral. They looked up with wide eyes as Kingston bore down on them. The cigarette flew into the air, embers glowing in the perpetual twilight as the men raised their weapons.

"Shit," Kingston said as he realised the guns were pointed at him. He dropped to the ground, covering his head with his arms as if that would protect him.

Bullets screamed over his head and the noise echoed around the buildings.

37

KENNEDY HISSED WHEN THE HUMANS' weapons roared. The Horde in front of him took the full brunt of the assault. Two were cut down in an instant and another fell as his legs were torn apart by the projectiles. The rest of the Horde stopped and turned back. Screaming in fear, they pushed and shoved each other as they ran back to the safety of the alleyway. Another Horde member fell as bullets opened his back, chunks of his flesh spinning away from his body.

The weapons fell silent. Kennedy could see two men in matching black uniforms kneeling by the wall. Smoke was curling around the barrels of their weapons. Behind them, two more black-clad humans were running towards their kneeling friends, armed with the same weapons.

Kennedy knew a lost cause when he saw one.

He waved his arm above his head and pointed back up the street. The Horde didn't need telling twice and they all ran back to the relative darkness offered by the side streets. Once he was sure he couldn't be seen, Kennedy turned to watch them.

Their efficiency was impressive. Now four of them watched the streets, but they weren't only focussed there. Two were watching for flanking movements and they were all talking to each other. He couldn't hear what was being said, but he could guess. Checking everyone was ok, checking no-one else was coming to harm them.

One of them jumped over the small wall and helped the human to his feet. Kennedy watched him being led away by an armed human. The black one was getting away and Kennedy didn't have enough men to attack. His hand went to his wrist, but he stopped himself. Did it have the power to teleport him and the black man? Kennedy didn't want to chance it, not yet anyway.

Kennedy thought about the dead Princes and Father's word. Whatever justice Father had planned would be terrible in its severity and Kennedy wanted to be part of it. The humans had killed all his brothers too.

He looked at the big building and wondered again just how he would get the Horde inside without mass casualties. The green area surrounding it would be red with the blood of the Horde if they charged.

Kennedy grinned to himself as a plan started to form in his head.

A much better plan.

38

Being surrounded by soldiers was a new experience for Kingston and he wasn't sure he liked it. Mindless following of authority didn't appeal – but then, no authority sat right with him. Of course, they had just saved his life, so he should be grateful.

One of the soldiers was talking to his men, clearly in charge. He certainly carried himself like he was. His sandy brown hair had the beginnings of grey in it, making him older than he looked.

"Back to the wall. Stay alert," he said, and three soldiers ran back to the perimeter. They resumed kneeling at points along the wall. All were training their weapons out to the streets and scanning their surroundings. Kingston had to admit it was pretty impressive. These guys had just shot a whole load of monsters and it hadn't phased them at all.

"You ok?"

It took Kingston a minute to realise the Captain was speaking to him. He was smiling at Kingston and for the first time, he began to think the day might end with them all alive.

The door to the Cathedral opened and the Captain led him

inside. It took a moment for Kingston's eyes to adjust; it was even dimmer inside the Cathedral than the perpetual gloom outside. The first thing he realised there were a few groups of people filling the pews. The second was none of them were soldiers.

"Where all the soldier dudes at?"

"We came in a Wildcat. This is all there is." The Captain looked like he was about to say more, but then turned away from them. "Make yourself comfortable," he said. "We could be here a while."

Kingston watched him go with his mouth open. "Seven soldiers. Hot damn."

A woman rose from the chair near him when he spoke and drew him into a hug. She looked awful, eyes swollen and puffy. Kingston held the hug, surprised at the warmth and care it held. Maybe it was time to stop being such a dick to her.

"Maybe eight," Danni said.

"Where's the rest?"

"Perhaps there's more on the way and this is the first wave in?" Danni said. "They call it a vanguard or something don't they?"

Kingston shrugged. He had absolutely no idea why anyone would send seven (maybe eight) soldiers to guard a van. "They have guns. That'll do. Where Carter at?"

He followed Danni's pointing finger and broke into a smile. He strode away from her, not waiting for her to catch up.

"Carter!" he roared, grin still in place. "I didn't think I'd ever be pleased to see some 5-0."

Carter and Linda both jumped awake. Carter blinked heavily and then his eyes focused on Kingston and Danni.

"You're alive!" he said, standing and stretching. The trials of the day were catching up with them all. Carter touched his face and winced, although it was no longer as red as it had been.

"Yeah man, just about."

Carter hugged Danni, who didn't push him away this time, then ruffled Ethan's hair. "How you doing, kiddo?"

Ethan gave him a thumbs up, but without smiling.

"What happened?" Carter turned to Kingston. "I saw those things run after you."

"Gave them the slip," Kingston said.

Linda stood and slid her arm around Carter's waist, lips thin as she watched Danni. "Hi, Kingston."

"This is Ethan. Linda found him." Carter didn't say anything else. His expression made it clear they weren't to ask the kid any questions.

"Hi." Ethan gave them a shy smile. Linda took his hand and led him further into the Cathedral.

"You did good," Carter said to Kingston, rubbing his face as if willing himself awake. He took care to avoid the wound. "We're alive because of you."

"The gang's all here." Kingston frowned. "Where's Charlie? I need me some fat boy banter."

Carter shook his head. Kingston's grin slipped and he looked away. He muttered something, but Carter didn't catch it. Probably 'those bastards' or maybe 'fat retard'. Carter was still unclear as to whether Kingston had *actually* liked Charlie or not.

"These soldier boys got any food?" Kingston changed the subject and hoped no-one noticed his voice break.

"Not much," Carter said. "They gave us tea when we arrived."

"Tea? Surely it's beer o'clock?" Kingston fished around in his pockets and pulled out a pack of cigarettes. "Oh, yes, nearly forgot about these bad boys. Anyone?"

"Beer o'clock? Surely you need a glass of milk?" Danni scowled at the cigarette and headed over to where Linda was sitting with Ethan.

"What the hell?" Kingston was perplexed. "The world is going to shit, and she's annoyed I want a ciggie?" He shook his head. "People today, too busy being woke and all that crap to enjoy one of life's simple pleasures. You want one?"

"No, I quit a couple of years ago. Best decision of my life really."

"Best?" Kingston said. "Seriously? Man, you need to get out more."

"You've heard of cancer, right?"

"Yeah, but it only applies to old folk." Kingston tapped the side of the packet, as if thinking of better times. "I quit about six months ago." He opened the pack and put the cigarette in his mouth. "Someone persuaded me it were a good idea."

"So, do you really want one now?"

"Man, we could be dead in an hour. Of course I want one now." He lit the end of the tube and inhaled deeply. "You sure you don't want one of Satan's finest nails?"

Carter threw back his head and laughed, drawing scowls form some of the groups sat near them. "I like that."

Kingston took another few drags and coughed before stubbing it out. More than half was crushed under his shoe. "Never tastes as good as you remember, does it?"

"Nope."

"Still better than that vaping shit though. What is *that* all about?"

Carter shrugged like he didn't care one way or another. Kingston was just making noise. He scanned the huge ceiling high above them. Even to his untrained eye, it looked spectacular. Around a hundred metres of stone, held up with what looked uncomfortably like ribs of more stone. He wasn't one to fawn over old buildings, but this was stunning.

They sat in silence for a moment, smoke lingering in the air between them. Carter breathed it in, relishing the second-hand smoke. Maybe Kingston was right, they were probably all going to die today, what difference would a cigarette make? Nothing really. How different would the boy's life have been with Carter to look after him? Maybe some of the rough edges wouldn't have formed and maybe others would have emerged instead. He knew plenty of cops with terrible relationships with their kids.

"What brought you to Exeter anyway? Shouldn't you be fleecing someone in Greenwich?"

"I never fleeced anyone," Kingston protested. "Most people I robbed were rich folk in need of their wallets lightening."

"Well, that's very good of you."

"It was good *for* me. I kept it all."

"Ok, so why come here? You running away?"

Kingston stared at him for a moment. As the silence stretched, he reached for another cigarette.

"Yeah, I was running away."

"You wanted out? Is that it? Leave the life behind?" Carter grinned at him. "You know it almost never works right?"

"I know. I came into some money." Kingston shrugged. "A lot of money. Enough to buy a new ID and shit and get the hell out."

"Why? I thought you and Keeler were tight." Carter frowned. Joe Keeler was the alleged leader of the Scorpions, with Kingston as his right-hand man. Keeler and Kingston had grown up together, been inseparable for years. Carter had lost count of the number of times they had provided alibis for one another.

"We were."

Carter noted the past tense but said nothing. He let the silence between them grow, waiting for Kingston to fill it. As ever with the young man, he didn't have to wait for long.

"Something happened. Something I can't change or put right."

Carter nodded. "You slept with someone you shouldn't have. Keeler's girlfriend? Something like that."

This time the silence was so long, he thought he'd blown it, forced the issue, but then Kingston nodded. He lit the new cigarette at last and inhaled deeply once more.

"Yeah, something like that. Keeler found us going at it one night. He wasn't supposed to be there, was supposed to be gone for hours out on a job. His car broke down, so he came home early. Shit man, it is what it is."

"I thought you and him had, like, a harem of willing volunteers."

"We did."

"So-"

"It was his brother, man. He caught me fucking his brother."

Carter felt his mouth open, but then he shut it, trying to hide his surprise. Kingston caught the look, however.

"I'll bang anything, man, I'm not fussy." He didn't make eye contact with Carter, just blew out the smoke again. "Keeler wasn't impressed, man. He always said he didn't care who you bumped genitals with as long as it was consenting. You know, do what you want behind closed doors and all that. Turns out it was a crock of shit. He reckoned I turned him – can you believe it? That's some straight up twentieth century bullshit right there." Kingston's foot was tapping on the stone floor, quicker and quicker.

"Keeler wanted me out of the picture. He beat the holy shit out of Stephen, did some real damage from what I hear. I didn't wait for him to come for me. I got the chance to take some money from a job, so I took it and came here. There's a guy I know out here. Owed me a solid, so I tapped him up to do me a new ID."

Carter shook his head. He didn't tell Kingston he was investigating the assault. *That poor boy.* He'd assumed it was gang related and had never been more wrong.

Kingston smoked more of the cigarette. "Thing is, I keep thinking about Stephen. Not the sex – well, not just that – but the way he speaks, the way he laughs. Christ, the way he smells."

"It's ok."

"So it looks like I'm gay," he said. "I ain't ever told nobody before."

"Nobody will care."

Kingston smiled through fresh tears. "I hope so, man. I'm just gutted I'll never get to talk to Stephen again."

39

ETHAN SAT on the floor playing with a plastic Jesus and a cow. Danni smiled, wishing she could join him. Anything to take away the grimness of the day. Linda caught her watching and smiled.

"Kids, eh?"

"I wouldn't know," Danni said. "Single, married to the job."

"Someone will come along. You're very pretty. Some hunky man will sweep you off your feet."

"God, I hope not," Danni blanched and cringed inside, hoping Linda wouldn't notice. She meant well, but screw that. Danni stood, turning away from the boy.

"You ok?" Linda asked.

"Yeah," Danni gave her a weak smile. "Just need to stretch my legs. I'm not great at sitting still."

Danni strolled over to the windows and made a show of stretching in case Linda was watching. Exhausted to the point of being too wired to sleep, the last thing she wanted was to have a conversation about her love life with someone as vacuous as Linda. She looked around, trying to find a distraction. Towards the rear of the Cathedral, she could see the Captain standing with two of his men, faces glowing in the light from a laptop.

"What are you looking at?" she asked, sauntering up to them with a casualness she didn't feel.

"Please return to your group," the younger man said, moving to cut her off. The one who had escorted her and Carter in.

"No."

That threw him.

"Miss, please-"

"Cut the crap, ok? I'm not your 'miss'. I'm a police officer, not some helpless bint you can order around." She prodded his chest. "Talk to me properly. I've been out there and *survived*. You have no clue what you're dealing with."

"We-"

"Nah, man, all you're seeing is my body. My face is up here and I'm going to talk to your boss."

"It's ok, Bawden, let her through." The Captain smiled at her.

"But, sir-"

"Leave it, Bawden, and for God's sake stop staring at her."

Bawden stood to one side, and Danni brushed past him, not even bothering to give him a filthy look. She'd met his kind before and refused to give him any kind of validation. The Captain held his hand out. "Call me Peter."

Danni shook it and introduced herself. "Well, Pete," she said, but he winced, so she added, "Sorry, Peter."

He looked like he was just trying to get used to the name. "What can I do for you, Danni?"

Straight to business. Danni was impressed.

"We're going to need more food for all these people."

She looked at the laptop screen and saw a man sat in a room with a bank of monitors surrounding him. "You've got contact with outside the wall?" she said, failing to keep the excitement out of her voice.

"Not exactly."

"What is that? The man, with the computers. That's nowhere I know in Exeter, so it must be outside. Your base, right? They sent you, so they can send more, right?"

"It's not going to happen," Peter said.

"Why not?" Danni put her hands on her hips, lips pursed.

Peter took his cap off and ran his hand through his greying hair. He was sweating, despite the coolness inside the Cathedral. He nodded at Bawden and the other man walked away from them, muttering to himself.

"Look, we have no idea what we're dealing with. None at all. There are scientists out there and they can't tell us how the wall is made. Shit, we don't even know what it's made *from*. Technically it's a dome, not a wall, but the apex is up in the stratosphere."

"But that's not possible," she said.

"Maybe not, but it's happening. Anyone or anything that touches the wall is instantly destroyed – we know this much. Three helicopters were scrambled when the wall came down." Peter shrugged. "We were the only one that made it through."

"Jesus," she whispered.

"Yeah. I lost some friends today." When he saw the expression on her face, he looked at the ground. "I guess you did too."

An uncomfortable silence enveloped them for a moment, both lost to a world of grief that would overwhelm them if they let it. Peter was the first to break the silence.

"Basically, the creatures let the wall down long enough to get a message out. It broadcast on every channel simultaneously. As far as we can tell, it's *every* channel in mainland Britain. All of them – even the obscure internet ones. We don't even know how they did it."

"What did they say?"

Peter gestured at the screen. "Be my guest, but I don't want this to be common knowledge, ok?" She nodded, and he pressed play.

A man stood, surrounded by tv screens, banks of computers and other machines she didn't recognise. He had long hair with a good build, and he appeared to be wearing a gown. She was reminded of the shapeless gowns they make you wear in hospitals. He was handsome from a distance, but that illusion shattered on closer inspection. She could barely see past his eyes, which were pitch black. She shuddered and it became worse when she heard his words.

"TO THE PEOPLE of this Island, I bid you welcome. It is long past time you knew of our existence. We were here before you and our claim to these lands predates you. However, we wish to exist, side by side, in peace.

"My desire for a peaceful cohabitation was shattered today. Several of my kind were butchered by the people of this city. My two sons – my children – were murdered in cold blood by the same individual.

"I have quarantined the city until my Horde finds the man responsible for the death of my children. Once we have him and our food source is secure, we will release any inhabitants who survive the search.

"Survivors will be granted safe passage out of the city. On this you have my word. Leave us in peace whilst we search for the justice we deserve."

AS SOON AS IT FINISHED, Peter closed the lid again. "It doesn't get any better, no matter how many times I watch it."

"They're looking for someone," she whispered. Her eyes flicked over to Kingston who was crying but smiling. Teenagers, just walking hormones. "Oh, God."

"Do you know who they are looking for?"

She shook her head, but far too slowly. He grabbed her arm – not with anger, but with an uncomfortable firmness.

"Danni, do you know?"

She shook her head again.

"I admire your loyalty, but this city is about to die. Thousands, probably *hundreds* of thousands of people are already dead. More will die because we don't have the manpower to stop these things. You should've seen it when we flew in. There are hundreds of them out there, and they are killing machines. If you know something, please, tell me."

"There is no way they are letting anyone go," she said, but in her head came the treacherous memory of the things running past her, chasing after Kingston.

"Probably not," Peter said. "By now, this video will have been seen by COBRA and I can tell you now, they will happily sacrifice one man if it means saving thousands. *I* would."

"Look, this message is full of shit. This all started way before the kids died." She filled him in with brief details of the murder case she'd been working on and the attack on the warehouse. "He's lying."

"Or he doesn't know what his troops are up to."

"I find that hard to believe."

"I don't." Peter rubbed his eyes. "Look, we both know they won't let us go. He says about securing a food source and from what I saw on the way in, that's us. I need to find this guy," he waved at the laptop, "and take him out."

40

CARTER LET the smoke linger around him. Lots of ex-smokers would make a big play of flapping their arms around to clear the air, maybe throw in a cough or two for good measure. Carter hadn't been above such over-the-top behaviour himself, but it just didn't seem worth the hassle today. So instead, he let the smoke drift around him, enjoying the taste and the memories it evoked.

Memories of when he met Linda. Thoughts of their long engagement and trying for a baby. He shook his head. Those memories weren't good. He glanced over at her, where she sat, watching the boy. It had shocked him to see her with Ethan. It was a stark contrast to the career woman he had argued with for years.

"So, what do you really think our chances of survival are?" These were Kingston's first words for several minutes.

"I was just beginning to relax," Carter said.

"Sorry, man, didn't mean to bring you down."

"Look around you. How many soldiers do you count?"

Kingston put the cigarette out and thankfully didn't reach for another: Carter could feel his resolve crumbling by the second.

"Not enough."

"That's an understatement. I count six guys."

"Seven," Kingston said and then, when Carter looked confused, started counting them out. "There are four outside on the wall, one by the door over there – although what the fuck he thinks he's going to stop there, I don't know – the guy what brought us the tea and the fella in charge."

"Ah, there were only three out there when I arrived," Carter said.

"Nah, man, you just can't count."

Danni sat down heavily next to them and glared at Kingston.

"What'd I do?"

"It's you," she said. "The creatures are after you."

"Me?"

"Back up, Danni. What are you talking about?"

She told them everything she'd seen in the video. "The guy who sent the video, he had those black eyes like the kids had."

"Who knows about this?" Carter said, looking around the groups in the Cathedral. Most of them were groups in their sixties, but there were some full of younger people. A couple of them looked like they could handle themselves.

"Just us at the moment. Peter, the captain, I think he's realised I know something."

"This crowd could get really unfriendly, really quick," Carter muttered.

"They wouldn't turn on me, would they?"

"Come on, really? You grew up on the streets. You would screw someone over for a fiver. What do you think these guys would do if it meant their *lives*?"

"I never did anyone for a fiver." Kingston looked hurt for a moment. "Tenner maybe, but then you're into big bucks."

"Do you take anything seriously?" Danni said. "The message

specifically says they would let us go if we handed you over. We'd have to leave Exeter, but we'd live."

"You're saying that like you've thought about it," Carter said.

"I ain't giving those things nothing," Danni said.

"So, by definition, you're giving them something," Linda called, coming over to them.

Kingston looked confused, but Carter smirked. Double negatives were not Kingston's strong point.

"Never mind." Linda rolled her eyes. "You lot look thick as thieves, what's up?"

"Nothing," Carter said. "Just discussing a bit of strategy if those things get in here."

"This 'Horde' doesn't seem to be clever," Danni said. "It will take them a while to figure out how to get in. The soldiers have some pretty awesome weapons outside so we should be ok for a while."

Linda frowned, but didn't say anything more.

"If they get in, it will be a massacre." She glanced over at Ethan, who had given up on plastic Jesus and was now thumbing through a bible. He looked bored as his lips moved whilst he traced the words with his other hand. She found herself smiling as she watched and then realised Carter was looking straight at her. Their eyes met, just for a second.

"Why did you call them that?" Linda asked suddenly. "The Horde? Is it their name? How do you know what they call themselves?"

"It's the name the army have given them," Danni said. "There's so many of them, I guess."

"It's a good name," Carter nodded. "Fits."

"The Horde." Linda shook her head. "Still, if they get in…"

She let the words hang in the stillness of the Cathedral. They were all quiet, contemplating what fresh carnage the rest of the day could bring. The earlier optimism at the arrival of the soldiers was dissipating rapidly.

41

KENNEDY RAN THROUGH THE TUNNELS, coat flapping behind him. He only slowed when the passage was too narrow, forcing him to squeeze through and duck below the low ceiling. He knew he was getting close when the rock started to change around him. Yellow stone gave way to the darker, harder rock the humans had built upon.

The Horde should be in position by now, out of view in the darker side-streets.

Kennedy waited for a moment, savouring the excitement coursing through his veins. This battle would be glorious. Today would live long in the Horde mind. He would become a legend.

The one who gave Father his revenge.

The one who gave the Horde a home above ground.

He examined the bracelet on his wrist and changed a couple of settings. He pushed the power up to max. This was a huge risk. Father had already warned him the bracelet was getting old and unreliable. What would happen on full power? How much of him would survive the transition from energy back to solid?

The face of the black man came to mind. His arrogant sneer as he had killed the Princes. His swagger as he had fled Kennedy and his hunters earlier. Kennedy would enjoy watching him suffer.

He pushed the button on his wrist bracelet and three spheres instantly burst through the rock, forcing it upwards in a tsunami of destruction.

42

THE SOLDIERS WERE TALKING in hushed but frantic whispers. Peter's expression was grim, but he was nodding in agreement to whatever Bawden was saying. The conversation went back and forth for a few minutes but ended with Peter pointing away from the main entrance. Bawden and the other man saluted then started talking to the survivors nearest them.

"Something's up," Danni said. She nodded at the soldiers, who were now making the group stand.

"They're moving us," Carter said. "Further inside."

Groups started moving slowly through the Cathedral as the soldiers approached. They were moving towards the rear of the room, where large wooden doors could be closed, cutting the room in half. It wouldn't delay the creatures for long, but any delay could be vital.

"Easier to defend," he muttered. "They're going to close us in there. It's a last stand sort of place."

"Is it a bad thing?" Linda asked.

He shrugged. "Maybe, maybe not. These guys know what

they're doing. Let's just let them get on with it."

"Really John? Letting other people take charge? That's not really you, is it?"

"I knew it!" Kingston said. "You never do anything you're told, right? You're more like me than you think."

Carter scowled. "I don't like being told what to do."

"He's understating things," Linda said and laughed. Seeing her face light up with the smile meant, for the first time, Danni could see what Carter saw in her.

The ground shook. Tapestries and flags hanging around the perimeter fluttered but didn't fall. Candle sticks fell to the floor, their noise dampened by a growing rumble.

"Earthquake?" Kingston said.

"In Exeter?" Danni raised her eyebrows. Kingston shrugged, like *What do I know?*

Gunfire erupted outside the walls, shattering the eerie peace of the Cathedral. Round after round erupted from unseen weapons. Someone inside screamed, a loud shrill sound that could be heard despite the rumble and it broke the paralysis gripping everyone. Groups of people were standing, moving further into the hall with terrified looks. Panic was a heartbeat away. Peter and the other two soldiers ran towards the doors, yelling for everyone to get back. He caught Danni's eye as he ran past.

"Get everyone back there. Close those big doors! Now!" He didn't slow as he shouted the instructions at her and didn't wait to see if she would comply.

Chairs were sent flying by the panicking crowd, which meant some people tripped or stumbled, slowing the whole group. Linda ran straight for Ethan who was frozen on the spot, whilst the others made for the wooden doors.

Ethan watched the panicking grown-ups with a calm expression. Linda felt a surge of pride and wondered where it had come from. Was this how parents felt all the time?

"Come on! Follow them!"

Ethan held his arms out and she swept him up without slowing. He buried his head in her shoulder, and she held him tight, hand on the back of his head so he wouldn't see anything.

A soldier charged into the building, pausing to turn and fire an indiscriminate burst back through the doorway. The noise from the weapon was deafening and echoed off the ancient ceiling.

"Help them," Carter said to Kingston. "Go!"

He pushed the other man towards Linda then turned and ran towards the soldier. It was Mclean, the one who had been brutal about Charlie's death. Danni saw the crush of people all pushing to get into the adjacent chamber and ran after Carter.

"What's happening?" he shouted as he neared Mclean.

"Hundreds of them," Mclean panted. "The ground exploded – like an artillery shell had hit. Then they rushed us. So many. We don't have enough rounds."

"Where's everyone else?"

"Out there," Mclean said. "Captain told me to come in here, set up and get ready."

Carter felt his legs go cold. He knew the answer but couldn't help asking the question. "Get ready for what?"

"They're coming in," Mclean said. "So many of them and those sphere things-"

The roof exploded. The beautiful, ancient roof shattered in the middle, raining chunks of stone into the Cathedral itself. More screams rang out as people scrambled for cover, although Carter didn't know where exactly they were hoping to run to as tonnes of rock fell from the ceiling. People jumped out of the way of large stones, but others were not so lucky. Gut-wrenching screams were drowned out by the thud of stone hitting the ground.

Stones stopped raining down, revealing the black dome obscuring the sky above them. Dust did nothing to improve the poor visibility and the thuds of stone had given away to screams of terror and groans of pain. A large mound of rubble cut a swathe across the room, separating them from the others.

Danni, Carter and Mclean saw a small group of four people, those too slow to flee before the ceiling had come down, and they were now scrambling up the mound. Danni looked up at the ceiling and saw the remaining roof looked precarious, with dust and small fragments of stone tumbling to the ground. No more big lumps of stone fell, so she guessed it would hold.

For now.

"Look," she said, pointing at the top of the rubble. Three blue spheres smashed into each other on the summit. Was it her imagination, or did the spheres look bigger than last time she'd seen them? Tiredness, adrenaline and fear were combining to warp her memory. She hoped,

A bright flash lit the room for a second and when it faded, a large man stood on top of the rubble mound. His tail swung back and forth behind him, like a cobra waiting to strike.

"Oh no," she said. "Don't-" she started, but it was far too late. The group on the rubble all stared at the new arrival, frozen with terror.

It pounced.

Its tail swung and two of the group flew away from it, faces dotted with spikes. Flesh was already melting away and their screams soon became wet, gurgled cries. It punched a third, the thing's hand sinking into the woman's chest before he pulled it free. Even at this distance, Danni could see the gore and the lump of flesh in the thing's hand. The woman collapsed, twitching and then was still. The fourth member of the group fainted, just as the thing kicked his head, snapping his neck.

The thing looked at the three of them, but turned away, scrambling up and over the summit with far more agility than the humans had managed.

"What in the hell was that?" Mclean roared. His weapon hung loose in his trembling hand.

"Trouble," Danni said. "It took out my entire police station this morning."

"By itself?"

"Yep." Danni shuddered as memories of the earlier carnage flooded her. "You can't kill it. It will just change into those sphere things."

"He's going to kill everyone," Carter said, voice stricken. He was trying not to picture the thing ripping Linda's heart out. "We've got to stop it."

43

MORE BY LUCK THAN JUDGEMENT, Kingston was in the clear when the ceiling collapsed. Stone thumped to the ground and he covered his head, drawing his legs up as he lay on the floor, making himself as small a target as possible. Smaller shards of stone bounced off him, but none were large enough to hurt.

Standing as soon as the rain of stone ended, he surveyed the devastation. Near him, an arm protruded from the rubble, its owner buried and presumably dead. The pile of stone cut the ancient hall in half, but it would be easy to scale it to get to the other side. Carter and Danni would be able to get back to them and he felt relief. A circular hole in the roof just revealed the ever-present dark dome above their heads.

A familiar face appeared in the gloom, covered in dust, looking like a wild-eyed ghost. She still had hold of Ethan, who didn't seem to be hurt.

"What's that?" Linda pointed to the top of the rubble. Then: "Oh no!"

Three blue spheres crashed together on the summit. The thing stood there looked like the stuff of nightmares with its tail swinging ominously behind. It jumped out of sight and soon fresh screams filled the air.

A crowd of people were trying to push their way through the doors, and they were all shouting at each other. The sense of panic was fierce in the air. Any second now, someone was going to snap and then they would turn on each other.

The other doorway was less crowded as it was nearer the fallen rubble.

"This way!" Kingston pulled Linda after him. Ethan still held her hand and was dragged along with her.

"That man had a tail," Ethan said.

"Yes, sweetheart." Linda pulled him closer.

A roar sounded above the noise of the screams and shouts of the survivors. Linda looked up at the rubble, and saw the tail come into view first, swaying high above the powerful figure now standing on top of the rubble. He pointed right at them and roared again. Linda felt her bladder loosen but didn't break pace. The door was just a few metres away now.

Deep down she knew the door would not save them. That thing could burst through rock over a metre thick, so a wooden door wouldn't even slow it. However, the door felt like safety, like a blanket on a cold night. She had to get the boy to the other side. If she did, maybe the army would have enough time to come and save them. Of course, she knew the army wasn't coming; the gunfire outside said they had enough to deal with and might all soon be dead. She knew an unassailable truth.

No-one was coming to save them.

44

THE DOOR FLEW open again and Peter and Bawden stumbled in, carrying another soldier between them. The third man was bleeding heavily from multiple wounds covering his body. Peter pushed some chairs out of the way and lowered the man to the floor.

"Come on Gareth," he said, checking for a pulse. His expression made it clear he hadn't found one.

"We need help. One of the big ones has got in." Carter gestured at the four corpses and then pointed at the rubble. "He's gone over there. We have to help them!"

"They're all going to die!" Danni cried, and scrambled up the rubble pile.

Peter blinked heavily. Things had gone from bad to worse to catastrophic in a heartbeat and now he was trying to collect his thoughts. His team were all dead, except for Bawden and Mclean. So many of those damn creatures – where had they all come from?

"Sir?" Bawden said.

"We need to barricade this door." He pointed at the chairs. "Get them stacked in front of both doors. Do it now."

Mclean and Bawden started to pile the chairs up against the door Peter had just come through. They could all hear the roar of the creatures outside, but none came to the door.

"The others?" Carter demanded.

"I'm with you," Peter said. He slipped the magazine out of his weapon and checked the rounds. "Let's go."

Carter led the way, scrambling over the rubble as parts of it slipped under his feet. Shards of stone trickled back down, sounding like rain as it fell. He soon crested the mound, where Danni was waiting and couldn't believe what he saw.

"Holy shit," Danni said.

The thing was in the middle of a crowd of people. They had been trying to get through a doorway, but in the crush, it was easy pickings for the creature. With one swing of his tail, five people fell to the floor, screaming as the spikes and acid tore through their bodies. Any that his tail didn't hit, he punched or kicked. He was a spinning machine of death. The air was thick with screams of the dying.

Gunfire rattled out from next to them, deafening them both momentarily. Bullets tore into the thing, opening his back and making blood fly from him instead of the corpses he was butchering.

"No!" Carter shouted, but it was too late.

Three blue spheres burst out of the space where the thing had once stood. They streaked up, straight through the hole in the ceiling and disappeared.

45

"WHAT THE HELL WAS THAT?" Peter roared.

They scrambled down the other side of the rubble. As soon as they reached the bottom, Carter had to turn away from the carnage. Years of front-line police work had given him a cast iron stomach – or so he had thought.

Nothing could have prepared him for the pile of bodies in front of him. 'Bodies' was a generous description, as many were separated from vital parts such as legs, arms and heads. Blood squelched in the carpet underfoot and ran freely across the stone floor where the carpet ended. Carter's foot touched something, and he looked down. A woman's head stared back at him. Her eyes and mouth were open, locked in a never-ending scream. He shuddered at the thought of what her last few moments must have been like.

"It seems to be their leader," Carter said. "Those spheres appear whenever he's shot and it's how he gets away. You think you've got him," Carter made an explosion noise, pulling his hands apart and shrugged. "Then he comes back."

He examined the bodies more closely now, looking for a familiar face. His heart thudded loudly in his chest and he could hear the blood whoosh through his ears. Nausea gnawed at the pit of his stomach, but it eased when he didn't see Linda amongst the dead. He closed his eyes for a second and was granted an image of her choking under tonnes of rubble. His eyes snapped open, shattering the image. Kingston didn't appear to be amongst the dead either, which filled him with unexpected joy.

"Have you ever seen anything like this?" Danni said, voice hoarse. Carter shook his head, but Peter nodded.

"Yeah, in Afghanistan and once, back home, in Kent. Devon too."

When it was clear nothing more was forthcoming, they continued to search for survivors.

"What about the ones outside?" Danni was first to break the heavy silence. "Why aren't they attacking?"

"We caught a break," Peter said. "All the rubble will slow them down, so we should regroup. Prepare for what's next."

One of the heavy wooden doors was shut, but the other was blocked by the corpses. Grimacing, Peter strode through the carnage to the large wooden door and started dragging the bodies out of the way. Swallowing bile, Carter helped him and then Danni joined in. It took them several minutes to move enough bodies and limbs but eventually they could push the heavy door closed.

Once on the other side, they took stock. The back of the Cathedral had several smaller rooms around the perimeter, with a smaller chapel style area in the middle. Pews lined this middle area and an altar stood at one end. Small groups were huddled there, many crying, and more in shock. Carter counted no more than thirty. Jesus. Everyone looked grimy and most were smeared with blood – whether their own or someone else's, Carter couldn't tell.

Then his eyes settled on a familiar face and relief washed through him.

Linda sat in the middle of the chapel, hugging the children. As soon as Linda saw him, she disentangled herself and crushed him in a hug. Despite informing him of a few new bruises, the hug felt good.

"I thought he'd got you," he said.

"No," Linda sniffed. "He ignored us. Just slaughtered all those people."

"Like a fox in a hen house," Peter muttered.

"I know," Carter said, "we saw. He's gone now."

"For how long?"

"I wish I knew." Carter looked up at the roof, his eyes drawn to the gaping hole. "We have to be ready to fight them."

"What's the point?"

"I don't understand," Carter said.

"Why fight, John?" Linda looked deep into his eyes, the blue mesmerising him even in the gloom. "Why? Those things are going to come in here and we will all be killed."

"You don't know that."

"How many people have died today? Now what? We're huddled in here, in the dark, waiting our turn."

"We're not waiting our turn. We're surviving."

"Christ, John, do you believe that?" Linda waved her arm at the various shell-shocked groups in the room. "Is this surviving? I don't think so. This is waiting." She took a deep breath. "If we stay here, we will all die."

"The doors are barricaded."

"Yes, but the bastard came through the roof. The fucking roof John."

"We have guns now."

"How many bullets? How long before it all runs out?"

"I don't know."

"What happens then?"

"I don't know," he said again.

"We all die, that's what happens then."

"Keep your voice down," Carter said. "You're going to scare everyone."

"*I'm* scared, John."

"I think we all are, Linda." Carter hugged her, holding her to him until she relaxed into it. "We'll figure something out." Deep down, he knew she was right. The situation was dire, but he wasn't about to give up. They'd been through too much to just roll over and die. They had to fight back but he just didn't have a clue how. "It's ok to be scared, babe."

"It's stupid," she said. "I'm not even worried about me, but Ethan-"

It took him a moment to realise she was crying, and he held her tightly again, feeling completely and utterly impotent.

46

Kingston sat alone in a cold, stone room, with his head in his hands. His cheeks felt hot to the touch and tears brimmed in his eyes. He had barely taken in his surroundings, just fled, leaving the others behind, and hid in this room. He hugged his legs to his chest, with his head nearly resting on his knees. At least his feet were still.

He had to stop running. Had to make a stand. He'd never run from anything when he was a Scorpion, but now he'd run from London straight into hell, and he'd kept on running, deserting people who had saved his life. Christ, he was such a coward. For all he thought he was tough, it turned out he was just a scared little boy.

He thought of Stephen, his handsome face, strong body and hands. He remembered every second of their time together, but then cringed. What had he done when Keeler had found them together? He'd run away.

He'd left Stephen at the mercy of his brother. Kingston could have stayed, talked Keeler round, maybe even taken the beating instead. Even as the thought formed, he knew it was more bravado, more bullshit. Kingston hated pain.

Christ was on a cross in front of him, watching with mournful eyes and anguished expression. As Kingston gazed at the cross, the sadness and shame inside him multiplied. Tears rolled down his cheeks, clearing tracks through the grime.

He would find a way to make it better with Stephen. They could go abroad somewhere together, far away from the intolerant shits in London. Maybe put a bullet in Keeler's head for good measure.

No.

No more killing.

What a day.

Kingston wiped tears in his sleeve and sat back, looking around the room for the first time. He didn't get religion. Priests gave him the creeps and the less said about those nutters with sandwich boards who raved about the end of the world the better. Although, maybe those guys (and they were *always* guys – like men had a monopoly on religious insanity) had a point: today sure did look like the end of the world.

Maybe it wasn't too late to get a little God. Save my soul.

He snorted. Ridiculous. Was there a heaven for all dead things? He tried to think of the various people he had known who were now dead – and there were a lot of them. Were they in Heaven? Hell? Still, if human souls went to Heaven, what about animal souls? Dogs? Cats? Shit, what about all the flies? The spiders? The thought was crazy and following the logic, why would there be a heaven for humans just because they believe? Seemed crazy.

He wiped the tears from his eyes and lay down on the cold stone bench, thoughts churning through his mind, until finally, impossibly, sleep took him.

47

DANNI FOUND Kingston fast asleep and nudged him with her foot. He opened his eyes and glared at her.

"Yo, wakey, wakey."

"I'm so tired." He rubbed his eyes. "Good to see you're still alive."

"You too."

They smiled at each other for a moment, but Kingston broke eye contact to stare instead at his feet.

"So, you looking for me?" he mumbled.

"Not really, well, not just you. I'm trying to see how many we've got left."

He winced at her bluntness. There was a toughness to Danni, that was clear, but sometimes she overdid it. He saw it with the younger members of the gang, always trying to prove something, usually to themselves.

For her part, Danni was examining the room.

"It's pretty solid in here," she said, tapping the walls. She swung the door and looked at the thickness of it.

"No way out," he said. "Gives me the creeps." Kingston cast a nervous glance at the cross.

"Only one way in. Easier to defend than out there."

"Really? How long till those things come back? I'm not planning on being here when they do."

"Where are you going to go?" Her expression was like the one his mother used to wear, just before he ran away.

"As far away from here as possible," he muttered.

"Good luck. Hundreds of monsters and a wall which destroys everything it touches might have something to say about that."

"I don't want to die." His voice wavered on *die*.

"Nobody does."

"If they take me, all of this stops, right?"

"I doubt it. They were killing us long before today. We just didn't know about it. I bet if we looked in our archives, we'd find loads of disappearances or murders. Today was inevitable."

"Yeah, I might have made it worse."

"You can't think like that," she said. "It was always going to happen at some point." She sat next to him and took his hand, surprised at its smoothness.

"I shouldn't have killed those kids."

"You or them." She shrugged. "I don't think you should think of them as kids. They're monsters."

He didn't look as certain.

"Bottom line, Kingston, whether you run or not, they *are* coming in. They might *want* you, but they're going to kill us all."

"What do you mean, they want him?"

They both started at the sound of the new voice. Linda stood in the doorway, hands on hips, face furious. Behind her, Carter looked crestfallen. Ethan peered out from behind her legs. Neither Kingston nor Danni had heard them approach.

"Those things want him. Why?" Linda demanded.

"I maybe killed a couple of their young." Kingston still avoided eye contact, shoulders slumped.

"They've been killing us all day, so what?"

"The creatures have sent a message," Carter said. "They're claiming they did this for justice, but they were killing people long before anything happened today."

"Exactly." Danni nodded.

Linda's face relaxed, her expression changing from fury but then she frowned. "So what are they saying? Hand *him* over and we all go free?"

"Something like that," Carter said.

"No," Danni said. "We're not giving anything to those things."

Linda rested her hand on Ethan's shoulder. "One life for many."

"They will still kill us all."

"You don't know that."

"We do," Carter said. "Just look at what's happened today."

"We have to take the chance."

Kingston sat, still slumped on the bench, eye's wet. "She's right. I give myself up and you lot might survive."

"It's not happening," Carter said.

"Christ, John!" She jabbed a finger at him. "This lowlife is part of the gang you spend so much time moaning about. He's going to end up in prison anyway."

"He was leaving that behind! Weren't you?"

Kingston nodded.

"For fuck's sake, John, people don't change. You know that." Linda pushed Carter's hand away when he tried to reach for her. She stomped away, footsteps echoing around the large chamber, leaving the three of them standing with mouths open.

"Well, that's not good," Danni said.

They all ran after Linda.

48

KENNEDY REFORMED with a bang and collapsed, panting. The roar of blood in his ears was fading now, replaced by a dull ache. It had been exhilarating to take so many of the humans down at once. He had let the bloodlust come over him and he relished his destructive power.

The humans hadn't stood a chance.

Kennedy grunted mostly at the memory but also at the dull ache. What was that? He could still taste the blood and hear the bones snapping as he tore through the humans. Their bodies were so soft. How had they become such a dominant species? Stupid too, the way they had tried to push each other out of the way. Didn't they know a calm line would have saved most of them?

No discipline.

He took in his surroundings. Putting so much power into the bracelet had cost him some control. Once he'd left the Cathedral he had flown in a large arc, eventually coming down through the roof of a building nearby. He was surrounded by clothes and those ridiculous plastic human-sized statues the humans clothed for whatever bizarre reason. Must be some kind of religious worship thing. Humans really were odd.

He dusted himself down and started to move through the racks of clothes, eventually emerging onto the streets. Glass crunched under his feet and he felt cooler air on his skin. A large group of the Horde were waiting for him outside the building, and they hissed in deference when they saw him. A hundred and twenty-eight of them. Another good number. *A sacred number.* Kennedy shook his head to try and clear the ringing sound in it. Everything sounded muffled.

Why was his ear still aching? He had been reformed for at least a couple of minutes now; all pain should have eased. With growing trepidation, he raised his hand and ran it over his head.

His hand slid straight over a smooth scalp. His right ear was missing, gone into the ether when he transformed. Kennedy roared in frustration. The Horde moved back a step, heads bowed, fearing his wrath. Kennedy took a deep breath and calmed himself. At least it was only an ear; it could have been worse.

He sent a command to the Horde assembled in the streets surrounding the Cathedral. *Windows,* he told them. *Like doors, just different. Go through them.* Once it was received, he paused to wonder why Father hadn't given the Horde more sense. But of course, you don't need intelligent foot troops – you just need lots of them. He could only give simple commands – *go here, eat this, kill that* – but Father could give far more complex commands. He should be here.

Kennedy turned back to the top of the street. In the distance, the Cathedral loomed over the surrounding buildings. He grinned at the members of the Horde, who were now getting closer to him as they realised he wasn't angry with them. More Horde swelled their ranks, no longer a sacred number, but a large one never-theless.

His attack had been for two reasons: weaken the humans resolve and confirm *he* was there. It had been a resounding success on both counts. Now, finally, he would lead a triumphant attack. With a roar, he led the charge at the Cathedral.

49

"THEY WANT KINGSTON," Linda yelled as she ran into the main chamber. "That's who they want. He killed the boys from the message."

Peter swore to himself. This was not what he needed. Bawden and Mclean were pushing the big door shut, sealing them in again. They had finished barricading the doors and headed back to Peter.

"Slow down," Peter said. "What are you talking about?"

"He told me, he told me everything," she panted. Footsteps echoed on the stone, getting closer. "Him!" she spat, pointing at Kingston as he arrived.

Peter took a step towards the young man. "Is this true?"

"He goes nowhere," Carter said.

"Stay out of it, John."

The disappointment in his eyes was something she would never forget, and she felt a pang of guilt. Was this really the right thing to do? Was she really going to give up Kingston? She glanced at Ethan, face solemn and unsmiling, the way no kid should be. Kingston's life for his.

No brainer.

"So, you killed two of them and they did this?" Peter asked. All the chatter in the Cathedral stopped and he felt everybody's eyes on him.

"They had already attacked us," Danni said. "The warehouse was the night before." She looked at Linda and her mouth turned into a sneer. "They were already killing us before he was even here. This is just retro-active justification. It's bullshit."

"You're not going to hand him over." Carter repeated.

Muttering now from the groups. A young man with broad shoulders and a farmer's tan stood and Carter glared at him. This could get ugly.

Peter was frowning, his eyes distant as he ran through the options.

A bang shook the doors. Linda gasped and took a step backwards.

"Relax," Peter said, "that's the outer doors. We have a bit of time yet. And, we have some tricks up our sleeves." He nodded at Bawden and Mclean, who scurried away without a word.

"The crypt things," Kingston said suddenly. Peter turned to him. "These little rooms around the edge. We could hide in them."

"Crypts on the perimeter? Do it," Peter nodded. "Good idea."

Kingston started to move to Ethan, but Linda's expression made him stop.

"Perimeter's a much better word than edge," he muttered.

The remaining adults started to file into the crypts, and Carter noted there were depressingly few of them. Several of them stared at Kingston with disgust on their faces. Kingston stood nearer to Carter, letting the man's body shield him from the glares. The Horde were slowly whittling down the numbers of humans in the Cathedral – and probably Exeter overall – but the ones here would happily hand Kingston over.

Another huge bang echoed in the large chamber.

"Incoming!" Bawden shouted and then the air was filled with the roar of machine guns. The sound was deafening, and Carter covered his ears. Bawden and Mclean had mounted two large-calibre machine guns on tripods near the thick wooden doors. The design of the Cathedral meant the walls supporting the doors were constructed from ornate stone, with gaps that must have held windows at some point in the past. The gun barrels aimed through these openings and now, bullet casings rained onto the stone floor with a tinkling which sounded not unlike rain.

"Move!" Peter roared at Carter, but Carter shook his head. The words were drowned out by the noise. "Go!" Peter pointed and shouted, just as the weapons stopped firing.

"Have it!" Bawden screamed.

Large stained-glass windows to his right exploded and creatures leapt into the room. They were jumping through the glass, cutting themselves as they shattered the panes of glass. The first wave of creatures landed heavily, oozing blood from a multitude of wounds. The machine guns roared again, cutting them down before they could stand. More came through the windows, shattering the remaining glass until none remained.

"Running low!" Bawden shouted, just as Mclean called the same. Peter swore and pushed Carter away.

"Run," he said, and checked his weapon.

Carter and Kingston ran to the nearest crypt, where Danni was holding the door open for them. She let the door swing shut as they fell into the small room. A statue of a knight lay under an intact stained-glass window, and a cross decorated the wall. An old man stood in front of the knight, terror etched onto his face. Carter glanced at the windows but was relieved to see they were too small for the Horde to come through.

The wall exploded inwards, ruining the windows and

stonework as a huge hole appeared. His stomach lurched as he saw three blue spheres emerge from the wreckage, sailing ahead of the bricks. They sliced through the old man in three different places, sending a shower of blood and gore splashing over them and the walls. The man crumpled to the floor, most of his head missing.

Splinters of stone sprayed into Carter's face, and several cut into him as he covered his head with his arms. He could make out the figures of Kingston and Danni through the dust and knew they were also on the floor.

The spheres collided with a flash and the air was filled with a stench like battery acid and sewers.

"You," the creature snarled. It picked Kingston up with one hand, like he was an errant toddler about to play with fire.

Kingston didn't move or resist. Blood covered his face and his head lolled to one side. His eyes were closed, but Carter could see his chest rise and fall. His own legs refused to obey, and he lay on the floor trying to stand up. Everything hurt and he was in no shape to fight this creature.

"Father wants to see you; he has plans for you and Mother." Its voice was more cultured than expected, but the threat was still very clear. The thing clambered over the rubble, emerging from the Cathedral, still carrying Kingston in one hand.

Carter dragged himself across the ground and used the rubble to haul himself upright. Behind him, Danni started groaning and he felt a surge of relief as she coughed up dust. He didn't wait for her, though, but stumbled over the wreckage and out onto the green.

Outside was a mess. The helicopter was never going to fly again: flames flickered inside it with the rotor blades bent to almost vertical. Horde jumped up and down on top of it, oblivious to the heat from the flames but relishing the damage they wrought. More Horde ran from the side streets, heading straight for the main entrance to the Cathedral. None of them even glanced in Carter's direction.

A huge hole had opened in the ground between the helicopter and Cathedral. Around the hole were the bodies of the rest of the soldiers. Their saviours. All dead. Carter sank to his knees, exhaustion overwhelming him as he watched the creature carry Kingston towards the hole and then jump in.

Danni rested a hand on his shoulder and coughed.

"They got him, Danni." On the grass near the hole he could see the soldiers discarded weapons. "I can't let them take him."

"He's dead."

Carter shook his head. "No. I could see him breathing. That thing didn't kill him."

"Why not?"

"I have no idea, but right now, he's still alive. He might not be in another thirty minutes."

"Are you suggesting-?"

Carter tried to grin at her, but it gave him a manic air. "No-one in there is going to save him. They all think this is his fault."

"But Linda-"

He ignored her, instead clambering down the remainder of the rubble and then striding across the grass. Weariness still played with his muscles, but he felt energised now. Somebody needed his help.

"I've got to try," he muttered.

Danni jogged to catch up with him. "Wherever he's going, the leader is going to be there, right?"

Carter nodded. "Yeah, probably."

"Ok, well it's long past time for him to get got."

Carter considered this for a moment. Danni's faux toughness made him smile but he was scared and wanted the company.

"Well, let's get those weapons then."

Danni found two grenades on one of the men's belts and pulled the belt free before tying it around her waist. They picked up the machine guns and a spare clip each. There was nothing else: the soldiers had used it all. She peered into the hole, seeing the smooth sides leading into a tunnel hidden underneath the Cathedral green.

Without speaking, they slid into darkness.

50

KENNEDY MADE good progress through the tunnels. The human –
much heavier than a Horde member –didn't slow him. He ducked
when the tunnel roof sloped inwards but didn't care if he hit the
human's head on the rock. It gave him a strange sense of satisfaction.

He flexed his hand, not liking the way it felt. The tips of his
fingers felt odd – vulnerable. The claws were gone, and his fingertips felt bare and soft. Missing an ear, now his claws – what was
next? Kennedy scowled. He had to stop using the band. How many
times until something vital didn't rematerialize?

Before long, the stone gave way to the familiar metal of the
travel tube and home. Kennedy allowed himself to smile now.
Father – and Mother – awaited.

51

BAWDEN STOOD near one set of the large wooden doors, with McLean by the other. They kept up a cacophonous stream of rounds as the creatures poured over the rubble or leapt through the windows. The growing pile of corpses didn't stop or slow them at all.

Peter stood near Bawden, directing fire whilst holding his own weapon ready to cover the guys as they reloaded. They were burning through rounds at a ridiculous rate and Peter tried not to let his concern show.

Eight Horde congregated at the bottom of the rubble pile. He tapped Bawden on the back so he stopped firing.

"Grenade," Peter yelled as Bawden changed magazines. The grenade bounced near the group of eight and rolled to a stop by their feet. A creature examined it, grunting and nudging it with his foot. It exploded with a thump, chairs disintegrating in the explosion, throwing fresh dust and splinters into the air. The group were flung off their feet and they landed heavily, most missing limbs. The survivors made pathetic mewling sounds whilst they died.

"Ignore them." Peter grimaced at the ringing in his ears. "Watch the windows." He sprinted over to McLean and said, "Cover the rubble."

More deafening roars echoed around the chamber as the creatures and weapons shouted. The hail of rounds meant the creatures were kept at bay, and the pile of corpses increased steadily.

Then the inevitable happened.

"I'm out," Bawden bellowed. He started to rummage in his pack for more, but it was too late. A creature cleared the space between the gun and the Horde and landed on Bawden. He pulled a handgun out of his pack and pressed it to the creature's head, pulling the trigger. The thing fell to the ground, blood splashing out of the exit wound at the back of its skull.

Another creature filled the space, then another. Bawden fired twice, downing two of the things, but more were pouring through. One of the things grabbed Bawden's gun arm and bit down on it, clamping its jaws on the thick muscle of his forearm. Bawden screamed, dropping his gun and another creature jumped on him, sending them all toppling backwards.

Peter thought about shooting the creatures, but instead lined up a shot and took Bawden's head off. It was a small mercy, quick death over prolonged agony.

Moments later, McLean stopped shooting and pulled his rifle off his back. "Time's up, Captain." If he'd seen Peter shoot Bawden, he didn't say anything.

Across the hallway, the creatures gathered around Bawden's corpse with yet more coming behind them. So far, the creatures were ignoring them. Peter pulled McLean back, motioning for quiet. The other man nodded, and they edged backwards until the wall of the central crypt blocked them from view.

They were in the oldest part of the Cathedral. Crypts lined the outside, with an inner sanctum between them and the creatures. This had several pews and a small altar in it but was currently empty. All the humans were hiding in the crypts.

More and more of them appeared at the end of the corridor. They were moving with caution now and not with the frenzy of their earlier actions. It was like they knew this was the end of their hunt and wanted to savour it. A creature shuffled forward, closing the gap between them. McLean shot it in the face. It was immediately replaced by another. And another. And another.

Peter and McLean backed up, shooting any Horde that took a step forward. It wasn't long before Peter felt cold stone against his back. They were at one vertex of the corridor. From their right, more movement. Nowhere else to go, now. They were trapped.

Horde members continued their slow advance in front of them, and more came from the right.

"Here I am, stuck in the middle with you," McLean muttered. "We're screwed."

Both sets of Horde slowed now, hissing and snarling at the trapped humans.

McLean lifted the last grenade from his belt, pulled the pin and threw it to the right. Then he charged forward, firing at the other group of Horde. Creatures fell, limbs twitching as blood pumped out of the wounds. The survivors started to shuffle backwards, away from the screaming man.

Peter covered his head as the grenade exploded, shaking the wooden doors and pushing more dust into the air. The thick doors held firm, but as the dust cleared, he could see more Horde coming towards him. He didn't have any grenades, and in any case, he wasn't sure the doors would withstand another explosion. He fired at them, but there were too many, so he headed after McLean.

McLean had succeeded in pushing them back almost to the

main chamber, but then his weapon clicked. He reached for another mag, but none remained. Yelling in frustration, he threw the SA80 at the nearest creature. It bounced off the thing's head, making it stagger. He started to reach for his pistol.

Each movement was too slow compared to the Horde.

One pounced on him, raking teeth across McLean's neck. As he screamed, McLean shot it point blank, but another took his arm and yet another punched him, snapping his nose. The creatures swarmed him, and he would be dead long before Peter could reach him.

Peter had too little ammo left to give McLean the mercy he'd given Bawden. He stopped, panting hard. Horde filled the end of the corridor now, filling the gaps made by McLean. Behind him, more Horde advanced, their hisses filling the air and becoming the only sound he could hear.

52

LINDA SAT on the floor with Ethan on her lap. She hugged him, wishing she could change his wide-eyed look for something more joyful. The whole room had been reverberating with the noise of the guns, but now it was silent outside. Linda fought the urge to open the door and look. John was out there somewhere, but she felt the need to stay with the boy. John could take care of himself.

She hoped.

They heard someone running outside, then slower steps receding from the door. Ethan let out a low moan, and Linda covered his mouth with her hand. He made eye contact, shaking his head to apologise silently for making noise. Her heart broke and tears welled in her eyes. Kids should never say sorry for making a noise. The air became heavy and still in the room as they both held their breath. Linda felt the walls closing in on them, felt the weight of the roof pushing down on them.

She felt bile rise in her throat and was powerless to stop her limbs from trembling. If the creatures found them, it would be carnage.

Annihilation.

What would she do to save this boy? Just minutes before she had been prepared to hand a man over to these things so everyone else would live. Would she lay down her own life to save this kid?

All those arguments with John about his need for children. How she used to tell him it was a pathetic attempt to validate his own life. He thought himself less of a man because he didn't have his own kids. How she hated colleagues bringing their mewling babies into work. All that had changed now.

At that point, she knew she would do anything to keep the boy alive.

Anything at all.

53

KENNEDY REACHED the control room and threw Kingston to the floor. He grunted and opened his eyes for a moment, but soon closed them again. The human cut a pathetic shape on the floor.

"I have him, Father."

Father turned from his screens and looked at Kingston with cold eyes. "This is him?"

"Yes."

"You are sure?"

"Yes."

"He doesn't look like much, but he must be a good warrior to have beaten my sons."

Kennedy said nothing. It was almost certainly not a good idea to point out how easy it had been to capture the human. Father was still grieving his sons so highlighting their weaknesses, even indirectly, would not be a smart move.

Father kicked Kingston with his toe, eliciting a groan from the prone man. "Wake up," he commanded.

Kingston didn't move.

"Why isn't he moving?"

"The humans do not obey like we do," Kennedy said. "He is asleep. He will wake soon."

As if on cue, Kingston groaned again. His eyes flickered open, but this time they stayed that way. His pupils dilated as he focussed on the room and the thing standing in front of him.

"What is that smell?" Father asked, a sense of wonder in his voice.

"Fear," Kennedy said. "Or perhaps he has soiled himself."

"I haven't pissed myself." Kingston rubbed his head, wincing as his hand came away covered in blood.

"It speaks!" Father said and he broke into a grin.

"Who the hell are you?" Kingston tried to crawl away from Father's malevolent gaze, but his limbs wouldn't cooperate.

"You may call me Father."

"Father? Jesus, who you the daddy of?" Kingston hoped he sounded braver than he felt. He knew, of course, that this thing in front of him was the one who wanted revenge for the killing of the two boys. His sons. A low moan escaped Kingston's lips, and he started to tremble.

Father laughed. "He is a fine specimen, Kennedy. Mother will toil all night with this one."

"What are you talking about?"

"I am Father, but Mother helps us to propagate. With your help, she will feed us too."

Kingston couldn't think straight. The ringing in his ears muddled his thoughts. Tears swam in his eyes, making two Fathers dance in front of him. He didn't understand what Father was saying, but working in a kitchen, making meals for this lot didn't sound too bad.

Kennedy picked Kingston up, dragging him to his feet. Kingston protested and struggled but couldn't break the thing's grip. His limbs felt too heavy, his exhaustion absolute.

"Take him to Mother," Father said with a wave of his hand. "Time to end this."

54

KINGSTON TRIED to bury the rising panic. Father was possibly the most intimidating thing he had ever seen – given the creature holding him was the second, it was no mean feat.

At a distance, Father could be considered good looking. But up close, nothing could be further from the truth. He had long hair, like a man on the cover of the awful romance books his mum had read for a while. It was not the luscious locks of those men though, but greasy and lank, and his hairline started halfway over his scalp. His eyes were two dark pits, like the kids. No white at all, nothing to show where sclera ended and the iris or pupil started. His nose was upturned, like a pig, but the nostrils were narrow slits, more like gills on a fish. His cheeks were high enough to make models jealous and two cherry red lines for lips, more like scars, finished the look. Thick lesions covered one of his cheeks, angry red welts that looked like they were spreading.

The one holding him, Kennedy, was hugely subservient to the man. Everything about his body language confirmed the suspicion:

there was no question as to who was in charge. Kennedy kept his head bowed, making him look smaller and weaker than Father, even though he could snap the other in half. Kingston was now being carried down a long corridor, past plain metal panels. Lights glowed in the ceiling and a low background hum made everything seem to vibrate.

Soon Kennedy stopped by a door which slid open, revealing a large room, well over fifty metres long. Two rows of metal pods sat in front of him, in lines of four. Each pod had a flat base, and curved sides that swelled before tapering to a point at least two metres above him. They looked like sleek, metallic rugby balls which had been cut in half. Wires emerged from the top of each pod, snaking away to connect at a central point then disappearing into a large tube.

Above his head was another walkway with an identical setup and the racks of eight were repeated three more times along the length of the room. Four rows, each with two sets of eight and repeated above throughout the room. Kingston had always been good at doubling numbers and he counted it up. There were two hundred and fifty-six pods in the room.

This was it, Kingston realised. This was where the Horde came from, but it didn't make sense. There were a lot more than two hundred and fifty-six creatures running amok in Exeter.

Away from the symmetry of the room, a huge machine dominated one wall. A massive pipe rose from the top of it, and wires ran from them to the thick pipes connected to the pods. Kennedy dropped him by the large machine, forcing the air out of Kingston. He gasped for breath.

"If I had my way," Kennedy rasped, "you would have been dead a long time ago."

Kingston moved backwards on his hands and feet, scrambling

until his back hit something solid. Panic gripped him hard, and he couldn't breathe. Sharp pains ran riot across his chest. Is this how Charlie felt at the end?

"This is Mother," Kennedy said, gesturing with his hand.

Kingston looked to where Kennedy was pointing. He couldn't see anyone, and it took him a moment to realise the creature meant the machine. Lights flashed across its surface with illegible text scrolling through various displays on three different panels. The whole thing hummed and glistened with a damp sheen which wasn't in keeping with its futuristic look.

The centre of the machine was dominated by a large opaque glass panel. It slid to the side as he watched, revealing a white cuboid, blinding in its intensity. It had the sterility of an operating theatre. Tubes hung loosely from the ceiling – one filled with red liquid, another blue and yet another yellow.

Kennedy pressed some buttons on the machine and a female voice said something unintelligible. When he was done, lights came on along the corridor. These lights were much brighter than the low lights illuminating the way this far.

"She is ready." Kennedy bowed.

At first Kingston thought the big creature was talking to him and his second thought was he didn't want to know what she was ready for. Then he realised Father had entered the chamber.

"I have called off the Horde. They may feast on the dead."

"Yes, Father," Kennedy bowed again.

Father knelt in front of Kingston and grabbed his chin with strong fingers. He forced Kingston to make eye contact. "You have caused me immeasurable pain. You are responsible for everything that has happened here today. I take my retribution on you and justice will be served."

"What the hell you chatting about?" Kingston heard the waver in his own voice and swallowed hard. His street bred toughness had deserted him.

"Today will live long in Horde memory. No longer will we have to hide and now, thanks to the sacrifice you are willing to make, we can live in peace."

"Let everyone go," Kingston said. "You promised. Let them all go. No-one else dies."

Father's lips pulled into two thinner lines than normal. An attempt at a smile. "You will die many times."

Kingston's panic fled to be replaced with outright terror. After everything, he so desperately wanted to stay alive. To hold Stephen one more time. To thank Carter for keeping faith with him, not just today. To make amends for a lifetime of wrong decisions. What the hell did Father mean? How can anyone die more than once?

Rough hands grabbed him, and he was forced into the open pod. Kingston tried to grab the edges of the door, but Kennedy was too strong, and his fingers rattled on the frame without gaining purchase. Kennedy pushed him hard and Kingston stumbled, crashing against the rear wall.

Kingston collapsed as Kennedy retreated. The door slid shut without a sound and he was alone in the sterile chamber. He couldn't tell where the wall ended and the ceiling began. The light was so bright, it hurt his eyes.

He stood on legs that threatened to give way, keeping his back to the wall. What the hell was this? It was silent, but warm in the room though it felt very far from womb like. The coloured tubes hung in the middle of the room, in line with his chest. They writhed like snakes, waving back and forth despite the lack of a breeze.

Kingston frowned. This didn't look good.

The red tube suddenly darted forward, hitting him right in the centre of his chest. Kingston screamed as the tube punctured his skin, burrowing in. Instant cold spread through his torso. He could hear blood rushing in his ears, bringing a tidal wave of pain. The blue tube stabbed forward, entering him a few centimetres to the right of the red tube, and whilst the pain was not as great, it was still significant. Kingston could hear himself screaming, but it sounded far away, as if underwater. His confused brain was shutting down, protecting him from whatever was happening. The final, yellow tube slammed into his temple and the cold spread through his brain. Every fibre of him howled in agony as the strange fluid pumped into him.

Darkness crept into the corner of his vision and dark circles appeared every time he blinked. The cold spread now, and he could no longer feel his legs. Pins and needles shot up his arms. He wanted to fall, to curl into a ball and scream, but the tubes held him fast. Silent tears coursed down his cheeks and his throat was raw from screaming.

Kingston closed his eyes as he felt the darkness overwhelm him. *Don't quit!* This was not who he was. He didn't roll over and give up, not for anyone. He had so much to live for. *No!*

He opened his eyes. He was on all fours, coughing and spluttering on the floor of the cavern. With the back of his hand, he wiped drool away. It felt cold on his skin and he realised he was naked. He couldn't understand where his clothes had gone or why he was free of the wires. Two holes marked his chest where the tubes had been, and he rubbed his head. His hand came away sticky with a cocktail of oily yellow fluid and blood.

He coughed and tried to stand. Father's feet swam into view, horrible maligned, clawed things with webbing between the toes. The claws looked the same as the spikes on the ball at the end of Kennedy's tail.

"What did you do to me?"

"I'd worry more about what I'm *going* to do to you," Father said. He punched his hand into Kingston's chest, splintering the ribs as his hand sunk through flesh.

The last thing Kingston saw was his still beating heart being ripped from his chest.

55

WHICHEVER WAY PETER TURNED, death awaited. Horde crowded both ends of the corridor, shuffling closer to him. The pistol in his sweaty hands was woefully inadequate. Who to shoot first?

There were more Horde than he had rounds for. Could he clear a path? Push them back like McLean had nearly managed? Doubtful. The Horde would follow him and maybe he could lead them away from where everyone was hiding. He hadn't felt so powerless since Afghanistan.

That's it.

He squeezed the trigger and walked towards the nearest Horde. It fell to the floor, screaming and he shot another. He kept shooting, feeling no satisfaction as they fell. This was a futile gesture, after all, merely a postponing of the inevitable. Behind him he could hear the rest of the Horde approaching and he knew he should keep a bullet back for himself.

Another Horde member fell but wasn't replaced by another. Peter stopped firing, confused by the creatures' inaction. They were standing still, swaying like weeds in a breeze.

"What are you waiting for?" he screamed and shot another.

The stench of cordite and creatures filled the air. No-one and nothing moved, except for the swaying creatures. Peter's heart hammered in his chest. Was this how he was going to go? After everything? Afghanistan. Huntleigh. Now this.

He stepped closer to the Horde, standing almost face to face with the nearest one. It gave no indication he was there at all.

"What the hell?"

As one, the creatures turned back to the main hall and ran, streaming past him and heading for the windows. They jumped through without a sound, leaving Peter alone.

56

SILENCE.

Thick, glorious silence. Not punctuated by gunfire or screams for what seemed like the first time in hours. Linda gently extricated herself from Ethan's hug and stood.

"I'm going to look."

Ethan shook his head violently.

"It'll be ok," she promised. "I'll be quiet."

Linda slowly turned the handle and inched the door open. She expected a mass of claws and teeth to greet her but the corridor was empty. Exhaling a breath she hadn't realised she'd been holding, she stepped into the corridor. She kept her back pressed against the wall and eased the door closed. The click as its latch caught sounded like a cannon.

Nothing appeared.

She crept along the corridor, strides getting wider by the step as she gained in confidence. Upon reaching the end, she peered around the corner and saw Peter walking towards her.

"Peter!" she cried.

"Hi," he said, but his face was grim. He looked exhausted, covered in blood and grime. His pistol hung loosely in his hand and she could see the end of it trembling. "Are you on your own?"

"No, I have Ethan back here. We're ok. What about you?"

He shook his head. "Just me. I was about to give up checking these rooms when I saw you." He pointed down the corridor. Four more doors.

Peter strode past her and continued to open crypt doors. He told people to come out when he found them. Depressingly few people emerged from the shadows. He continued, opening doors and smiled when Ethan ran past him. The boy hugged Linda tightly and the small group of survivors all followed him as he walked.

The very last door he opened revealed a ruined wall. Large stone blocks had been blown into the room and blood coated the walls and rubble. A corpse lay on the floor, holes in its body. The source of all the blood, presumably.

"What happened in here?"

Linda peered past him. "The one with the tail. The ball things."

He nodded. "It fits, but-"

"Where's John?"

"And the other two – Danni, Kingston." Peter looked out over the green, taking in the massive hole, corpses and burning helicopter. There was no sign of any Horde.

"Maybe John is out there," Linda said.

Peter didn't look convinced. He pointed at the hole in the ground. "That's where the thing came from. We should go down there, find this Father and end this."

Linda's pale face and wide eyes told him all he needed to know about what she was thinking.

"With what?" Peter muttered. He slid the magazine out of his pistol and grimaced. "A firm handshake and a stern word."

Linda realised he was talking more to himself than anyone else. "I need to find John," she said.

"My duty is to the people still alive here. We don't know where he is or whether he has anyone with him. Our best bet is to wait here. If he's alive, he'll come back here. You are more than welcome to go out there and look for him by yourself." Peter's expression was grim, lips thin with determination.

She shied away from him, reaching for Ethan.

"We need more ammo, before they come back," Peter said to the group crowding the doorway behind him. "Help me gather some supplies. It's all we can do now."

57

FATHER WIPED the blood from his mouth with the back of his hand. He licked his teeth and paused, sensing something there that shouldn't be. He worried at it with his tongue for a moment but then dragged out a small pink lump. He flicked it into the air and caught it in his mouth.

Kennedy put the arm he was holding down. The hand was still intact, but he had removed enough flesh for white bone to be visible. "Our food supply is secure, what would you have me do now?"

"I will send a message to the humans. They are free to go, but the city is ours."

"You are letting them go?"

"For now," Father said with a wan smile. "Maintaining the barrier is exhausting. I need to rest, but if they try to trick us then it will not end well for them."

Father stood and kicked at Kingston's corpse. "I see why you've been tempted. They are tasty."

Kennedy didn't dare say anything.

"I have been wrong to make us wait for so long. We cannot live alongside this filth. All this time we have been superior to them and I am sorry I doubted you, my friend. I must rest, then we will show the humans our true power."

Kennedy burned with pride. Father had called him friend for the second time and also apologised! Truly today was a special day. He smiled until Father left the room, then resumed eating what was left of Kingston's arm.

58

"This city is ours. We have food and shelter and have served justice to the human who caused us suffering. The Barrier will be removed but I can reseal the city if you do not obey my simple rule: this city is no longer for humans. Leave us in peace and we will extend you the same courtesy."

Father stopped recording and rubbed his head. He didn't think he'd ever held the Barrier over such a range or length of time before. He had usually used it to stop people finding their home. He transmitted the message and sank back in his chair. The humans were aware of his power now and so wouldn't attack the city. His Horde were safe for now, but perhaps they could expand their lands in a couple of days, once everyone was up to full strength. He could produce new Scouts from mother too. Feeding them would no longer be a problem.

Exhaustion hit him, and thanks to a full belly, he sank into a deep sleep.

The Barrier was down.

59

LONG AND NARROW tunnels stretched away from them. Carter took the lead, holding the weapon like he'd seen in thousands of films. Danni looked more comfortable carrying hers, and she brought up the rear. Torches attached to the underside of the barrels illuminated the way. The cone of light didn't push enough of the darkness away, but he was grateful for it all the same.

He inched forward, expecting Horde members to come roaring down the tunnel. He was acutely aware of his own breathing, the sweat on his back and the echo of his footsteps. They were walking as slowly as possible to reduce the sound of their steps, but each one still sounded like a gunshot to him.

Eventually, after walking for a period of time that could have been two, fifteen or thirty minutes—the dark had a way of swallowing time—they reached a junction.

"Which way?" Danni whispered and Carter winced.

"Choose," he shrugged. They took the left-hand tunnel, but the roof sloped lower and lower until Carter was nearly bent double. He looked back at Danni and shook his head. Retracing their steps quickly, they took the other path. This one also narrowed, but at least they could pass. Something the size of the thing that had taken Kingston could still come this way. It would be a squeeze, but it was doable.

A screech echoed through the tunnels, making them both jump, an inhuman sound chilling them to the core. Danni looked behind her, but the corridor stretched away from her, dark and empty. Another scream rang out and Danni swallowed.

"Is that Kingston?"

Carter didn't reply, but he set off walking faster now, then breaking into as much of a jog as the cramped conditions and darkness allowed. They soon reached another junction, but something was off about this one. Ahead of them the tunnel continued as it had done, all rough rock and jagged edges. The tunnel to the left was similar, but the rock looked smoother. Underfoot it was more worn than the rest of the passage. Moisture condensed on the walls, giving them an eerie sheen.

"This way," Carter said, nodding down the tunnel. As he did so, another scream rang out. There was an air of finality to the scream. "I hope we're not too late." He took another step forward, then another, forcing his rising dread away with action.

60

Kingston opened his eyes. Somewhere he could hear someone screaming but it sounded far away, like his head was wrapped in wool. With watery eyes, he tried to take in his surroundings but couldn't and everything remained blurry. He shook his head, trying to clear it. The fuzziness dissipated, and the room came into sharp focus.

He was still in the pod. Two tubes entered his chest and he ripped them out, grunting with pain as they tore small holes in his flesh. Fluid leaked out, blue and red liquid mixing with his darker blood. He wiped at it and then pulled the last one out of his head. Excruciating pain followed, forcing him to stagger, but the pain soon subsided to a dull throb. Kingston stood panting for a moment, then he reached for the door.

Cold air blasted him when he stepped out the pod, reminding him he was naked. A machine hissed to his right and he turned to the sound. Rows of the pods stretched out before him, all dark, but clearly occupied with *something*. A panel he hadn't seen before slid out of the side of his pod and he stepped back on unsteady legs. *What's wrong with me? Why don't I feel too good?* The panel had an all-in-one jumpsuit in the same tatty grey the Horde had worn. Kingston pulled it on, and it immediately offered some protection from the cold breeze blowing through the corridor.

Another scream rang out.

He whirled towards the sound. It had come from the end of the corridor. Kingston swallowed hard and turned away from the sound.

Remembering he was in the depths of the Horde's lair, he crouched and started walking away from the sounds. He passed more pods and resisted the urge to look in one. Whatever was in one couldn't be good. Maybe more Horde sleeping; maybe something else.

Something worse.

The corridor was long and, on his trembling legs, it took him an age to reach the end. Once there, he realised it wasn't a corridor, but he was still in the large room, filled with pods.

The 'corridor' he'd walked down was part of a bank of the pods. Above him, more pods were suspended from the ceiling, stretching vertically above him. He counted four rows rising above each bank of pods and he was overwhelmed with déjà vu. He'd seen this before, when he'd been next to a big machine. He couldn't see it right now, so where was it? How had he come to be away from it?

What was happening to him?

A light came on in the pod next to him.

Adrenaline made Kingston move quickly, rounding one of the dark pods and crouching next to it. Limbs trembling even more, he risked peering around the pod. The illuminated pod's door slid open, revealing a figure on the floor in the foetal position. It coughed several times and then forced itself upright on legs that shook more than Kingston's. Its black skin shone in the light from the pod, the light accentuating the figure's muscles. It ripped the tubes out, spilling the multi-coloured liquid onto the floor. The thing grunted, staggering in a way familiar to Kingston. With a start, he realised he was looking at another human.

"Hey," he whispered and approached the man.

The figure turned to look at him. "What the hell?" it said.

Confusion clouded Kingston's mind. This was impossible. The hair. The shape of the shoulders and arms. The tight muscles he was so proud of. The way he was standing.

Kingston was looking at himself.

61

LIGHT FLOODED THE CATHEDRAL. Peter looked to the windows, seeing sunlight stream through the windows.

"It's gone," he said.

Other survivors all looked up as the light streamed into the room. Many of them closed their eyes and turned their faces to the sun, letting the sudden warmth roll over them.

Linda stood next to him, with the kid near them. Ethan was smiling, something Peter realised he hadn't seen before then. It transformed his face, making him look his age at long last.

Peter returned to the crypt with the ruined wall and peered out, scanning the Cathedral grounds around them. Still the same large hole, ruined helicopter and trashed shop fronts. Near the shops he could see several members of the Horde, and he quickly ducked back inside. Were they coming? He risked another look and frowned. They weren't moving, just standing in the shade of the buildings, swaying but otherwise still. It was almost as unnerving as when they were running at them, screaming and shouting.

Almost.

"What's wrong with them?" Linda asked, making him jump. He hadn't heard her approach.

"I don't know."

"They're not moving."

"I can see that."

"We should go."

"Go where?" Peter said. "There are hundreds of them out there and not many of us in here. Where do you think we should go?"

"I-"

"We're not going anywhere in a rush. Last time the barrier came down it was only for a few minutes. I can't risk us being exposed out there."

They waited, both squinting at the sky, waiting for the darkness to return. Seconds passed then minutes. Peter ran back to his gear and pulled a radio out of the pocket. He pushed a button on the side and spoke into the handset. "Base 1, Base 1, come in."

Static greeted him when he released the button, just as it had since the moment the barrier had gone up around them. He swore and tried again, but still heard nothing but white noise.

"Damn it," he roared and threw the radio to the floor.

"Alpha 1, that you?"

Peter turned back to the handset and scooped it up.

"Base 1, Base 1, this is Alpha 1. You have no idea how good it is to hear your voice."

"Likewise, Alpha 1. Sitrep please."

Peter surveyed the remaining humans. All bedraggled, all tired. Most of them cut in some way. All of them damaged in ways that would never be seen.

"We need evac as soon as. Not good here. Come armed. Twenty civvies need immediate evac. Hundreds of hostiles around our position."

"Hundreds?" The voice was incredulous.

"Yes," he said. "You need to come in hard or there will be no survivors at all. We have children here."

"Roger that. Confirm location Alpha 1."

"Cathedral," he said.

"Support inbound, Alpha 1. Sit tight."

"How long."

"Twenty max."

"We might not have that long," Peter said, and he put the radio on the floor. The group of survivors had come closer to him when the radio had buzzed to life.

"Ok," he forced confidence into his voice. "People are coming here, now." Excited chatter greeted the news and he had to raise his hands to silence them. "We're not in the clear yet. We don't know how long the barrier will be down or if it will stay down. Try to stay calm and vigilant until my friends get here." He winced at the word *friends* but couldn't think of anything better. "The Horde are still out there. They've stopped attacking for now, but we don't know how long this situation will remain. There is light at the end of the tunnel-" another wince – "but we're in the home stretch. Don't stray too far from your safe places."

He turned his back on them and pretended to look for something in his kit bag until they started to disperse. Soon, Linda and Ethan were the only ones near him. Peter looked at his watch and only then realised it had stopped when he'd crossed the barrier.

Hurry, he thought. *For everyone's sake, hurry.*

62

"WHAT THE HELL?" Kingston mimicked the thing that looked like him.

"This isn't possible," the other Kingston said. "Who the fuck are you?"

Kingston began to feel ill. This was truly impossible. The thing looked exactly like him, down to the scar on his stomach from a knife fight that had nearly gone so, so wrong.

"You're one of them. You've copied me somehow, made me so you can go back to the surface and take over."

"What are you talking about?" the other Kingston said. "*You're* one of them, I'm me."

Something emerged from the darkness behind him, but Kingston didn't have time to shout a warning. He watched in horror as the doppelgänger convulsed, back arching. Blood spurted out of his mouth and he gurgled a noise that might have been a scream. More blood splashed onto the cavern floor, its dark viscosity spreading over the metal. Other Kingston tumbled forward, landing with a thump and a crack. Judging by the angle of his head, he was not going to complain.

Kennedy stepped over the corpse. He snarled and hissed at Kingston, blood dripping from his hands.

"No," Kingston said, his voice a whisper. His mind snapped, coherent thought rushing from his synapses.

"No?" Kennedy repeated.

"What have you done to me?"

Kennedy laughed. "Something wonderful," he said as he grabbed Kingston's shoulders. Holding him fast, he opened his mouth and closed it around his neck, sharp teeth slicing through the flesh and muscles making blood splash onto his face. Drunk on the taste, Kennedy started to pull Kingston apart, piece by piece.

63

FURTHER DOWN THE TUNNEL, they found an opening. Carter ran his fingers along the sides, the edges smooth and perfectly straight.

"Guess we found it," Danni said. She angled her torch beam down the corridor, playing the light over the walls. The corridor was too regular to be natural. Even though the tunnels under Exeter were man made, water had roughened the rock over time. This tunnel didn't have any irregularity.

Carter brushed the wall, removing a thin layer of dust. Underneath was a patch of grey, reflecting the light from his torch.

"Metal," he muttered.

"What is this place?"

"I don't want to say it out loud," he said. "It'll sound stupid."

Danni put her hand on the metal, surprised at its warmth. "Is this a spaceship?"

"Told you it sounded stupid."

They made their way down the corridor, and the lights hummed into life overhead. Previous blocks faded to black as they walked. The effect was a constant block of light which followed them down the corridor.

"Do you really think these things might be aliens?"

Carter shrugged. "It's as good an explanation as any. Whatever this is, it's clearly been here a while – like hundreds of years, at least."

"How do you work that out?"

"No way could they have built this in the last century without someone finding out. No, it's older than that."

"The tunnels were built in, like the 14th Century or something. It can't be that old. Can it?"

Carter shrugged. "We're way beyond what I understand here. I don't even like Doctor Who."

"This isn't good is it?"

He shrugged. "Let's find Kingston and be done with this. Let others worry about everything else."

Danni nodded. "The bastard with the tail gets got, no matter what." The corridor ended with another door, which slid open as they approached, revealing a T-junction.

"Which way?" she asked. A scream rang out, long and piercing until it was suddenly cut out. They exchanged a look, and then Carter nodded to the right.

The direction the scream had come from.

"I was afraid you'd say that," she said.

They both raised their weapons and crept down the corridor. Danni was aware of the weight of the grenades in her pocket. They might get some use yet.

Another door slid open and Carter slipped through first. He stood with his back to the wall as Danni followed, stepping to the other side.

"Oh my god," she said.

The room was filled with row after row of capsules. Each one of the cuboid capsules were dark, but they could see eight with open doors on the ground level. Carter inched towards the nearest one and peered in. Brightly coloured tubes hung from the ceiling, dripping strange liquid onto the pristine floor. Other than the tubes, the inside of the pod was empty, yet it stank of sweat and something rotten, a stench at odds with the appearance. He reached out and touched the ends of the tubes.

"Don't," Danni said, but he'd already got the liquid on the ends of his fingers.

"It's like oil. Same consistency, like when you fill your car with diesel and get some on your hands."

"You do that?"

"Not on purpose."

Yet another scream rang out echoing in the vast cavern. This was louder even than the last. They were getting closer to the source of the terrible sound.

"What was in these things?" Danni whispered once the echoes faded.

"I'm not sure we want to know," Carter said. "There must be hundreds of these things in here. Is this where the Horde come from?"

"There's not enough pods." Danni reached out to touch one but withdrew her hand without making contact. The dark glass unnerved her. Was there something moving behind it?

A light came on in a pod a few down from her. She raised her gun as the door slid open.

"Move!" Carter hissed, but even as he said it, he knew they were in trouble.

There was nowhere to hide.

64

KINGSTON GASPED as the cables popped out of him. Coughing, he fell as the door slid open. The cables swayed above him, dripping the remains of fluid onto him. He stayed on the floor on all fours, panting hard. Each breath hurt, but the feeling subsided and he started to breathe more easily. Stomach churning, he stood on unsteady legs, but they gave way and he landed heavily on his backside. He swore and tried again, this time using the smooth wall of the pod to help him stand.

Cold air on his skin made him realise he was naked, but then a panel opened on the side of the pod and a grey garment slid out on a pole. He pulled it on, gathering it around him like a blanket to ward off the chill. Something cold and hard pressed into his back.

"Don't move," a familiar voice said.

"Carter!" he turned to face the man.

Carter took a step back but didn't lower the weapon. "God, I could have shot you!"

"What the hell are you doing here man? This is where they live.

They're going to be here in a second." Kingston stared at the pod for a moment, frowning. "Wait, where am I?"

"The thing took you, remember?"

"Yeah, he put me in a machine. I met their leader," Kingston shuddered.

"Their leader is here?"

"He calls himself Father. He's like a bigger version of the Horde." Kingston stared down the corridor of pods, frown deepening. Something wasn't right. His memories were clouded, but this didn't look like the large machine he'd been put in. "I think I killed his kids, but-"

"We need to go," Carter said. "Before they find us."

"Yeah, but-" Kingston spun on the spot, taking in all the pods. "This isn't-"

"What the hell are you two snowflakes doing?" Danni hissed from the shadows behind them. "Let's get the hell out of Dodge."

"Come on," Carter said, putting a hand on Kingston's shoulder.

Kingston flinched at the touch and shook his head, like he was trying to clear it, not say no. "I don't get it. This isn't the machine they put me in."

"Kingston," Carter said, but didn't get a response. "Paul! Come on mate, focus. We need to get out of here."

"No, I-"

A hissing noise filled the air around them.

"Behind you!" Danni yelled.

Kingston turned and whimpered. The corridor was suddenly full of Horde.

65

KENNEDY SAT WITH FATHER, belly full. Contentment was not an emotion he was familiar with, but he liked it. With a hum of the machines filling his ears, he let his eyes slowly close. Today had been a good day. Finally, they were free of the tunnels and this self-imposed prison. Now, Father's caution in waiting so long for them to reveal themselves was paying off in more food than the Horde could eat. With Mother's help, their food for the future was secure.

Yes, today was a good day. A great one, even.

Father's message had been broadcast and now the humans would leave them alone. The city was theirs. Nothing could stop them now. The humans had seen what the Horde could do, so they would be foolish to break the terms Father had given them.

Wouldn't they? Doubt gnawed at him the way he'd eaten the bone just now.

Kennedy dismissed the thought. He should not question Father. What if they did break terms? Had Father spoken to any humans? Did he know what a pile of scheming, lying, odious things the humans were? None of them could be trusted – Kennedy knew this from his limited dealings with them. They were a hurtful, spiteful species and the world would be better if it were rid of them.

One step at a time. Take the city first.

Kennedy smiled to himself. Father knew what he was doing: he knew what was best for the Horde, even if it was too soon to take the Barrier down. He must have been exhausted, that was all. Maintaining a Barrier was tiring – he'd seen what it had done to the Princes – so keeping one so large? His respect and love for Father grew once more.

But what if the Humans didn't trust Father?

What then?

Kennedy sat up, eyes snapping open.

Father was all knowing. All powerful.

Kennedy watched him watching the screens. Some of the displays were dead, their feeds no longer working. The working ones showed parts of the city, deserted streets strewn with the debris of destruction and dead humans. But then-

"What's that?" Kennedy said. Something moved on one of the screens. Something big.

Father turned to the screen he had indicated. On it, a large machine crept down a street on two large tracks. It was green and brown, and a huge barrel emerged from the front of the machine, swivelling back and forth like a malevolent pipe. Behind the machine came more humans, all dressed in identical green and brown clothes, carrying more of the weapons he had seen earlier.

"What is this?" Father roared.

"They are coming for us," Kennedy said.

Father shouted and struck the top of his counter hard enough to dent it. "They did not obey! They have broken the terms of our peace agreement. Kill them," he hissed. "Kill them all."

Kennedy felt the push of the order in his mind and knew the Horde would respond without question. Now it would not just be the dead that would suffer. Then, with another roar, Father threw back his head and pushed his arms out wide. Kennedy felt the pressure build, but then his head snapped to the doorway.

Gunfire.

Here. In the Home.

With a moan, Kennedy set off towards the sound.

66

THEY ALL FELT the pressure in their heads and all sound became muffled for a moment. Danni gasped as the pressure built, squeezing her eyes shut, but then it was gone. The Horde in front of them were also affected by the pressure and paused so she managed to react quicker. Danni opened fire and the first two Horde fell back into their compatriots, making them all stumble. Kingston and Carter ran towards her, Kingston's eyes wild with fear.

"They've come for me," he shouted, voice at a higher pitch than normal. His earlier confusion had gone now, replaced with outright terror.

Carter fired at the Horde as they regained their footing. Bullets tore into them, making them spin as they collapsed to the ground. "Relax," he said to Kingston, "we got them all."

"We need to get out of here," Kingston said, pleading. "Please." He turned away from Carter with tears in his eyes and came face to face with the largest Horde member. The one with the tail.

Kennedy.

67

"RUN!"

Danni wasn't sure who shouted, but as soon as she saw the tail, she sprinted down the corridor. Footsteps behind her told her the other two were close behind. Gunfire roared again and she guessed Carter was shooting at the thing.

She skidded to a halt, turned and aimed. What she saw made her legs go weak. The thing was running hard at them, with the ball of spikes a mean metronome behind it. Its mouth was full of teeth and one of its hands was tipped with vicious claws. The other ended with what looked like normal human fingers.

Holding her breath and fighting the urge to scream, she pulled the trigger and bullets sped towards the thing. It exploded and three blue spheres emerged from the cloud, crackling with energy. They hovered for a second then shot towards them.

"Down!" she shouted and the three of them jumped to the floor. Danni grazed her chin as she landed and felt the heat of the spheres pass over her as she fell. As soon as she hit the floor, she scrambled forward then stood, watching the spheres streak away from them.

"No!" Kingston shouted as he tried to stand. Danni glanced at him but didn't want to take her eyes from the spheres, which were now arcing into the air.

Kingston was looking at the capsule she was standing next to, face coated in sweat. He retched, but no bile came out.

"What's wrong?" Carter rested a hand on the young man's back and could feel him trembling.

The spheres had disappeared into the gloom above their heads. Danni kept her head tilted up, scanning for their return.

"This is the pod I was put in," Kingston said.

"Ok," Carter said slowly. "But we don't really have time for this." He tried to keep focussed on Kingston, but the threat of the spheres was overriding any sympathy he felt.

Confusion squashed his features as he pointed at the machine and then back towards the pods. "I didn't come out here."

He touched the door of the nearest pod and it slid open, revealing an empty white space. Three wires hung limply from the ceiling but otherwise the pod was empty. Moving quickly, Kingston opened the next pod but this one was also empty.

"Guys," Danni hissed. "We don't have time for this." A blue hue was brightening the air above them, but she couldn't see the spheres. Not yet.

The third pod Kingston tried wouldn't open. He banged the door in frustration and the resulting clang reverberated through the cavern

"Kingston, what are you doing?" Carter hissed at him.

Danni scanned the pods now, tearing her eyes from the growing light. "Powers of two," she muttered. "It's a binary system."

"What?" Carter demanded. "This isn't the time for a maths lesson."

"Binary revolves around powers of two. Look at the pods. That's why the Horde were always in groups of eight. Wherever they came from, it's a maths system we understand."

"So what?"

"Maybe they're not aliens after all," she said with a shrug. "Maybe they're something else."

A breeze had picked up in the corridor now and the blue light intensified.

"He's coming back!" Danni said.

The door to the pod slid open. Kingston fell out, gasping and coughing as he hit the cold floor. He wiped his head, looking in horror at the blood and yellow fluid there. He tried to stand, but his legs trembled, and he collapsed with a cry.

Carter stared for a second, mouth open. Kingston was standing next to him on the verge of a panic attack and yet he was also naked on the ground in front of him. Both men were identical down to the tiny hole in their temples.

"What the fuck?" Carter said.

68

SPHERES SMASHED TOGETHER and Kennedy roared back into existence. Four humans were near him, one lying on the floor.

Him.

He swung his tail and it crunched into his head, snapping his neck, even as the acid started to do its work. Spinning, he sliced at the other black man's face, who recoiled in disgust.

Nothing else happened. His cheek should have been sliced to shreds. Kennedy howled in frustration. He'd forgotten his claws had gone. He had essentially slapped the black man.

Fresh bullets tore into him, forcing him to stagger backwards just as he pushed the button on his bracelet and burst into sphere form again.

69

"THEY'VE GONE!" Peter called. The Horde had moved as one, without warning, disappearing into the streets surrounding them. "Let's go, now!"

The survivors emerged, most still looking shaken. The sunshine made their various states of disrepair look worse.

"You told us to stay," Linda said.

"The situation is evolving. We have a window of opportunity. We go, now. If you want to stay, you can."

He clambered over the ruined wall, sliding down onto grass. Stones skittered down as more of the survivors emerged into sunlight.

"It's beautiful," Linda said. "I'm never going to take it for granted again."

Peter didn't know if she was talking about Exeter, which frankly, had looked better, or the sky which usually looked a lot worse.

"Where are we going?" Linda asked. Peter waited at the bottom of the rubble, helping the last couple of people across. He did a quick headcount and was dismayed to realise some had stayed behind. Twelve people stood with him now. There had been over seventy when he'd arrived at the Cathedral.

"Quickest way out?" Peter asked.

"No idea. I came from there." Linda pointed behind him to the narrow street she had walked down a lifetime ago.

"Let's go. Stick together and don't leave anyone behind."

They ran across the green, heading for the street Linda had indicated. Halfway there, Peter frowned and held his head as sudden pressure built. Everyone else in their bedraggled group was doing the same.

"Oh no," Linda cried. She pulled Ethan to her in a crushing hug.

The sun faded from view as the wall reappeared, casting dark shadows around them. Peter skidded to a halt. What did this mean? They weren't far from the Cathedral. Should they go back?

A scream in the distance made his mind up, but before he could turn back, a large group of Horde appeared at the top of the road, heading straight for them.

70

DANNI BREATHED hard and released the trigger. The spheres streamed into the air again, arcing high above them. Kingston was holding his face, but more in surprise than pain. There wasn't a mark on him. "What the hell?"

"You got lucky," Danni said.

"He had claws, before," Carter said, voice somewhere between awe and fear.

Carter knelt by the man who looked like Kingston. His eyes were open, staring into nothing. Half of his face had melted, and his skull was crushed just like the man back in the station so many hours ago. Other than the bashed in head, he looked exactly like Kingston.

"They're making me. Why are they making *me*?" Kingston's voice was stripped of the bravado it had earlier in the day. Now he sounded exactly like he was: a scared teenager, way out of his depth.

"I think we should get the hell out of here," Carter said. Blue light was growing behind Danni. "Now," he yelled.

Danni turned just as the spheres coalesced and reformed into Kennedy. She screamed and tried to raise her gun, but it was like moving through treacle. Kennedy's tail swooped over his shoulder, stabbing her with the ball of spikes. Danni let out a howl as the tail ripped her shoulder open. She fell back onto the pod, her blood mingling with the other Kingston's. Green ooze swelled in the wound and she screamed again as the acid went to work.

She staggered forward, trying to put some distance between her and Kennedy, but the tail swung again, this time connecting with her side and sending her stumbling into the pod. Danni tried to remain standing but couldn't; the pain was too great. Her legs gave way and she slumped to the floor, crying in agony. She didn't want to look at her shoulder: she knew it was bad. It felt like it was on fire, waves of pain coursing through the joint. She'd lost the gun but had no idea when. Darkness encroached at the side of her vision and she couldn't move her arm.

The door to the pod slid shut, a smooth movement punctuated with a soft click. She barely heard it over her own screams. Danni remembered the man from earlier, her colleague whose name she didn't know. His screams following his meeting with the spiked ball hadn't lasted long, and she knew hers wouldn't either.

She fumbled at her belt and gripped the grenade. The pipes above started to weave as if they were searching for her.

"Time to get got," she whispered between gasps.

She pulled the pin and closed her eyes.

71

Kingston watched in horror as Danni took the full force of the spiked ball and staggered into the biggest of the pods. Before he could move, the door slid shut.

"No!" he yelled and scrambled for the gun she'd dropped.

"Mother has her now," Kennedy grinned.

"No," Kingston said again and pulled the trigger. He aimed for Kennedy's right arm and the bullets flew towards it with a deafening roar. Bullet after bullet smashed into the creature's arm, turning the shoulder joint into a mess of torn flesh. He couldn't control the pull of the weapon and it started to veer up, bullets smashing into the pipes overhead. Multi-coloured rain fell as the pipes shattered.

An alarm rang out, deafening them even as Carter joined in, his bullets tearing into the thing's head.

Kennedy danced like a puppet on strings, until eventually the strings were cut. He lay twitching on the ground, blood spreading around him. He tried to move his hand to the bracelet, but he was too slow and it wouldn't obey. *Him*. The one who had killed the princes was standing on his free hand, pinning it to the ground. Kennedy had no strength left as cold fire spread from his multitude of wounds and his breathing became ragged.

"What have you done to me?" Kingston's face was contorted with fury.

Kennedy tried to laugh, but it died in his throat. "What you deserved."

Kingston shot him between the eyes, watching as his brains splashed onto the ground behind him.

"Fuck you," he said and kicked the corpse.

Carter approached with small steps, keeping the weapon tight to his shoulder and pointed at Kennedy.

"Get back."

"Why? He's dead."

"Spheres. Every time we've killed him, he came back as those spheres."

Nothing happened. The only movement near Kennedy was the spread of his blood over the cold metal floor.

"Danni," Carter whispered. The elation at finally killing the creature faded as he looked through the small window into the pod. Why did this one have a window but none of the others did? He didn't have time to wonder about that now: Danni was in trouble.

Wires from the ceiling waved above her, darting forward but she was just out of reach. Black lines ran over her face, tracing the veins just under her skin and showing the rapid progress the poison was making. Her shoulder was a mess of melting flesh and her chest was concave. Acid melted her clothes around the wounds and continued to sink through her flesh, eating muscles and revealing bone. As he watched, her chest stopped rising.

"No!" he roared, slapping the window. Now the wires had stopped weaving above her and hung twitching like they were in a breeze. Something rolled free of her hand, tumbling across the floor.

"Run!" Carter yelled as soon as he saw the grenade, struggling to make himself heard above the klaxon of the alarm.

He grabbed Kingston's arm and they set off at a sprint, heading towards the entrance. Kingston let himself be dragged, Carter seeming to know where he was going. Kingston didn't want to stay down there a moment longer. A light pinged on in a pod as they passed, but Carter didn't slow.

The explosion was loud and hot, far louder than it should have been. Carter risked a look back over his shoulder and saw the pod containing Danni was ablaze. The door flew off its housing and fire was already spreading over the top of the pod. Flames licked along the wires, glowing brighter and brighter as they spread and took hold. In the distance, he could hear some of the Horde shouting, but he couldn't see them. Thick smoke swirled through the air, filling the space.

Soon they wouldn't be able to breathe.

"Faster!" he shouted, but neither of them had more energy. They were going as fast as they could and then they heard another explosion, followed by the screech of metal on metal. He looked again, and saw the fire had already spread further, devouring pods like they were dry logs.

The door was twenty feet away now. Smoke was making them both cough, crowding out the air they needed. Gasping, Kingston stumbled. Another explosion ripped the air and now the heat washed over them.

"Come on!" Carter screamed and pulled Kingston back to his feet.

Then they were out of the room and into cleaner air. The door to the cavern slid shut behind them, sealing them from the heat and the smoke. Thick locks slid into place with a loud bang. Both sank to their knees, gasping for breath. Stale air had never tasted so sweet.

Kingston dragged himself to the window and watched the inferno lick the glass. No heat made it through the door; it remained cool to the touch despite the raging firestorm on the other side. Flames consumed everything, nothing left untouched. Bodies writhed in the furnace, and one lurched towards the glass, mouth open in a howl. For a moment, its features became clear. Same nose. Same eyes. Same mouth. Kingston put his hand to the glass and turned his head away. He couldn't watch himself burn.

"They're all gone."

The voice came from behind, but it wasn't Carter. He turned quickly and his blood ran cold when he saw who stood there.

Father.

72

LINDA SCREAMED as she turned away from the Horde. *To have come so close! To have survived through so much today only to die with help on the way.* She could hear the gunfire and shouts in the distance, but they sounded so far away.

"Run!" she yelled at Ethan, glancing back over her shoulder. With the Horde closing in, he looked tiny – far too young to be running from monsters. A group of adults had pushed past her but now turned back, feet scrambling on the pavement and faces full of fear. It was far too late. The Horde pounced and screams rang out. The soundtrack of the day.

She pushed the boy ahead of her, back towards the Cathedral. Ethan ran as fast as he could, but his stride just wasn't long enough to cover the ground.

Peter appeared at the corner, raising his pistol. Linda thought for a moment he was going to shoot her then the gun burst to life. Bullets rushed past her so close she could feel the heat of their passing.

"Back to the Cathedral," he roared. He fired again until the gun clicked empty. Peter surged forward, picked Ethan up, and then started running to the Cathedral. With the extra weight, he was slowed but still moved more quickly than most.

Another scream, another cut short. The Horde were gaining on them. Linda tried to keep up with the captain, but her legs were burning and her chest heaving. At last the days' strenuous activities caught up with her. She felt a sob escape her lips as she heard Peter swear.

From the other side of the green came more Horde, streaming in large numbers out of the side streets. They were blocking the route back to the Cathedral.

There was no way through; nowhere to run.

Peter stopped, putting Ethan down so the boy could run to Linda.

She let Ethan hug her and held him close.

"Don't look," Linda whispered into Ethan's ear. "Hold on to me and don't look."

The Horde had them surrounded and seemed to know it. They stopped, a circle forming around the small group. It was as if they were taking their time, savouring the kill. One of them darted forward and grabbed Linda. She let go of Ethan and turned to the creature, lashing out with a fist. The creature looked completely surprised for a moment, but then it grinned at her.

"Take me but leave him alone!" she yelled and punched again. Its head whipped back, and she punched again and again. Bones broke – both in her hand and the thing's face – but she kept punching and screaming at it. The creature stumbled and fell, blood pouring from various cuts on its face. As she followed through with the punch, Linda looked up, screaming in triumph.

Three more Horde were waiting for her.

"Oh no," she said softly and turned her back to them. Ethan held his arms out towards her, tears streaming down his face. She hugged him, feeling vulnerable and helpless as the Horde shuffled closer.

"I'm sorry, kiddo, I'm so sorry."

Linda pulled him closer, holding his head tight to her own, crushing him with the hug and her love. She could at least protect him from the sight, if not the sound. Their time would come soon enough.

73

"You," Father said. "You've killed them all."

He moved so quickly Carter didn't see the kick, but he felt it. Father's foot connected with Carter's chest, sending the man tumbling onto his back. Something cracked, and Carter screamed. Every breath like fire and he knew a couple of ribs had been broken.

"We hid for centuries, waiting for the right time." Father kicked again, but this time he hit Carter's leg and the pain wasn't so bad. Carter rolled into the foetal position, arms covering his head as best he could. "Centuries! Down here in the dark since we arrived, waiting for your technology to match ours so we could join you."

Father turned his attention to Kingston, punching him. His fist connected with Kingston's nose making blood spurt onto the grey overall. Kingston's legs gave way and he collapsed to the metal floor, holding his nose.

"We would have given you everything we know. But you-" he knelt next to Kingston, forcing him to match Father's malevolent gaze. "You killed my sons."

"I didn't know." Kingston's ruined nose made it sound like *dibn't doe*. "They attacked us."

"No," Father said. "They would not hurt a thing."

"I think you know nothing about your people." Carter was crouched over, holding his ribs with his free arm. He inched forward, the effort of each movement etched on his face.

"I forbade touching humans," Father said. "Until *you* hurt my sons."

"No," Carter said. "Your people were hurting us long before we even knew about you."

Father frowned. "No."

"Yes. You and your people are monsters."

Father kicked Carter in the ribs again and Carter heard bone crack. Fire raced through his lungs as Father punched his face. Again and again, blows rained onto Carter's head. He felt the edges of the world go fuzzy, black spots appearing at the edge of his vision. Everything seemed so very far away, and he couldn't even raise his arms to protect himself. Every blow made his head ring like a hammer hitting an anvil.

He heard another loud crack and thought *this is it.*

Game over.

74

KINGSTON WATCHED Father hit Carter and whimpered. He was next. Once this thing had beaten Carter to death, it would be his turn. Failed again. He couldn't do anything right. Couldn't run any more. Carter didn't deserve to go like this – trying to save him. He reached out and closed his hand around the barrel of the gun.

The feel of the weapon energised him, adrenaline flooding him, making him forget his wounds as he stood. Father was still hitting Carter, oblivious to the young man behind him. Kingston swung the weapon, the butt smashing into the back of Father's head. A loud crack greeted the connection and Father screamed. Kingston swung again and again, each hit making Father stagger away from Carter. He turned to face Kingston and the young man smashed the weapon into his jaw. He hit him again, this time breaking his nose. Father tried to raise his arms to protect his head, but Kingston's blows were too persistent, too strong. Father sank to his knees and Kingston continued to beat him. Kingston swung the weapon over his head and brought it down repeatedly. Father's face was bleeding, skin splitting under the assault. Bones broke and his black eye popped out of its socket, swinging back and forth on its tenuous connection to the optic nerve. Still Kingston swung the weapon, sending blood spraying through the corridor with every upswing. The sound changed from a satisfying crunch to a dull thump and then a wet slap.

"Kingston," Carter's voice was thick with pain. "He's had enough."

Kingston stopped, breathing hard. He was covered in Father's blood and he wiped his face, looking at his hand with revulsion. Father was neither breathing nor moving.

"This was not our fault," he said, wheezing.

"We should go." Carter's nose was at an angle on his face and would not be straight again without surgery. He made a slight whistling noise every time he breathed. "There might be more. Let's get the hell out of here before they see what we did to the place." He pointed at the door. Flames still burned the other side of it, but the door was not getting hot. "No idea how long the door will hold, but I don't want to be here when it breaks."

Carter tried to stand but clutched his chest. Kingston caught him, dragging Carter's arm over his shoulder to support him.

"I got you, man, I got you."

They started to make the long journey back to the surface.

THE HORDE STOPPED MOVING, stopped hissing and sunlight flooded into Exeter as the Barrier disappeared yet again. When the warmth hit her, Linda looked up, relishing the feeling on her skin. She glanced over to the Horde, but they were still stationary, only the strange swaying motion giving any indication they were alive.

"Peter," she whispered. The creatures hadn't attacked or moved once they'd closed in on them. Why not? What was going on?

"I see it," he said.

Gunfire erupted around them and they saw the rearmost ring of Horde fall to the ground. Still the creatures didn't move.

"Stop!" Peter roared waving his hands. Soldiers were running into the green, shooting at the Horde as they went. Taking a breath, Peter pushed his way through the remaining Horde to the edge of the ring. Despite the slaughter of their brethren, they remained swaying.

"Sir." A soldier saluted as soon as he saw Peter, but he couldn't hide the surprise in his voice. "We thought you were a goner."

Peter did a three-hundred-and-sixty-degree turn, surveying

the destruction around him. People were coming out of the Cathedral – the ones who had chosen to stay behind – crying and hugging each other. Ethan emerged from the Horde with Linda, holding hands. His little face was pale, eyes wide. He was going to need a lot of therapy after this. They all were.

"So did I," Peter said. "So did I."

EPILOGUE

CARTER SAT ON THE BENCH, lost in thought as the rain hammered down around him. London stretched out before him and he could see all the familiar, comforting sights: St Paul's, The O2 and the Shard all dominating the skyline. Greenwich observatory sat on his left, beaming the meridian line across the park as dusk approached.

He sat alone, the weather too inclement for the park to be full of people like it should be at the height of summer. He was soaked through but didn't care. Water seeped into his shoes and his coat had given up any pretence of protection half an hour ago. Someone on the news had said the poor weather was due to Exeter and what the Horde had done, but Carter just thought it was heavy rain for the time of year.

"Carter."

A voice behind him. Faint, barely heard above the rain. It had been a good few weeks since the press and paparazzi had left him alone – onto the next big story – so he wasn't too concerned. Besides, the voice sounded familiar.

A man stepped out from the tree line near him. It had been a few weeks since Carter had seen him, and those weeks had not been kind. He'd lost a lot of weight and shaved his head. The first scratchings of a beard graced his chin, and with the gaunt look, he was almost unrecognisable.

Almost.

"Kingston," Carter said and found himself smiling. He hadn't seen the young man since leaving Exeter over a month before.

"Hey, man," Kingston returned the smile, but it looked out of place on his face. "Just wanted to check in before I go."

"Where are you going?"

"As far away from here as possible. Somewhere no-one knows me."

"Keeler still after you?"

Kingston shook his head. "Given everything, he gave me a pass."

Carter nodded. "Anywhere in mind?"

Kingston laughed. "Yeah. Somewhere big. Try and start again."

He had been given a rough ride in the media following the Liberation of Exeter. Many news outlets – and more families – had blamed him, and only him, for the slaughter of tens of thousands in Exeter. Some had speculated they could have lived side by side with the Horde if only Kingston hadn't killed their young.

Carter defended Kingston, pointing out the Horde had already killed – and eaten – lots of people before Kingston even arrived in Exeter. Carter received a couple of death threats himself for that. Danni and Peter had emerged from the chaos as heroes. Danni was going to have a memorial garden dedicated to her when they finally rebuilt Exeter. As to Peter, well, *that* was classified.

"How's Linda?"

Carter shrugged. "Good, or as good as you can expect. She got a book deal."

"Are you keeping Ethan?"

"At the moment. There's a long process for adoption – especially as they are still trying to trace his parents. We also have to show we're ok as a couple. You know, no issues." He pointed to his head and shrugged.

"That's good, that's good." Kingston's voice caught for a moment, and Carter thought he might cry. "You guys will make great parents."

"Hey, come on, we're alive."

"Yeah, but-"

"Many aren't." Carter was more forceful this time. "We'll be unpacking the day for decades, man. Life is full of ifs and buts, but *we* know they weren't good, the Horde. We stopped them. Me. You. Danni."

It was his turn for his voice to break. Danni would still be alive if she hadn't followed him. Maybe she would have been killed by the Horde in Exeter if she hadn't come with him. Maybe Father would have enslaved the whole of the UK if she hadn't destroyed Mother. She might have survived and gone on to be the greatest detective in the UK. He shook his head – that sort of thinking did nobody any good. Survivor's guilt, his therapist said. Well, he had plenty of that.

Kingston's face was full of anguish. "I keep thinking of being down there."

"Don't," Carter said.

"I think about it all the time. Am I *me*?"

They locked eyes for a moment, but a movement behind Kingston drew Carter's gaze. A young man stood by the tree nearest them. He tapped his wrist. *We got to go.* He still bore the scars of his beating, but it was a miracle he still had his faculties.

"The me who went to Exeter was falling in love with him," Kingston pointed at Stephen. "Is it still me?"

"Come on man, seriously?"

Kingston shrugged. "I don't even know if I actually like smoking or not. Are these lungs clear of any sign of it? The cravings I get, are they memories or my addiction. Who am I now?"

"If they're not your memories, then whose are they?" Carter said. "All we are is memories, right?"

Kingston nodded, but didn't look convinced.

"You can't think about it," Carter said. "Just live."

"I can't think about anything else."

Carter nodded, water dripping off his nose. "Look, take care of yourself, ok? Be the best you can be. You have a second chance. Go for it."

"You're staying in London?"

"Probably. I'm off work for a while, seeing a shrink. Linda's book deal is in the six-figure region, so I don't need to work." He shivered and stood. "You want a coffee? My place isn't far. Linda would love to see you. Ethan too."

Kingston raised an eyebrow. "Ethan maybe," he snorted. "Nah man, we just got to get going."

"Don't dwell on things, ok? Move forward, always forward."

They stood in silence for a few minutes, watching the rain bounce off the grass, flowers and trees. Heavy clouds shrouded the city and this rain was not going to stop for a few more hours. Eventually, Carter turned to Kingston and offered him his hand.

"Take it easy. See you around."

With that Kingston shook Carter's hand for the first, and last, time.

THE END

ACKNOWLEDGMENTS

Writing a book is never a solitary task, even if putting the words down is. First off, I would like thank Dawn and D&T Publishing for taking a chance on this novel, Patrick C, Harrison III for the edits and Don Noble for the cool cover.

I seem to have been writing this book for five years, and over that time lots of people were generous enough to spend some time looking at various drafts. So, in no particular order, thanks to Katie Samuel (hope you like your death scene!), Shani White (sorry about yours) and Rich Evans (you're in the next one…). You all saw the roughest version of this, full of bloat, but still encouraged me to keep going. Justin Park and Graeme Reynolds both gave me the confidence to think this was actually any good, so thank you both! Kev Harrison also helped me get it over the finish line and was kind enough to provide a cover quote too. You should really check out his stuff if you haven't already. Thanks also to Jim Mcleod from GingerNuts of Horror and Tim Lebbon who have been kind enough to give cover quotes.

The police sections were aided by Dan and Ben, both of whom were very generous with their time. Obviously, any mistakes in this final version are down to me. I have taken some liberties with the geography of Exeter for the sake of the story.

I started going to conventions around the time I finished the first draft of this, and my writing circle has grown considerably as a result. Everyone I've met at a convention deserves thanks, either for having time for a chat, making me feel welcome or giving me advice. There are too many people to list here, but I'll go with the first two to welcome me: CC Adams and Phil Sloman. Both are great guys and writers.

Finally, my wonderful family for putting up with me during the frankly torturous process this book went through. Josh and Ethan continue to make me proud every day. Tinu, you are my One, but you already know that.

Until next time!

Dave Watkins
July 2022

ABOUT THE EDITOR / PUBLISHER

Dawn Shea is an author and half of the publishing team over at D&T Publishing. She lives with her family in Mississippi. Always an avid horror lover, she has moved forward with her dreams of writing and publishing those things she loves so much.

D&T Previously published material:
     ABC's of Terror
     After the Kool-Aid is Gone

Follow her author page on Amazon for all publications she is featured in.
     Follow D&T Publishing at the following locations:
     Website
     Facebook: Page / Group
     Or email us here: dandtpublishing20@gmail.com

The Exeter Incident by David Watkins

Cover by Don Noble

Edited by Patrick C. Harrison III

Formatting by J.Z. Foster

Corinth, MS

Printed in Great Britain
by Amazon

25530139R00225